# DORNA

# DORNA

*Based on a True Story*

SAEED GHAHRAMANI

Print ISBN: 979-8-9864765-0-6
Kindle ISBN: 979-8-9864765-1-3
Epub ISBN: 979-8-9864765-2-0

Cover Design and Formatting by ebooklaunch.com

*In loving memory of my learned friends*

Ebrahim Aminzadeh

And

Nosrat Modarres

Love's pain is but one tale—no more. Wonderful is this
That from every tongue I hear, the tale is not repeated!

—Hafez

# Contents

# Acknowledgment

While writing this novel, several people helped me either directly or indirectly. Lili, my beloved wife, deserves an accolade for her patience and encouragement; so do my wonderful children, Adam and Andrew.

I learned a great deal about the times, life, and character of Dorna from my remarkable late friends Ebrahim Aminzadeh and Nosrat Modarres. I am indebted for sharing all they knew and had learned from their relatives about Dorna.

Special thanks are due to my colleague and friend, Professor Ann Kizanis, a perfectionist who has eagle eyes. Ann read, very carefully, a considerable part of the novel and made many valuable suggestions.

The editor of this novel, Maxime Mckenna, presented ideas for revisions that were insightful. It gives me a distinct pleasure to thank Max for all his enthusiastic editorial help.

# CHAPTER 1

## PAST IN THE MIRROR OF THE PRESENT

### 1

To what ocean can I tell my pain and yet not cause a tsunami? To what river can I confide, which would withstand overflow? To what rock can I reveal my story, which could resist a total shatter? Strangers would be devastated, to say nothing of the acquaintances; I know that no true friend's heart could bear hearing my story. I will not get any consolation, no matter whom I confide in, no matter to whom I spread the pages of the many chapters of my life; a life that has been intertwined with suffering, torture, and pain. My friends and relatives would probably feel only pity toward me with facial expressions filled with sadness and with eyes full of tears. So I confide in my pen alone and let it write, let it use all my spirit and subsistence as ink. Let it write until the inkwell of my existence is dry. My life will come to an end, but my story may survive. For many years, my feelings have been prisoners of my calm manners and reserved appearance. However, the time has come for my pen to write the real story of my life and reveal all my innermost thoughts and secrets.

This is not only my life story. It is the life story of thousands of Azerbaijani women tormented at the hands of domineering husbands. And by no means do I want to stereotype men. Only God knows how many men have existed who are decent and honorable human beings. Instead, I am challenging and condemning those societies that allow certain men to exercise authority and power over women, mainly because of applying the law of jungle to the human society.

I am not sure if this book will ever be published. I am writing it for people who are not yet born or who are very young. If the book is published and you are reading it, please be advised that it has been a long time since I have gone, and at this time, I cannot guess the state of mind of the readers of my book. Whoever you are, let us hope that the current state of affairs (social, political, and cultural) have advanced and progressed, and human minds have blossomed so that gender equality is no longer an issue. It does not really matter who you are, an Azerbaijani or any other Iranian, a Middle Easterner outside of Iran, a European, an African, from Asia or Australia, or one of the inhabitants of the Americas. Whoever you are, you need to know what happened to *all* your fellow humans. In Iran, they say that those who do not learn from the past are condemned to repeat it. I am just presenting the life of a woman as an example of the millions who lived through important junctures in Iranian history. I want you to know that women in my generation were cursed, doomed, and damned. What we went through is more than enough for all future generations of all societies all over the world.

In my day, women were the captives of men. The individuality of a woman was ignored, and we were totally dependent upon our fathers, brothers, and husbands. There were exceptions, but by and large, we were not allowed to be creative, reach high levels of education, write essays, or be self-confident. Like Virginia Woolf years before, we Iranian women experienced the harmful influence of a male-dominated culture on our creative and imaginative lives.

# 2

My name is Dorna, and I am fifty-four years old. During my lifetime in Iran, specifically in the northwest region of Azerbaijan, women have gained a good deal of freedom. We have female actors and singers, politicians and parliamentarians, physicians and engineers, and even soldiers. Not long ago, women could only travel abroad accompanied by their husbands, fathers, or brothers. Today, in 1975, women need only their fathers' or husbands' *permission* to travel alone all over the world. Female athletes compete all across the country, and we have come a long way since the days of my youth, when I was a hostage to my husband's every whim. But we still have some road ahead of us until we reach a gender-blind society. Even though we have the right to vote in Iran, still in many countries in the world, including a few European countries, women do not have the right to vote.

In my younger days, very few girls were allowed to go to school, and fewer had their parents' permission to continue to high school and earn a diploma. I was very lucky to go through a rigorous curriculum and finish high school successfully. Moreover, I even earned a bachelor's degree from Tabriz University. And because of that, I feel obliged to write my story.

While I hope this memoir will one day see the light of day, I do not dare submit it to a publisher myself, since I have written it as a woman who has unleashed her feminine sensitivity and even sensuality when necessary. I learned this style from the poems of a great Persian poet, Forugh Farrokhzād. She was daring. I am not. Forugh's appearance in the social and literary life of Persia was one of the greatest phenomena of Iran's twentieth century. She was the embodiment of the collective tongues of all Persian women throughout history who had not been able to describe their womanly emotions and desires. Forugh founded a new language in which women could openly express that which their bodies prescribe and pronounce. With her poems, through imagery affected by a feminine life experience, she rose up against the oppression of a traditional male-dominated society.

> I have sinned a rapturous sin[1]
> in a warm enflamed embrace,
> sinned in a pair of vindictive arms,
> arms violent and ablaze.
>
> ...
>
> Lust enflamed his eyes,
> red wine trembled in the cup,
> my body, naked and drunk,
> quivered softly on his breast.

---

[1] "Sin" from Selected Poems of Forugh Farrokhzād, translated by Sholeh Wolpé, (Fayetteville, Arkansas: The University of Arkansas Press, 2007).

I have sinned a rapturous sin
beside a body quivering and spent.
I do not know what I did O God,
in that quite vacant dark.

Forugh embodied an explosion and articulation of the painful complexes, tense moral fiber, and the silence of Iranian women. She singlehandedly ended the deprivation and exclusion of female artists, poets, and thinkers from the cultural and intellectual life of Persia. At age thirty, by full immersion in the condition of suffering fellow human beings, she killed her old self and became a spokeswoman against injustice, misery, poverty, and affliction. On February 13, 1967, at age thirty-two, she died in Tehran in a tragic car accident. She was fourteen years younger than me. I am very lucky to have read her life's work.

No one thinks of the flowers.
No one thinks of the fish.
No one wants to believe the garden is dying,
that its heart has swollen in the heart of this sun,
that its mind drains slowly of its lush memories.

Our garden is forlorn.
It yawns waiting
for rain from a stray cloud,
and our pond sits empty.
Callow stars bite the dust
from atop tall trees
and from the pale home of the fish
comes the hack of coughing every night.

Our garden is forlorn.
...

I plant my hands in the garden soil –
I will sprout,
I know, I know, I know.
And in the hollow of my ink-stained palms
Swallows will make their nest.

# 3

My older sister, Dena, and her husband, Habib, have a magnificent house, and on a fall day back in 1960, there was quite a hubbub in their front yard. All friends and relatives, old and young, big and small, had already arrived. Auntie had invited everyone. They had all gathered to help prepare for a huge celebration that was happening the next day. The guests had divided the tasks among themselves, and they were all busy doing their parts. Children were playing. I was the only one idle. I could not concentrate on anything. A deep sorrow was ruling my heart. I was worried.

They had told me that a guest, whom I had never known or met, was coming from afar and that this big party was in honor of that guest. Seemingly no one knew who the guest was, except that he or she was extremely important to Dena and Habib.

What bothered me was that, until that day, my sister had never kept a secret from me. I had no choice but to wait until the next day to find out the answer to the big riddle.

Dena and Habib's house was very large with high ceilings and spacious rooms furnished with beautiful, expensive Persian carpets, works of art, ornaments, and the type of furniture that could be found only in aristocrats' mansions. The front yard was a two-acre lot of land covered by beautiful gardens full of gorgeous flowers, dazzling plants, and spectacular trees. All the annuals, perennials, and shrubs, together with the breathtaking eucalyptus trees and weeping willows, had left no room for melancholy, and yet I was full of gloom, feeling that I was trapped in a huge cage. The air I breathed felt heavy, and the light of the sun did not rejoice my heart. The lump in my throat had become tight, insistent, painful. The depth of my distress was pressing me hard to rip my dress off and run outside the house barefoot.

# 4

Ms. Mahin's melodious voice, singing happy songs, could be heard from anywhere in the house. It was her style and habit to sing when performing housework. She was sitting outside in a corner of the front yard and scouring out the large bronze charcoal samovar with red brick powder. This was the seventh samovar she was cleaning and the most expensive in Habib and Dena's collection. It was a precious work of art made by Russian craftsmen, and it was engraved with a seal of Emperor Nicholas I, dating it to sometime in the first half of the nineteenth century. Another relative, Badri, was sitting in the middle of the front yard beside the attractive pond. She had just finished washing two huge sixty-six-pound capacity copper cauldrons and was listening to Ms. Mahin's song and whispering the song's lyrics. Sometimes she got excited and sang loud, creating relaxed moments of concordance between her own singing and Ms. Mahin's:

> I've splashed water on dusty narrow roads
> No dirt ever blows where true love abodes
> When my angel comes and goes
> A river of love and devotion flows

Ms. Mahin and Badri's harmonious singing was suddenly interrupted by the bleat of a sheep tied to a eucalyptus tree. It, too, seemed to want to sing along, and everyone present in the front yard laughed with delight. But I was saddened for the unlucky sheep, which I'd learned would be sacrificed the next day in honor of the mysterious guest. I tried to console myself with the knowledge that, on such occasions, my sister and brother-in-law gave the meat of the sacrificed animal away to the poor and needy.

I went over to the sheep, whose color was pure snow, its face cherubic and innocent. I petted its head, chest, and the base of its neck. Then I whispered in its ear, "You, poor animal, I am so sorry for you. I wonder in whose honor they are going to slaughter you tomorrow. You and I have one thing in common: neither of us knows who that person is."

Afterward I went to the kitchen. My sister's loyal houseman, Verdi, was there. Since he was everyone's favorite, and everyone's uncle, we all called him Uncle Verdi. He had lived with Dena and Habib a long time and performed all the general duties in the house. After years of working for my sister and brother-in-law, Uncle Verdi still had thick hair, but it was completely gray. His shoulders were hunched forward, and he had bad posture, as he was always bent forward at the waist. He tried to stand straight with chin in and shoulders back, but his manful stride often failed.

Ignoring his old age, he directed all his energy toward pulling out large amounts of charcoal from the huge storage area that was built in one corner of the kitchen and usually contained up to four hundred pounds of charcoal. He used an instrument very similar to a dustpan, but much larger, to pull the charcoal out and move it to the patio. Uncle Verdi had already placed long grills out there in a lengthy row. He put the charcoal briquettes on the bottom grills and arranged them in a pyramid. He was getting the grills ready for over a hundred skewers of chicken and just as many skewers of lamb, which would be grilled the next day. The charcoal dust had covered Uncle Verdi's gray hair and happy face, so that from his face, one could not see how tired he was. But his eyes could not hide what his face did. He was exhausted and needed to rest.

While in the kitchen, after talking with Uncle Verdi for a few minutes, I greeted his wife, Houri, who was in charge of setting up several tables for serving tea in the large reception room of the house. Like Uncle Verdi, Houri had also gotten on in years, but she still had a great deal of energy. When she saw me, she laughed, raised her eyebrows, closed her eyes, and said, "I pray to God that nothing untoward will happen tomorrow." Then she left. Her statement made me more anxious, and her laughter confused me. I left the kitchen bewildered.

In a room next to the kitchen, my niece, Neda, was sitting on the floor. There was a large tablecloth spread before her with dozens of sugarloaves on the spread. In those days, sugar usually came in big solid lumps shaped like a cone, usually six inches in diameter and twelve inches high weighing around two pounds each. A cone of sugar was (and still is) called a sugarloaf.

Neda was breaking the sugarloaves into manageable chunks with a small adze and then, using a special pair of scissors, snipping the chunks into cubes. When she saw me, she brought the three middle fingers of her right hand together, kissed them, and blew the kiss toward me. I responded with the same gesture and left. Neda was a love of my life. She was raised to be an independent lady, knowing what needed to be done and willing to do what was required. Her outward beauty reflected the beauty of her soul: pale pink lips accented her flawless complexion, her large brown eyes were kind yet wistful. She was determined, strong-willed, hopeful, with a youthful expectation still alive in her. She was wise beyond her young years, worldly-wise more than "book smart," but also very intelligent.

Elsewhere in the house, people were setting tables with porcelain plates, sterling silver forks and spoons, exquisite crystal glasses, and bone china egg cups. Others were filling up the leaf-shaped salt and pepper shakers and the large crystal sumac dispensers. My aunt was in full control. She oversaw every aspect of the preparations for the big party. Even though Auntie was in her seventies, she was still a forceful manager. She regularly checked everyone to make sure that they had no needs, and she gauged their progress and energized them with words of encouragement. All relatives and friends loved her and followed her instructions with enthusiasm.

Although I usually love such hustle and bustle before a reception, my anxiety and curiosity had excited bitter feelings in me.

It was late afternoon when a boy knocked at the front door. Uncle Verdi opened. The boy told him that Hāji Samad would arrive in ten minutes and left. Uncle Verdi announced in a loud voice that Hāji Samad, the cook, would arrive shortly, and at that, all the women and girls covered their hair with scarves. They had already covered the rest of their bodies with nice, full-body dresses and long, thick cotton socks.

Upon his arrival, Hāji Samad shouted in a loud voice, "Oh God, Oh God," and then he fake-coughed to get everyone's attention. This was a common practice to alert the women and girls that a man outside the circle of close kinship was present. Auntie greeted Hāji Samad and told him how honored she was that he had agreed to be the cook for the next day's festivities. Hāji Samad did not usually cook for parties, he only cooked at his own restaurant, which had several traditional Persian dining rooms and was located in the Tabriz Bazaar. But Dena and Habib's parties were an exception, because Hāji and Habib had an intimate friendship. Habib's Persian carpet showrooms were only a block away from Hāji's restaurant, and they had known each other for decades. They had even traveled together to Mecca and had successfully performed all of the rituals of pilgrimage, thus earning the honorific title of Hāji. Hāji Samad was the best cook in Tabriz. Both he and Habib had impeccable reputations around town.

Hāji Samad was accompanied by a boy in his late teens, and the two went directly toward the kitchen. There were quite a few bags of rice there, which Habib had ordered directly from Rasht, a northern city in Iran, known to produce some of the best long grain rice in the world. Rasht's rice is usually longer grained and fluffier than the best basmati rice. Its grains have a most pleasant aroma, and they are long and slender, bone-colored and identical, and hard and firm under your teeth. Hāji took a small pot, poured enough rice for ten people into it, and then carefully washed the rice, drained it in a colander, and placed it in a cauldron.

When cooking rice, all prominent cooks use rock salt. A master like Hāji Samad was no exception. The teenage boy accompanying him took chunks of rock salt from a large gunny sack and, one at a time, wrapped them in pieces of muslin cloth before handing them over to Hāji, who placed the wrapped pieces among the rice. Hāji and his assistant repeated this process until they had prepared enough rice to be cooked the next day for all guests. By the time they were done, they had filled several cauldrons, eventually covering the rice in each cauldron with cold water until about three and a half inches over the top of rice. Then Hāji Samad set to marinating 150 pounds of lamb fillet, 150 pounds of ground lamb, and 80 chickens in his secret marinade.

The most popular dish in Iran, also known as the national Persian dish, is *chelow kebab*. It is a simple dish, and no matter what, it is almost always delicious. However, when a true expert makes it, it is extraordinary. For us Iranians, nothing is more flavorful and luscious than a good *chelow kebab*, which consists of a plate of steamed, saffroned long-grain rice with a raw egg yolk on top, grilled tomatoes on the side, and two or three pats of butter, complete with a pair of lamb, beef, or chicken kebab skewers. We sprinkle sumac over the kebab, mix the rice with the butter and egg yolk, and eat.

Hāji Samad's *chelow kebab* was known across the country, and he had earned his culinary reputation by word-of-mouth alone. He cooked the tastiest rice, and it was well known that Hāji Samad's kebabs melted in your mouth. All those who visited Tabriz, as tourists or for business, made sure to dine at least once in his restaurant.

When Hāji had prepared everything for the next day, he stood straight, stroked his mustache thoughtfully, and told Auntie, who was keeping him company, that he would return with several assistants, early in the morning the next day, to cook the rice and grill the kebabs.

Auntie thanked him and praised his new assistant. Hāji said that the boy was not his assistant, but his son, and her humble servant.

"It was God's will that, after eight daughters—eight flowers from the Garden of Eden—I become the father of a son who will carry my surname forward to future generations," he said.

Auntie suggested that he sacrifice a sheep in his boy's name and divide its meat entirely among the very poorest families. She said that such a sacrifice would protect his boy against all harm and from all evil. Then she took three dollars out of her purse and gave it to Badri and asked her to give the money to a charity in the name of Hāji's son.

Hāji was very impressed by such generosity. He thanked Auntie, his face beaming with a smile, and said, "This boy will keep my name and reputation alive. Let us hope that, God willing, one hundred years from now, my restaurant still offers the best *chelow kebab* in Iran. For the sake of continuity, I will soon transfer the deed to my restaurant to this boy, my son, the apple of my eye and my heart and soul."

As Hāji was talking about his son, he caught sight of a long-haired, massively built, tabby-colored Persian cat with a round face, sitting on its paws in a corner of the kitchen and watching the platters of meat. Hāji stopped talking about his son, and pointed his forefinger at the cat, and told Auntie and Badri, "Tightly close the door to the cellar, or else, tonight, this clever and shrewd cat might throw a party and invite his friends over for a lavish dinner with an endless supply of meat!"

Then he burst into laughter, and while his gold teeth came into view and his fat belly shook like a willow tree, he said goodbye and left with his son.

# 5

I was killing time in the front yard when Dena called me aside to hand me the dining floor cloths she was holding. These were special calico cloths that we spread on the floor and upon which various food items were laid. The guests sit around them, often crossed legged, and dine. Dena asked me to spread them in the banquet hall and other rooms on the second floor of the house. She told me that she would have more cloths delivered to me upstairs in a few minutes.

I hanged the cloths she gave me over my forearms, and when my hands were free, I gripped hers tightly and said, "Dena darling, I beg you, for God's sake, tell me who the guest is."

Ignoring my plea, Dena simply replied, "Auntie has asked us to spread the floor cloths and tablecloths today. Tomorrow, we are going to be extremely busy. No one can decorate the dining rooms more elegantly than you can. This is one of your fortes. It has always been that way. Use your creative ideas to set up the dessert tables. I know that desserts are your passion. Arrange the dessert pieces for an unforgettable catered look."

She freed her hands gently and smiled. Right then, Auntie passed by. She paused, and Dena winked at her. I opened my mouth to ask her a question, but she did not let me talk.

"Dorna darling, may God sacrifice my humble life for your exalted being," Auntie said. "We have too much to do. Just hurry up." Then she quickly moved away.

Dena walked away as well, and she was not far from me at all when she muttered, "This Guest is too precious for all of us, a lot more than you can imagine."

Carrying all the dining cloths, I climbed the stairs to the second floor. In the upstairs vestibule, a full-length mirror leaned against the wall. It caught me by surprise, and I froze in front of it.

My miserable past had aged me. I was not yet forty, but I looked much older. Looking in the mirror, I saw no trace of the person I once was. Even dyeing my prematurely white hair had not helped me restore my real age.

Only God knows how long I was staring at my reflection when the cuckoo clock on the wall struck the hour. The sound brought me out of my trance. I looked at the clock and its pendulum. I thought that I, too, might be a pendulum, hanging from a doomed and ominous fate.

I made a point never to avoid telling myself home truths: no matter how unpleasant the facts about me were, I tried to accept them. It was my way of coming to terms with the ugliness and bitterness of my life. But there was one exception. I could not accept my name. Dorna, in Farsi, means crane. The long-necked and long-legged bird is a symbol of beauty in Iran, and I got upset each time someone told me that my name befitted my beauty. They did not know that I wished there were a way for me to throw out not only my name, but also my entire past, along my beauty.

Suddenly, I had an urge to take a vase and smash it against the full-length mirror and then go around and shatter all of the other mirrors in the house. However, I knew that it was not the mirror but rather something inside me that I needed to break. I turned away from the mirror and walked toward the banquet hall.

The house was clean and tidy. There were Persian carpets spread in every room, and each carpet, with no exception, was a work of art. I lifted up a corner. The cleaning people had even swept underneath.

I caught sight of a colorful floral carpet colored in lively, joyous greens. The color green agitated me. It reminded me of a life full of serenity and creativity. My sister, Dena, had such a life, and I envied her. Thanks to Mirza Hadi, there was nothing green in my life anymore.

I thought again of the next day's party. It was only two days ago when, in my presence, Habib told Dena that, this party should become the biggest and best they had ever thrown. I Hadn't understood why Habib cared so much about this party, why it needed to be so perfect, and above all, why they wanted to keep me in the dark about the special guest.

Through the window, I heard someone playing a violin. The melody was familiar: I had heard it many times, years ago. The sound came from the neighbor's front yard, and I was curious to see who was playing. The window was placed high up. I was not tall enough to reach it, even on my toes, and all of the chairs, couches, loveseats, and sofas had been moved downstairs in preparation for the party. The banquet hall and all of the other rooms on the second floor had been emptied of furniture.

There was a small storage closet at the end of the hallway. I rushed there and found a wooden ladder, which I leaned against the wall. I climbed it and opened the window. A pleasant breeze caressed my face. Outside, the trees were vibrant, and the wind picked up their red, orange, and gold leaves before depositing them gently on the ground in a spectacular carpet that crunched under the feet of passers-by.

From my vantage point, it was not hard to see the man playing the violin. His back was to me. He had a full head of dense salt-and-pepper hair, and he sat around a table with three other men who listened to his music. He was playing with remarkable skill, and I had no doubt that he was a professional musician, a phenomenal one.

When he had finished playing, he stood up and turned around. I saw his face. I recognized him. Oh my God, it was him—none other than Nima himself. I was overcome with fear. A chill swept over me. My forehead broke out in a cold sweat. I came down the ladder and laid on the floor.

# CHAPTER 2

## FALLING IN LOVE INSTANTLY

### 1

It was 1938, the day of my seventeenth birthday. I was full of jubilant delight, overwhelmed with the unself-conscious arrogance of youth. I was told much more often than I wanted to hear that I was the luckiest person in the world, and God had not created anyone more fortunate than I was. All girls wanted to be me, and I was tired of so many envious glances. I was known to be one of the most beautiful girls in Tabriz. I had long, wavy, luscious, chestnut-brown hair, almond eyes, and a straight, proportional, prominent nose. At that young age, my heart-shaped face, graceful neck, tan complexion, soft skin, full lips, and long legs had made me a sensual, exotic girl. I drew everyone to myself. At times, I felt like people saw me as an innocent young person, and at others, they found me a confident, worldly woman.

In those days, high school was out of the question for most of girls. Parents confined their daughters to their homes, preparing them to be wives and mothers. They told their daughters that a woman's life goal must be to raise healthy and successful children and to help her husband realize his ambitions. An overwhelming majority of parents thought that high school would make their daughters leery of tradition. They were afraid to be accused of raising daughters who were non-worshipers, indecent and impertinent, or even worse—brazen hussies. So instead, they destroyed their daughters' futures and raised them to be sex objects for husbands and to be cooks, house cleaners, washerwomen, caregivers, babysitters, hostesses, and the like.

My father was as different from most as chalk is to cheese. He was a truly broad-minded person for his day. His biggest regret in life was that he did not have formal education beyond elementary school. Nevertheless, he was an extremely well-read person, a self-educated man who had mastered Persian literature and poetry. He followed world politics religiously, and in Tabriz, he was considered to be a patriotic leader, even though he had no official political positions. Masses of people listened to his ideas and attended his lectures. My father was a true activist. To him, my right to higher levels of education was impossible to violate. He did not give a damn what others said about his choice to let me attend high school. He was not afraid of their taunts or of being thought far too permissive.

My older sister, Dena, on the other hand, had no drive to study beyond grade six. She did not fret over lost opportunities, nor did she believe that, for girls, education was a pathway to a brighter future. My father was greatly disappointed at her attitude. But this had not diminished his love for her. Dena was too perfect not to have unlimited and unconditional love of the entire family.

Dena was and still is absolutely beautiful, totally put together, with not a hair out of place. Back then, she dressed with flair, like a conservative woman of means, with her rich and beautiful clothing. If she had become an actress, she would have been a star. She had a beautiful polished smile that lit up her face—with dimples in her cheeks and a slight dimple in her chin—and a set of perfectly straight white teeth.

Naturally, with such attributes, Dena had as many suitors as there are leaves on trees. But none adored or admired her more than Habib. He was the most persistent and had asked for Dena's hand in marriage for two years before my father concluded that he was the right husband for her. Dad was convinced that Habib was a God-loving, trustworthy, and hard-working man. Once I overheard him telling mom that, "Habib is capable of undertaking challenging tasks. He is open-minded, and he is neither passive nor socially apathetic. He has inherited a very large and beautiful house, as well as his father's carpet business, which has a nice, decent showroom in the Tabriz Bazaar. He has been able to maintain the business with competence. I will help him extend his business, and with his perseverance, God-willing, he can soon become a major carpet merchant in Tabriz." Dad had got to know Habib well, and I sometimes wish he would have lived to see his son-in-law become one of the most successful and respected carpet merchants in all of Iran.

I remember the day my father told Dena that he wanted her to marry Habib. Dena was carried away with joy. However, as expected from a dignified and noble girl, she pulled herself together, kissed dad's hand, and told him, "As you wish father, of course! Your wish is my command." For the rest of us, it was a significant moment to see dad's reaction. He held Dena's face between his palms and kissed her on the forehead. We were glad of dad's decision, since all of us, except him, knew that Habib and Dena were already very madly in love.

Dena had made our father understand that she was not interested in high school in a smooth and graceful way, and dad had reluctantly accepted that. However, the situation with my brother, Sina, was different. Sina was prone to vice and depravity, and when father realized that fact, he was forced to remove Sina from high school. This utterly devastated father.

When it came to education, I was dad's sole hope. I alone was able to keep him happy and proud. Every year, I was the student with the highest grade-point average in my class. I was the light of his life.

Being from a rich and prominent family and one of the most beautiful girls in town, I inevitably attracted suitors. It had become a routine for my father to sit down with suitors and their parents, only to announce to them, "Dorna is studying to become well educated so that she can rub shoulders with people of high society—not become a housewife." Once, when a suitor had responded, "What a waste!", dad had angrily thrown him out.

As much as my father loved me and Dena, to him, Sina was something else. He cherished Sina above all others. I cannot imagine a love greater than that of my father's for Sina. And yet, Sina was never ashamed to disgrace my family with his behavior. During the school year, Sina skipped his classes to sneak into the neighbor's orchard, to go skinny-dipping in well, and above all, to gamble.

Sina played the game of Astragals. He joined other gamblers, who gathered at deserted buildings in no-traffic neighborhoods. They all squatted on the ground in a circle facing inward and played that ancient game for money with three astragalus bones, or knuckle bones, found in the ankle of a sheep, goat, or calf. To some extent, these animals' knuckle bones resemble a six-sided unbalanced die, except that two of its sides are rounded, and of the remaining four sides, two sides are broad and two sides are narrow. When an astragalus is tossed, it cannot land on any of the rounded sides. So, there are only four possibilities: to land on one of the two broad sides or on one of the two narrow sides. The game begins by a gambler throwing up three astragalus bones randomly. Depending on which side of each of the astragals come up, of all possible outcomes, only a few are winners and a few are losers. In a large majority of outcomes, the player neither wins, nor loses. Of course, since the knuckle bones are not balanced, the possible outcomes do not occur with equal probabilities.

Playing Astragals, like any other form of gambling, was reproachable and deserved rebuke. But it was an addictive game, and addicts were constantly faced with a severe temptation to play. Some pathological gamblers had lost all of their wealth and had incurred substantial debt through Astragals. Every time someone reported to my father that Sina had been seen playing Astragals, it was like a dagger through dad's heart.

In reality, my father's house was a mansion, but he did not like it referred to as mansion, so we all called it a house. It had a huge front yard comprised of many islands with flowers, shrubs, and trees. A small stream wound through the entire length of the beautifully manicured grounds. Adjacent to our house was an orchard with hundreds of mixed fruit trees. A nine-foot stone wall had been erected at the boundary line between the two properties. When the stream met the wall, a small circular opening allowed the water to pass through.

Every week day, my father went to work, and whenever my brother knew that my mother was away from home, he would skip school with some of his friends, and they would enter the front yard of the house covertly and follow the stream toward the opening. Then they would crawl through the opening to the neighbor's orchard, where they ate freely from the fruit that grew there. Occasionally, the caregiver of the orchard saw the kids and followed them. If he caught one, he grabbed him by the ears and dragged him down to the front gate. But if the caregiver caught my brother, he continued to drag him along all the way to my father's chamber in the Bazaar. It made my father angry that his only son skipped school, trespassed on the neighbor's property, and stole fruit from the orchard. Dad would yell at Sina, and when he was finished, he would sigh and say something like, "You, wicked idiot, I have set my hope on you to replace me someday. What a desperate and forlorn hope!"

There was also a mill near our house, and behind it was a fifteen-foot-deep well whose water was used to run it. In the summer afternoons, especially between noon and four o'clock, there were always a bunch of teenagers playing by the well. These were exactly the types of kids that my father did not want Sina to hang out with. Regardless, Sina frequented the well and kept playing with those kids. The boys would take turns skinny-dipping in the well, where he and the other boys, one at a time, would get their wrists fastened with rope and would take turns lowering each other down into the ice-cold water of Tabriz. As you might imagine, this activity was dangerous and once in a while an accident occurred, sometimes ending tragically.

Sina failed seventh grade, was held back, and then failed that grade for a second time. After that, my father accepted that Sina would never be an educated person. So, he took him out of school altogether and, at that young age, put him to work full time as an aide, errand boy, and performer of odd jobs. By working for my father from childhood, it was almost guaranteed that Sina would learn all aspects of dad's business and that eventually he would take full control over its operation. When Sina turned nineteen, dad made him marry and start a family. Father thought that Sina's profound responsibilities at work and his obligations to his wife would leave him no time to get into trouble.

# 2

On the morning of my seventeenth birthday, I stepped out of the house and set off for school. I walked through several interconnected narrow alleys until I reached the main public square of Tabiz, a huge plaza with the spectacular municipal building at its center. The clock tower chimed eight O'clock.

That morning, the square was crowded. My school was at the other side of the plaza, and it was impossible for me to walk through such a crowd to get there. I asked why so many people were present at the plaza, but nobody answered.

A man standing farther away overheard me and came over. He explained that two men were thrashing each other violently with vicious blows to the body. They were knocking one another on the head, face, and neck and insulting each other with the most obscene language.

I asked why no one intervened. The man shook his head and replied, "Not only is no one trying to stop them, but the crowd is instigating trouble. They are nasty trouble makers, cheering the fighters on, saying things like, hit the 'son of a bitch' in the face, scratch the 'son of a whore's' eyeballs out, and punch the 'bastard' in the nose." The man then apologized for repeating the indecent language.

In those years, Azerbaijan was in a state of disorder and confusion and many people wanted the province to remain that way. It was very different from the heroic rebellions of past and future Azerbaijanis, which were for freedom and democracy in Iran, against the royalist dictatorship and foreign domination. At that time, the common people found the chaos entertaining. In particular, they got very excited whenever there was a brawl. My ignorant townsmen could not understand the implications of civil unrest and its unpredictable consequences.

The crowd suddenly seemed to double, then triple. People were pushing each other hard, and the situation was becoming dangerous. But I was determined to get to the other side of the plaza, no matter what. I did not want to be tardy or miss my first class, a two-hour-long math class. My classmates would lend me their notes, but it was hard to figure out everything from their notes alone. Plus, if I borrowed them, then I would owe them a favor in return, and I hated to owe anything to anyone.

I was standing there, watching the enormous crowd and thinking about the impossibility of estimating how many people were there, when someone called me by my last name, "Miss Moin-al-Tojjar!" I turned my head toward the voice. It was an elderly man in his late sixties or early seventies standing at the threshold of his shop. When I looked at him, he motioned me into his store. I rushed toward him but hesitated to enter. I had never entered a store by myself. For shopping, I was always with my mother, my father, or with our houseman, Mashdi. But I realized that if the crowd continued to grow at the rate that it was, I could get trampled.

"Miss Moin-al-Tojjar, please don't be a stranger," the shop owner said. "Come inside, avoid the crowd."

It was a notion store but carried stationery as well. The shop owner looked very familiar, and I recognized him as Hāji Morad, whom I had seen at my father's Ramadan parties.

Ramadan is the ninth month of Muslim year, during which time Muslims fast every day from the first light of dawn—almost ninety minutes before sunrise—until sunset. Shortly after sunset, they have an early supper at the end of the day of fasting. Every year, my father gave a big party during Ramadan and invited all prominent merchants and shop owners of Tabriz to our house for the early supper.

Two Ramadans ago, during my father's party, Dena and I stood in the vestibule and peeped through the curtain into the dining room. There, Hāji Morad caught our attention by eating with his right-hand fingers. He had put his fork and spoon aside and instead used his hand to take pieces of meat, mix them with some rice, press the mixture to make it lumpy, and put it in his mouth. After chewing each mouthful, he licked all five fingers clean. Dena and I had fun watching him, and each time he licked his fingers, we burst into laughter.

Inside the shop, Hāji Morad pushed a stool toward me and said, "Please sit down, my daughter. Make yourself at home."

I sat down, and while he fingered his worry beads, Hāji Morad said, "Your grandfather of blessed memory showed a paternal interest in me. He was the one who paid for the goodwill of this shop. I could never afford it on my own. I owe him my life. He took me under his wing and supported me until I was able to become the breadwinner of my family, God bless his soul. He then helped me start that family."

Hāji Morad knew that the time was not right for such talks. However, since he wanted me to feel comfortable, he was talking uninterruptedly and, while talking, sputtered saliva, and that made me feel sick to my stomach. I avoided looking at him directly.

"The prospects are bleak," he continued. "It is a dangerous situation. Stay here until the police are able to disperse the crowd. Make yourself comfortable."

I liked Hāji Morad. He was so appreciative of what my grandfather had done for him. My parents had taught me to be careful about the people who bite the hands that feed them. But Hāji Morad was not one of them.

A large number of army troops arrived in the plaza to quell the disorder. In Tabriz, policemen did not carry guns; they only had a baton for self-defense and for keeping the peace. There was no way for the police to end the turmoil with batons. Bringing in the troops was the only way to disperse the people and restore peace.

The hard-handed soldiers at the scene demonstrated a stunning show of force. They fired warning shots into the air and hit the crowd hard with the butts of their rifles. To scare people away, they took a few into custody.

Hāji Morad had locked the shop. Through the half-glass door, we could see outside. We heard loud bangs, the sounds of gunshots. I trembled; I had turned as pale as death, and Hāji Morad told me calming and encouraging words.

Soon, people scattered, and within fifteen minutes of arriving, the soldiers had cleared the plaza and its surroundings. Hāji Morad waited a little longer before unlocking his shop door.

I rose from the stool and was ready to leave, when an incredibly handsome young man in his early twenties, carrying a briefcase, entered the shop and exchanged warm greetings with Hāji Morad. The young man was tall and stood straight, I quickly forgot all of the drama of that morning. My fear disappeared.

Suddenly, he turned around, and our eyes met. His large, ocean-blue eyes ignited a feeling that was unknown to me until that moment. I immediately looked away. I knew that what had happened between me and that majestically handsome man was not a mere passing glance; it was a bolt of lightning that had struck me square in the heart.

I was at an age where I naturally spent a great deal of time thinking about sex. However, up until that moment, I had never lusted after a real person. The men of my fantasies were imaginary, virile men. Of course, talking about such topics was as taboo as it could get. But my fantasies were my own private possessions, and they were not anyone's business to know. Since they occurred naturally and were out of my control, I was not ashamed of them.

That day, in Hāji Morad's shop, for the first time in my life, I felt lust for a real man. My body ached. Was it just lust or was I in love? It was too soon even to think about it. Nothing, not even the most intense lascivious fantasies, had so aroused my desire.

I was in a state of shock, standing there, frozen and dazzled, gazing at this young man. His condition was no different. He stared back, stunned and speechless.

Dripping with sweat, I saw myself in a wall mirror that was hanged in the shop, my face, ears, and neck had become red in color.

Suddenly, the sound of Hāji Morad's voice reverberated throughout the shop.

"Good morning, Mr. Nima!" he said. "I bet you need reed pen, inkpot, and ink."

Then, without waiting for a response, Hāji Morad pulled off of various shelves in his shop a reed pen, an inkpot, a glass-container filled with black ink, and a sheaf of wax paper and put them on the counter and said, "God bless your father, Mr. Nima, you always remind me of him."

Mr. Nima smiled, thanked Hāji Morad, and put all that he had purchased in his brown leather briefcase. After he paid, he shook Hāji Morad's hand, and left.

I was already very late for school, but I lingered in the shop, hoping that Hāji Morad might tell me something about Mr. Nima.

"May God bless Mr. Nima's father," Hāji Morad said. "He was a famous calligrapher." He pointed to a beautiful calligraphy art piece on a scroll mounted to the wall. "The calligrapher who wrote this was Mr. Nima's father. He was a true artist. Mr. Nima is also a superior calligrapher. He has inherited his calligraphy and painting talents from his father. He teaches arts, namely, calligraphy, painting, and music, at a vocational school."

I looked closely at the calligraphy piece that Hāji Morad had pointed to. In that beautiful hand-written piece, what attracted me the most was a poem by Hafez. Hafez (sometimes written Hafiz) is without a doubt the greatest Persian poet ever. His poems are the pinnacles of Persian literature. The poem written on the scroll read:

> A thousand breaches in my faith, with Thy dark eye-lashes, Thou hast made:[2]

---

[2] *The Divan-i Hafiz*, translated by H. Wilberforce Clarke (Bethesda, Maryland: Ibex Publishers Inc., 2007), p. 642.

Come, so that, out on account of Thy languishing eye, a
Thousand pains, I may pluck.
Ho O fellow-sitter of my heart from Whose memory, friends have
passed:
Not a day be mine, the moment when, void of recollection of
Thee, I sit.

My watch told me that I had already missed the first hour of my math class, and that I would be late for the second hour. I thanked Hāji Morad and left, heading toward school.

The road to school felt difficult. My legs were weak, and my heart beat like crazy. Why was my heart suddenly pounding so hard, so fast, and so loud? Is this a sign of love? I thought. Does love actually occur at first sight? The Hafez poem that I had just read was lodged in my brain. It was as if Hafez had written it for this exact moment of my life.

I finally made it to school and found my math class. The math teacher hated tardy students. She had once said ominously, that for tardy students, she would become "a nightmare their mother had never told them." She looked daggers at me and told me to go sit down. I was relieved. It was the first time I could remember her not embarrassing a student for tardiness. In that moment, I realized that she had a great deal of respect for me.

All day in class, my mind wandered. The teacher was talking about the derivatives of algebraic polynomials under a radical sign ($\sqrt{\phantom{x}}$). I knew that if a perfect square, such as 25 or 49 is under a radical, then we can get rid of the radical. For example, $\sqrt{25}$ is 5 and $\sqrt{49}$ is 7. However, if a prime number is under the radical, then the radical can never be removed.

I was like a prime number, hung up on the radical of those angry ocean-blue eyes of Nima's, a radical that could never be struck out.

The teacher was writing algebraic functions on the board and finding their derivatives. But, to me, they were not math, they were poems expressing my raging love toward a man whom I had seen for mere moments. I felt like I was floating on a chunk of wood in a stormy ocean, and for the remainder of class, my mind was caught in violent waves, struggling to survive and resisting to drown.

On school days, after regular dismissal, I usually walked home with friends from my neighborhood. But that day, I wanted to be alone! I did not want to talk with anyone. I needed to think about the new world that I had just wandered into. So, when class was over, I left school quickly and headed home.

Nima's eyes and physique had made my heart smolder. The whole world seemed dazzling, as if I had entered into heaven, the endless heaven with birds that sing sweet love songs among the branches.

All of a sudden, I found myself in front of our house. How I got there, I could not say. I knocked at the door, but no one answered. I knocked again, this time much louder, but nobody heard the knock this time either. Between the front gate and the first courtyard of our house was an eight-cornered foyer, which, for simplicity, we named using its geometric term, the Octagonal. Every school day, before my return home, Mashdi sat in the Octagonal waiting for me to knock. This was the first time that he had not opened the door. I began to worry. Mashdi was an old man in his seventies . . . "God forbid!" I murmured. There was nothing for me to do but to keep knocking, hoping that Mashdi would open the door.

Our house had three interconnected courtyards, all of which were completely enclosed by the walls and separated by large, heavy doors. The first courtyard was small about a half-acre, and consisted of three rooms, which were at Mashdi's disposal. He lived in one of them, and, whenever he had guests, they stayed in the spare rooms. Mashdi was in charge of the security of our house. For that reason, he cared about the security of the first courtyard more than that of the other two. The only way to enter our house was through the entrance door, which led visitors to the Octagonal and then into the first courtyard. He kept the entrance door closed, except when we had a public ceremony.

The second courtyard was much larger than the first. It had several huge rooms, a gigantic kitchen, and an assembly hall especially built for ceremonies commemorating the religious saints and holy figures, as well as social and political gatherings. Since my father was wealthy and highly respected, the people of the town expected him to hold cultural and religious ceremonies, and dad never hesitated to do so. When he did, we closed the door between the second courtyard and the third, where there was our mansion, the gardens, the creek, and all that I mentioned before.

I waited nearly forty-five minutes for Mashdi to open the door. I was disappointed that mom had not yet noticed that I was not home, because if she had, she would have asked Mashdi about my whereabouts, and consequently would have opened the door. I was tired of standing up for such a long time, so I went to sit down on one of the stone benches at the front of our house.

As I sat, I caught sight of a man staring at me from afar. I immediately stood up to get a better look. A dagger stabbed through my heart. My God, it was him, Nima, standing there, holding his brown leather briefcase. It was easy to figure out how he had found me. In the morning, he had followed me from Hāji Morad's shop to school, and in the afternoon, he must have followed me from school to my house. My God, how long had he stood there staring at me? Was he crazy? No, of course not; he was in love, also, and that is what love does to people. He knew where I lived and which school I attended: I was walking on air.

At last, I heard the door behind me open. I turned around. It was Mashdi.

"What a time to open the door!" I cried.

Mashdi thought I was angry at him. He panicked and started stuttering, "So, so, sorry, my la, lay, lady!" He had developed circles under his eyes, and his cheeks had sunk. He explained that he had taken a pill without knowing that it had a soporific effect. Poor Mashdi, he could never know why I yelled at him. No way would I have done that to him under normal circumstances. I loved him dearly, but I also wanted to stand there and watch Nima for as long as possible, and Mashdi had interrupted that.

"Mr. Mashdi, Mashdi dear, how do you feel?" I cried again. Mashdi was bewildered. Without waiting for his response, I passed into the house. I crossed the first courtyard quickly. When I got to the second courtyard, I could hear my mom and my Auntie talking to each other. They were engrossed in conversation; no wonder mom had not noticed that I had not gotten home yet. In the air was the sweet aroma of halva.

I found mom and Auntie in the kitchen, where a humongous copper cooking tray had been placed on the wood-burning stove. The tray was full of flour mixed with butter, and the two stood there taking turns stirring the mixture with a large whisk. My mother and Auntie always cooked plain halva made of a mixture of flour, butter, and sugar, flavored with rosewater and saffron. Halva is usually served during a funeral and the consequent seventh-day and fortieth-day religious ceremonies following the burial. It has religious significance, and it is usually served in all religious ceremonies and functions.

Near the stove, on the floor, there was a circular hole that was six feet diagonal and two feet deep. Such holes existed in some traditional aristocratic houses and were called, *basins of fire*. Our cook had loaded the middle of the hole with wood, leaving space for air circulation and room for flames to dance around. He had made a red, hot fire and had put gigantic iron pots on the fire to cook some dishes for the next day.

"Salaam," I said.

Auntie turned, her face wreathed in smile. She gave me a tight hug, planted a big resounding kiss on each of my cheeks, and said, "Salaam, Aloha, Bonjour, and Salute, all together to the lady of all the ladies."

Mom broke in, "Hurry up, Dorna! We need to add sugar and saffron to the roux. Go put your books and other stuff in your room and come back quickly to help."

"Our little beauty just returned home. She is tired," Auntie said. "Let her catch her breath and refresh herself. There is a fresh pot of tea on the top of the samovar. Let her have a cup of tea, it will perk her up." She held my hands in hers as she spoke. "Such fine, delicate, and dainty hands are too good for such a task as stirring flour in the pan. Such flushed cheeks, such a gentle and delightful face, which is softer than the softest rose petals—isn't it a shame that it be placed next to the fire to sweat? No, my dear sister-in-law, it is too soon for Dorna Darling to smell of burning wood."

Auntie hugged and kissed me again.

"We will not let you marry just any man who appears in your life," she went on. "The successful suitor will be the one who can afford to hire one hundred butlers, houseboys, and maids, all at your service, bowing to you day and night."

I smiled at Auntie and left the kitchen. Down the hall, I could still hear her saying, "We will not let her marry an ordinary man, not even if he is rich and distinguished, not to someone who lives far away, but to the richest, to the most noble, to the one who worships her beauty and charm…"

I got to my room, locked the door, and laid down on my sofa.

"Why does mom want me to learn how to cook halva?" I wondered aloud. "Does she think that I have a dreary life ahead of me and that someday I will need to cook halva for the death of all my dreams and aspirations?"

I needed to divert my attention from such dark thoughts. I began to think about Nima. Nima, with those angry ocean-blue eyes, was the sexiest man I had ever seen. In seconds, he was all that was on my mind. I was enamored with him. I wanted to embrace him and, with a preternatural strength, press his body against mine. I was overwhelmed with desire, and my body yearned for his touch.

I stayed in my room for a long while thinking about my love and future, humming to myself a poem of Hafez, which best described my psychic state:

> How happily Thou madest prey of my heart! Of Thy intoxicated eye, I boast:
> For, better than this, the wild birds, a person taketh not.[3]

# 3

Over the next month, I saw Nima almost every day. When I set off for school in the mornings, he would be waiting for me across the street and would follow me all the way, walking about fifteen feet behind. All day in class, I would have trouble concentrating: Nima was the only thing on my mind. He waited for me at the end of the school day, too, a couple of blocks away at a newsstand—he did not want to attract the suspicions of the other students. I would pass the newsstand on my way home, and again he would follow me all the way.

In the late evening, when I was alone in my room, I often drifted into fantasy. Not all of my fantasies were about sex, but when they were, Nima was always the man, the partner, and as ridiculous as it seemed, I always imagined him as my husband, to avoid any temptation to sin. I knew how easily one could get trapped into sinful actions. Wasn't that what happened to Adam and Eve?

---

[3] *The Divan-i Hafiz*, translated by H. Wilberforce Clarke, p. 289.

Years later, I read in Salinger's *The Catcher in the Rye* that a "woman's body is like a violin and all, and that it takes a terrific musician to play it right.[4]" After I read this, I realized that, way back then I had imagined Nima's body like a violin. I was the musician who played it, even though it took me a great deal of practice before I could play it like the terrific musician Salinger had in mind.

Nima always carried his brown briefcase with his right hand and always wore the same suit, which was not new, but it was clean and ironed. He never spoke to me, he just followed me all the way back and forth between my house and my school. He never came too close, either. It was as if he was an angel God had sent to watch out for me.

Even though we had never been formally introduced, we had made each other's acquaintance by gazing deep into each other's eyes. I had gotten used to having him walk behind me, and that presence had caused me to love him even more. Not knowing anything about his character, I idolized this man. To me, he was the second coming of Joseph, the eleventh of Jacob's twelve sons. In my culture, the prophet Joseph (known as Yūsuf) was an epitome of physical beauty and inner virtue. Nima's extraordinary, masculine good looks were identical to what has been attributed to Joseph. Perhaps Nima's resemblance to Joseph's physical traits had made me conclude that Nima was as exalted and as noble as Joseph. Did Nima really possess all these virtues? Was love revealing to me the truth about his character? Nothing ever hinted otherwise.

My school friends had left me alone. They knew that something was happening in my life, but they did not know what. They had decided that I could manage my issues if I was left to my own devices. While in class, all day, I was looking forward to the end of the school day to walk home by myself followed by Nima, who had a chasing competition with my shadow.

One morning, eager to see him, with my books under my arms, I walked out to the street. Nima was standing in his usual spot. Normally, he waited for me to pass by before he began following behind. But on that morning, he came forward and stood right in front of me.

---

[4] J.D. Salinger, *The Catcher in the Rye.* (New York: Little, Brown and Company, 1951), p. 104.

Calm and composed, Nima greeted me with a smile. My heart began to race. My hands shook. I didn't respond. My tongue couldn't move.

"Would you permit me to say something?" he asked. "Only a few words!"

I was in a state of shock. I looked down at my feet. I was afraid to look into his eyes, those angry ocean-blue eyes that could set the sky on fire. Who was I to resist them?

I swallowed my saliva, and in a firm voice, loud and clear, I told him, "I have no interest in what you want to say." Then I walked away.

When I had gained some distance, I came to my senses. My behavior had been inappropriate; in fact, it had been awful. I had violated my own principles. Prior to this encounter with Nima, I always thought that I was different from traditional girls and women, that I was a liberal thinker, free to strive for whatever my heart desired. Not even once had I believed or assumed that men were superior to women. Gender equality was embedded in the very fabric of my being. Even in my dreams and fantasies, I was consistently equal to men, if not superior to them. It had never been my body but *Nima's* body that was like the violin, and *I* the terrific musician who played it.

But in reality, I had proved to be as traditional as a girl gets. I was no Forugh Farrokhzād and nothing like the ones I adored during the later years of my life—Simone de Beauvoir, Eva Perón, and Virginia Woolf. I was a coward; I hurt a man I loved so passionately out of my concern for people's perceptions of me.

People already gossiped about me for daring to attend high school. If the news spread that I also had a boyfriend, I would have lost face in the whole town and brought disgrace upon my family. Our society vehemently disapproved of any relation between boys and girls, and I was ashamed that I could not stand up to such a stigma. At a crucial time, when I'd had a chance to act courageously, I bowed to backward traditions.

I should have known that, sooner or later, Nima would come forward and talk to me. I should have prepared for that moment, which I hadn't. But it was strange that Nima had waited as long as he had before trying to talk to me. What had he been waiting for?

Both of us had behaved childishly. Nima and I were playing a game, and since I was still only an adolescent and madly in love with him, I was having fun. Nima, on the other hand, was twenty-three and a teacher; he should have behaved more maturely. Following me back and forth between my house and my school for a whole month had been silly, too. Where was the pleasure in such chases day after day?

# 4

The walk to school was a blur. I do not know how I got there, but when I came to, I was sitting in my mathematics class.

No matter how hard I tried to concentrate, I couldn't. My mind wandered for the whole hour. At the start of my second class, I made up an excuse that I had abdominal pains, and my teacher let me go out right away. I went directly toward the trees in my school's yard and sat on the bench under the shade of an acacia tree. I tried to think logically. I thought that I had wounded Nima's pride with my arrogance. All he wanted was to tell me a few words, and I had not given him the opportunity to say what he had on his mind. I had behaved impolitely, and it was below the dignity of a well-mannered person, such as myself, to be so uncivil. I decided to undo my big blunder by acknowledging to Nima that my conduct on that morning lacked basic etiquette. I would apologized, and I was sure that Nima would forgive me, because he loved me. This decision put my mind at ease.

I attended the rest of my classes, and in the afternoon, when the school bell rang to dismiss us for the day, I left in a rush.

"Dorna, how is your abdominal pain, did it go away?" my best friend, Atoosa, called behind me. I pretended not to hear her, and I hurried to the newsstand, where Nima usually waited. But he was not there. My heart sank, and I had a sudden heavy feeling in the pit of my stomach. I began walking very slowly, hoping he would come, telling myself he must have been tied up with some important task. Otherwise, how could he forget his love?

As I walked, I looked behind me, and I stopped from time to time in front of different stores, pretending that I was window shopping. I took as much time as possible, and as I got closer and closer to my house,

I grew more and more disappointed. What if my worst nightmare comes true and Nima never comes to see me again?

I was immersed in such thoughts when a gypsy woman stopped me. Her bracelets and bangles jingled.

"My lady, your beauty reminds me of Venus," she said to me. "You walk just like an ambling partridge. Let me tell your fortune. I can tell you when the champion jockey of your dreams will finally sprint to you."

I responded that she was a day late and began to walk away. She followed me and grabbed my skirt. I turned around and saw a little child in a bag that was fastened to her back. The child was asleep. I gave the gipsy a coin, and she grabbed my wrist and said, "Don't run wild, my swift gazelle." Then she recited a poem of Hafez:

> ARISE, oh Cup-bearer, rise! and bring[5]
> To lips that thirsting the bowl they praise,
> For it seemed that love was an easy thing,
> But my feet have fallen on difficult ways.

The poem shook me. I pulled my wrist away and dragged myself home, exhausted.

# 5

That night, when Auntie said goodnight to everyone and went to sleep, I followed her to the guest room and asked her to sleep in my room. She had been cooking halva with mom all afternoon, and she had prepared pottage for twenty-five poor families to fulfill a vow she had made to God. Even though she was exhausted from all the hard work, she could not say no to me. I helped her carry her bedding to my room on the second floor.

In those days, we did not use beds. Except for my parents, everyone slept on mattresses made by sewing fabric together and filling the whole with cotton. Additionally, we each had a quilt and pillow, both stuffed with soft goose feathers. There were luxurious Persian carpets spread in

---

[5] Gertrude Bell, *The Hafez Poems of Gertrude Bell* (Bethesda, Maryland: Iranbooks, Inc., 1995), p. 65.

every room of the house, and at night, we carried the bedding pieces to the center of our bedrooms and spread them on the carpets. In the morning, when we woke, we triple-folded our quilts and mattresses, and, along with the pillows and bed sheets, wrapped them in special wrappers. We then put them inside a closet or in a corner of our rooms.

Auntie and I spread out our bedding pieces next to each other. Auntie said that her whole body ached. She prayed to fall asleep fast. Her prayer came true and soon, she was fast asleep and snoring softly.

I was not able to sleep. Nima had left me, and along with him, so had sleep. I tossed and turned in my bed for hours. It must have been insanity to have not seized that moment and grasped the opportunity to converse with my love. What else could it be? For a long time, I struggled with a vicious cycle of meandering thoughts about Nima, our love, and about my unforgivable behavior toward him. I could not break the cycle.

I crawled out of bed and sat down beside Auntie's mattress. I began watching her face. The moonlight illuminated her thin and bony face, a face that was pockmarked by smallpox scars. Without these scars, she would have been a very beautiful lady.

I wanted her to help me, even though she, herself, had never fallen in love with a man and could not probably understand how it was to be in love, especially so intensely. Auntie had been married once, to her best friend Taji's husband, Hāji Darab. Taji had had a daughter, whom she loved more than anyone and anything in the world. On her deathbed, she asked Auntie to marry her husband, Hāji Darab, after she was gone. She told Hāji Darab and Auntie that her worst nightmare was that her daughter be trapped at the hands of a wicked stepmother. She was absolutely sure that Auntie would give her child exactly the same kind of love and attention that she, herself, gave. Auntie and Hāji Darab honored Taji's wish, and they got married after Taji passed away. They had enormous respect for each other, but there was no love between them. Hāji Darab was still shackled by Taji's love even after her death, and Auntie had no problem with that. Auntie came to love Taji's daughter at least as much as she loved her own three daughters.

Auntie was the kindest person I knew. All her friends and relatives trusted her, and she was privy to their secrets, which she never shared with others. For that reason, she was known to be the keeper of secrets.

Until that time, I had no secrets to share with anyone. But at that point, I badly needed a confidant. I had to divulge my love story to someone so that I could lessen the burden of secrecy on my soul. It was clear to me that Auntie was my only choice. No one was more trustworthy than her.

Auntie stirred awake and sat up in her bed. She did not seem to realize that I had been watching her. She asked me to take the pitcher from the tray on the ledge and pour her a glass of water. Her mouth and throat were both dry as a bone, she said. I brought her a glass of water, which she swallowed in one gulp. She handed me the empty glass and laid down. I sat beside her mattress again and asked her to tell me a story.

"It is no time for stories, Dorna dear," she replied. "Go to bed and try to sleep. Plus, you are not a child anymore. You are old enough to tell stories yourself."

At that, I burst into tears. I had badly needed to cry. Auntie sat up again.

"How long have you been in love? Who is the lucky man?"

I said that I was not in love.

"The face is the index of the mind. Who is the man, my dear?"

"His name is Nima," I confessed. "He is an arts teacher and a calligrapher."

"So, he wields the reed pen, and as Americans say, the pen is mightier than the sword. It looks like this guy, Nima, cut into your heart by the nib of his pen and left a beautifully penned calligraphic word, *love*." Auntie did not have formal education, but she spoke intelligently, and I loved it when she waxed poetic. Listening to her calmed me, but I was still in tears.

"Dorna darling," she went on, "under the circumstances, you need to be wise as an owl and forget about Nima altogether. That is in your best interest, and I will help you as much as I can. I am sure that there will be many men in your life. You should not think that Nima is 'the one.'"

"No, Auntie, I cannot forget Nima. It is totally impossible. Wasn't it Hafez who said that when love appeared, it set the universe on fire? If that is what love does to the universe, who am I to resist it?"

Auntie got out of bed and walked to the window. She gazed at the night sky and shook her head dolefully.

"A horrendous storm is on its way," she said, "and I can hear the wind howl and the sound of howling from your brother, who is infuriated with you for falling in love. Now, tell me, what is more innocent and more natural than love? Our men, these paper tigers and cardboard cavaliers, treat us as anvils for their hammers. Yes, their blind zeal does harm to us, and their might often overcomes our right; however, until a time when our social might equals theirs, we will grin and bear the situation, but we will not give in to their demands. Love knows hidden paths, and a fence between makes love keener."

That night, I saw a part of Auntie that I hadn't seen before. I was impressed that she was aware that women all over the world struggled for social freedom and equality with men. It was unusual for a woman of her age to have deep sympathy for such movements.

# 6

All night, my tears fell into the lap of the night, until light flowed in the veins of darkness, the stars disappeared one after another, and the day shone from behind the mountain tops. My mattress was soaked through with all my crying.

On my way to school and back, I looked everywhere for Nima. Every time I heard footsteps behind me, I turned around hoping to see him. But I had no such luck. At times, my heart kept pounding so hard that I was scared it would come out of my chest.

I spent the day waiting for bed time, so that I could pour my heart out to Auntie again. Time passed slowly; the minutes felt like hours. At last, when it was time for bed, Auntie told me a long and exciting story. She was not tired anymore and was fresh and animated. In the story, a powerful king of a vast country had a daughter with a beauty that words fail to describe, the kind that, in the language of Shakespeare, "provoketh thieves sooner than gold." This princess had countless suitors from the nearest lands to the farthest, suitors who sent her large quantities of gold and precious jewels loaded on camels. However, the princess was madly in love with an ordinary man, tall and handsome, masculine and muscular, whom she had seen only for a few minutes from a distance. For that reason, she rejected all those noble and rich suitors, creating a riddle for everyone in the court of the king.

In the story, a wise and canny counselor of the king solved the riddle. He ordered a search for the man with whom the princess was in love, and after finding him, they put him in solitary confinement and tortured and starved him. Then in his wretched condition, they covered him in turmeric to make him look jaundiced and dressed him in an elegant white suit. When he was ready, the court minister informed the princess that they had located her love and that he was in the court. The princess was overjoyed. But when they brought the wretched man before her, he was everything but what she had imagined. There were no traces in him of the handsome man he had been. Utterly disappointed, the princess rejected him and, without saying a word, left the room. The man, who had no clue what was going on, was transferred to a dungeon, and one night, when he was in a deep sleep, they severed his jugular vein with a dagger, killing him instantly.

Despite how depressing the story was, Auntie impersonated the characters beautifully. I realized that, with this story, Auntie was trying to make me understand, indirectly, that if I insist on marrying Nima, I would be putting his life in real danger. A few days later, she repeated this message more bluntly: if my father and Sina, my brother, find that they are at the end of their tether, she told me, they would be capable of killing Nima.

# 7

Nima had disappeared altogether. It was as if he had metamorphosed into a drop of rain and was absorbed into the earth. I missed him so much, and it was frustrating that I could do nothing about it. I missed his brown briefcase, his ironed suit, his begging looks, and his footsteps behind me.

Sixteen days after I last saw Nima, while I was walking to school, a young boy almost ran me over with his bicycle. He was pedaling fast and had to break hard to avoid hitting me head on. He did swipe my leg, which caused me to drop my books. The boy laid his bike down, collected my things, put them together nicely, and handed them to me. Then he got on his bike and pedaled away.

A moment later, he came pedaling back. There was a letter inside the book with the green cover, he told me. Before I could say anything, he pedaled away again.

I froze. I was stunned that a child would give me a love letter. I saw Mashdi going home carrying fresh sesame breads.

"Mashdi, do you know that boy?"

"Yes," Mashdi replied. "That boy is Nasr, Mr. Mobin's son. He lives in the neighborhood."

"Did you note how impolite and reckless he was? Stupid roughneck boy!"

"Lady Dorna, I do not know what is wrong with him today. He is usually a well-mannered boy."

We each continued on our ways. As soon as there was no one around, I opened the book with the green cover. Inside was a fancy envelope. I lifted the seal and took out the letter. The beauty of the handwriting left me no doubt—the letter was from Nima.

*Greetings, greetings to the angel of all beauties, to the matchless beauty, the likes of which have never nor will ever set foot on this earth.*

*My beloved, my darling, I have so much to tell you. So much that even if all the reed straws in the world are cut and converted to reed pens and all the oceans are dried and filled with ink, I still would not have enough ink or enough pens to write all that I want to say. To describe my love and my longing for you, and my anguish at the possible outcomes of our relation with each other, I would need a blank book with limitless pages. In this short note, I cannot even allude to a brief account of our rousing and sensational love story.*

*From the moment that our eyes met in Hāji Morad's store, I have been restless. Tranquility has turned against me. In a nutshell, I am just crazy about you! Your love has astounded, disoriented, and dumbfounded me. Your glances have burned me. For you, I did what I thought I would never do for anyone: I spent hours waiting for you in the streets and hours following you around. You made me understand what love is, what it means, how it feels. Your love has given meaning to my life. Without you, I am no one and nothing, I do not even exist. With you I am somebody, and I adore my existence.*

*My beloved, do not leave my letter unanswered. Nasr, Mr. Mobin's son, is an honest and trustworthy messenger. He will visit you again. Please do not keep me waiting. Remember what the great American poet Ralph Waldo Emerson wrote: "How much of human life is lost in waiting."*

*I do not say goodbye, because you are always with me, day and night.*

*Love with all my body and soul combined,*

*Nima*

When I finished reading, it dawned on me: I had found my lost love, the love of my life. I kissed the letter, folded it and placed it back inside the envelope. Then I put the envelope inside one of my books and rushed toward my school.

# 8

That is how I received my first letter from Nima. The messenger, Nasr, whom I had despised so much, was endeared in my heart. The beauty of Nima's handwriting and his enchanting prose made me want to frame the letter. But where would I hang the frame? I did not even know where to hide the letter so that it did not come into the wrong person's possession. I was terrified that my father or my brother, Sina, might learn about it. "If that happens, they will debilitate me in every way that they can imagine." I thought. "They will make my worst nightmare come true by withdrawing me from school and consigning me to a homebound life."

Our maid had a habit of poking her nose into everyone's affairs. She was also a kiss-up. She loved to report to my father even the slightest misdeeds. I was sure that when she came to clean my room, she would check everything, even the pockets of my clothes. A natural place to hide the letter was under the carpet in my room. However, she dusted under the carpet regularly, making it impossible for me to hide anything there. Dreading that our busybody maid might find it, I decided to carry the letter with me everywhere inside one of my books.

# 9

Now when I left the house, I looked for Nasr, who brought me love letters from Nima regularly. I had yet to respond to any of them. Whether consciously or unconsciously, I did not want to put anything in writing. For a girl to write a love letter was a notorious profanity, and I was cautious not to leave behind any evidence for something that society considered taboo. I knew that, sooner or later, I would have to react to all those passionate words of Nima's, even though I didn't know how.

Finally, I bit the bullet. With my left hand, I wrote an address on a piece of paper, gave it to Nasr, and asked him to tell Nima to be at that address shortly after school let out at 4:00 P.M. I am right-handed, and by writing with my left hand, it would be difficult for someone to prove that I had written the address. The place I had chosen to meet with Nima was under a sycamore tree beside a stream in a secluded place. I loved that spot, and some days, when I needed to be alone, that's where I went. I knew that hardly anyone visited that place, so it was a perfect location for me and Nima to have a secret rendezvous.

I will never forget that very special day. Frenzied with love, my anxiety was at its peak. My palms were sweating, and my heart was beating too fast and too hard—it fluttered and seemed to skip beats. I felt eerie sensations inside my head, and I was nauseous and light-headed.

At four o'clock, when the school bell rang to dismiss us for the day, I thought I might have a panic attack. I took deep breaths and recited a poem of Hafez to calm myself down. The main theme of the poem was a requiem for those who are not alive with love, written as one would write a requiem for the dead (think of them as if they are already dead). I recited it all the way to the rendezvous point.

Nima was already there, leaning against the sycamore tree beside the stream. He was as gorgeous as ever. I stood right in front of him. I was mesmerized by his beauty, speechless. He seemed calm and relaxed, and there was a pleasant smile on his lips.

I was younger than him, so according to our tradition, I was supposed to greet him first, which I did not do.

"You know, I had always wondered whether or not angels greet people!" he suddenly said, breaking the silence. "Well, I just learned that they do not."

We both laughed. This put me at ease.

In that first secret rendezvous, Nima did most of the talking. He told me how excited he was that I was accepting his letters from Nasr and how, by doing that, I had built up his hopes. He complimented my beauty and spoke of his love for me, a boundless love that had shackled his soul. He was more mature than his age let on. He chose words very carefully and spoke distinctly. The tone of his voice was hypnotic, a tranquilizer for my soul. I even found his sentences poetic. To me, and probably only to me, his way of speaking had rhythm and rhyme.

Those moments, with Nima and I alone on that secluded spot, were some of the best moments of my life. I wanted to stay there with him forever, but I was also cautious of the time. I could be late only for so long. My mother expected me home within an hour of school dismissal. She knew that I usually stayed and chatted with my friends after school and that we often stopped for ice cream on our way back home. However, if I was too late, mom would send Mashdi out to look for me. I absolutely did not want that to happen. It was a pity I could not stop time, and it was amazing how quickly time passed when Nima and I were together.

# 10

Every weekday, after school was dismissed, I rushed to the secret spot. Nima was always there before me. We felt attached to one another; in fact, we were madly in love, and every moment we were together was a delight. My sexual desire was in full force. Even though Nima and I did not have any physical contact (not even a simple handshake), just looking at him could arouse sexual drive in me.

I fantasized frequently about him. One of my fantasies resembled a poem of Hafez: in my mind, it would be midnight, and wearing only a long-torn shirt, sweating and intoxicated, I go and sit by Nima's pillow.

Flushed on the chest and neck, with lips luscious and smiling enticingly, I begin to stare at him lustfully. Nima bends his head to my ear and says something like, "What nature pours in my cup, I drink. I would be an infidel to love if I did not worship such dazzling beauty." Then he continues, "Passion of your body fuels the fire of my lust, and as the tempted, I bear the consequence of such a heavenly sin."[6] Having forgotten the world and ourselves, ravaged by desire, Nima would then engulf my body, and we would spend that most intimate hour of the night together.

It might sound strange that, at that young age, I had fantasies based on images in the poetry of Hafez. But that is how it was. I had no exposure to sex scenes in movies, books, or magazines. With no such exposures, how creative or imaginative could I be? As difficult and mysterious as the poetry of Hafez was, those verses that I understood, or that I thought I understood, I adored. That is why it was natural for me to fantasize about the images that I was familiar with, even if they were too mystical. No matter how sophisticated those poems were, they did the job.

# 11

My secret rendezvous with Nima went on for three months. During this period, there was nothing about ourselves that we did not share with one another. The trust between us was so unbelievably comforting, the chemistry I felt with him as intense as it got. It was as if we were a single soul inhabiting two bodies.

Our time together was full of joy. My heart rejoiced whenever I saw him, and I was happy in life. But one day, as the Persian poets might say, the sorcery-playing dome of the universe sucked the happiness out. What happened was inevitable. I was madly in love and, as they say, love is the noblest frailty of the mind.

On that day, Nima asked for my permission for him and his mother to pay a visit to my parents and formally ask them for my hand. This started a turbulent storm in my heart. It scared me to death. It marked the beginning of the end of my relationship with Nima. In my heart of hearts, I knew that my father would never agree that his angel, the apple

---

[6] William Shakespeare: "The tempter or the tempted, who sins most?"

of his eye, should marry a poor arts teacher. Love had blinded Nima even more than it had blinded me. He did not realize that our love was forbidden, that we belonged to different classes. How could I or anyone blame Nima for not paying attention to such things? Love knows no laws; it regards no conditions.

I did not respond to Nima's request. A long period of silence ensued between the two of us. We both stared at each other with curiosity until Nima finally spoke.

"I have no wealth to give you," he said. "Let my whole existence be the gift I give you on our wedding day. Let our passionate and deep love be the guarantor of our prosperity. May we live in wedded bliss until we die. My love for you has no bounds. It had a beginning, but it has no end. Without you, I have no purpose. *With* you, I reach the stars and beyond, the limitless, timeless, and boundless celestial sphere."

I wanted to stay and listen to Nima. I never got tired of hearing him talk, of seeing him look at me. But it was almost time for me to leave. The hands of my watch were too cruel to move more slowly. They seemed to rush, and they left me no choice but to go. I thanked Nima for his words, said goodbye, and hurried home.

# 12

That night, I couldn't sleep a wink, nor could I dismiss Nima from my thoughts. Auntie, who was still sleeping in my room, breathed heavily in her sleep. Before bed, I had related to her the latest in the ongoing saga of my relationship with Nima.

As I tossed and turned, an idea came to me. I woke Auntie up and told her that I knew how to get my father agree to meet with Nima and his mother.

"Can't this wait until tomorrow morning?"

"No, Auntie," I replied. "I want you to promise that you will help me, so that I can finally sleep. You know that dad has enormous respect for your husband, my uncle Hāji Darab. If you tell him that Nima and his mother are close friends of Hāji's and that Hāji is very impressed with Nima and thinks Nima would make a wonderful husband for me, then I am sure that dad would agree to receive Nima and his mother."

Auntie yawned and said, "Okay, my dear, I will do that. You are right, there is no way your father would let Hāji Darab down. Now go to sleep."

I was hoping against hope that my father would like Nima so much that he would not mind Nima being poor. I had not read Shakespeare then to think that, "All orators are dumb, when beauty pleadth," but I instinctively knew that when someone is as handsome as Nima, everyone might fall under his spell. If Nima managed to enchant my dad, his heart would soften, and he might realize that his daughter could find happiness in Nima's company.

There is a saying, mostly about women, that beauty carries its dowry in its face. Why couldn't that apply to men as well? Why did my father need to find a rich husband for me? He was so wealthy that he could help a poor son-in-law become rich in no time. A person of his intelligence should be cognizant of beauty. He should understand that if Nima had no treasure house of gold, it was because he had a treasure house of inner and outer beauty.

I wanted so badly for my father to realize that.

# 13

It took a few days before Auntie finally persuaded dad to meet Nima and his mother. It was not easy. Following the tradition, Nima's mother had already requested a time to meet with my parents. She had indicated that she and her son were planning to make a marriage proposal. Upon my father's agreement, my mother asked Mashdi to go to Nima's residence and invite mother and son to pay a visit the next day at 6:00 P.M.

Nima and his mother arrived on time. Mashdi led the way through the first and second courtyards of our house and, in the third courtyard, ushered them up the stairs into a large reception room on the second floor. He asked them to make themselves at home until his Excellency, Mr. Sadr-al-Din Moin-al-Tojjar (my father), his wife, and his sister joined them. Mashdi told me afterward that he thought the grandeur of the house had intimidated the guests.

Shortly after, I watched dad, mom, and Auntie go into the reception room and close the door. I was on cloud nine that Nima was at my house, and at the same time, I had a great deal of trepidation. If things went well, and my father agreed to the wedding proposal, according to our tradition, he would call for the tea to be served by me, the future bride.

While they talked, I went to the kitchen and poured hot tea into five glass teacups. Along with an ornate silver sugar container, I placed the cups on a large antique tray made of silver and rushed up the stairs to the reception room.

I put my ear to the door and began to eavesdrop. Nima was talking about learning calligraphy from his father, about his education and love for music and teaching. When he paused, dad told him that he thinks violin is the most difficult instrument to learn. Then he went on to talk about some of his favorite violinists. Their conversation had not yet reached the subject of marriage.

As they talked on, the tea grew cold. I rushed back to the kitchen, emptied the cups, filled them again with hot tea, and ran back to where I had stood before. I put my ear to the door again and heard Nima tell my family that he and his mother were living in a small rental house. That infuriated dad, and he began yelling insults. He told Nima to cut his coat according to his cloth. I heard him say to Auntie, "Look, sister, this empty-handed hungry man, who does not even have a nice morsel to eat, has dared to ask for my daughter's hand."

There was a pause. Then he spoke again, this time to Nima.

"Look at you, the covetous violin player, you want to bite off more than you can chew," I heard him say. "You do not even have the wherewithal to take a wife of your own class. I suggest that, in your free time, you go play violin as a street peddler to collect some change. Perhaps then you might afford a bird of your own feather to flock with." His voice grew louder. "You have no business in Moin-al-Tojjar's house," he cried. "Get out at once."

The next thing I knew, the door burst open, hitting me hard on the top of my head. The tray of teacups toppled from my hands, scalding me all over with hot tea.

As dad shoved Nima's mother out of the room, she dropped her walking cane. Instead of picking it up for her, my father pushed it down the stairs. Nima, whose face had turned pale, held his trembling mother in both hands and helped her down the stairs.

Dad yelled at them uninterruptedly and made them more nervous. He called Mashdi, and pointing to Nima and his mother, shouted, "These hungry stray dogs have come to the butcher shop for meat. Do not even throw them a bone."

I could tell that Auntie and mom were badly embarrassed. They tried hard to calm dad down. Nima's mother could only walk very slowly, meaning she and Nima would have to endure a lot more humiliation from my father before they reached the main exit door of the house.

This was a side of dad I had never seen. He had turned ruthless, with a heart of stone. I couldn't bear to watch the rest of the fiasco. I squatted in a corner and stayed there until long after Nima and his mother had gone and dad had calmed down.

# 14

Auntie found me in the front yard. She asked me to join her and my parents for dinner. I had no appetite, but she took my hand and pulled me along. I did not resist.

In the dining room, the dinner table was set and the food had been served, but no one was in the mood to eat. Dad was blaming Hāji Darab, Auntie's husband, for having forced him to agree to allow a "wretched fiddler" to come into his house and ask for his daughter's hand. Auntie was begging dad to forget the whole thing. Hāji Darab did not have the faintest idea what had gone on, and Auntie was scared that dad would confront him.

My mother tried to change the subject. "May God protect Dorna from the evil eye," she said. "She is the most beautiful, the sweetest girl in Tabriz. We should expect many young men to ask for her hand in marriage. We cannot be disrespectful toward them. That sort of behavior is beneath our dignity."

"All those young men do damn wrong to overstep the bounds," my father exclaimed. "They should all go to hell. There is only one man in Tabriz who is sufficiently competent and merits to become my son-in-law, and that is Mirza Hadi,[7] the only son of Heshmat Mirza."

Auntie, mom, and I looked at each other with surprise. This was the first time dad had ever mentioned that he'd had a husband in mind for me.

"Mirza Hadi is highly educated and has an advanced diploma from Paris," he went on. "I will only hand off my little girl to someone from a noble and aristocratic family. Mirza Hadi will be perfect."

---

[7] Mirza is a title used as a prefix or suffix to identify a person as a member of the noble class.

My father explained that a couple of years ago, when Heshmat Mirza was still alive, the two men had agreed on their children's union. Mirza Hadi currently lived in France, but he was set to return in the summer of 1940, right when I graduated from high school.

"Dorna and Mirza Hadi will be married then," dad said. "I gave Heshmat Mirza my word, and my word is my bond."

Listening to my father, I realized my dreams were all crushed. I wanted to hitch my wagon to a star, as Emerson says, but how could I, when my father so easily crumbled my future before my own eyes? When you are a prisoner of your traditions, when you are confined in the valley, how can you hope to get over the hill?

Auntie remained silent. She was keeping a low profile, hoping that dad would forget about Nima and would not mention him to her husband.

But mom was unhappy about my father's plan: Mirza Hadi was known to be a self-indulgent playboy.

"Heshmat Mirza is dead, so whatever agreement was between you and him is null and void," she said. "You should look after Dorna's welfare. Mirza Hadi is a degenerate."

"Stop all this nonsense," my father interrupted. "Mirza Hadi is one of the wealthiest men in all of Azerbaijan. He will be able to fulfill Dorna's every wish. In Tabriz, he is one of only a few people with a Western education, a man of noble birth with blue blood flowing in his veins. Listen carefully: the die is cast. As soon as Dorna graduates from high school, she will marry Mirza Hadi, and you shall see, every girl in Tabriz will envy her."

With that, he left the dining room, and shortly after, mom followed. Auntie and I went to my room. We didn't speak. I got into bed and thought about my situation, torn between the love of my life, Nima, and the man I was going to be forced to marry and live with for the rest of my life.

My father had inflicted not one but two calamities upon me in one night.

# 15

After that accursed night, I still went to the secret rendezvous spot almost every day after school, hoping I would find Nima waiting there for me. But he was never there. Each time, I leaned against the sycamore tree beside the stream of water, exactly where Nima used to stand, and cried hard for a long time. Then I would go home, where I went straight to my painting room and tried hard to immerse myself in painting.

Every day, as I was walking back and forth to school, I was frantically looking everywhere for Nima with no luck. I never blamed him for trying to avoid me. My father had badly wounded his pride in front of his mother. Dad's reaction to his request for my hand in marriage was morally and socially reprehensible. It was as if my father was suddenly and temporarily possessed by a demon.

A month after that accursed night, Mashdi reported to my father that he had seen Nima loitering in our neighborhood. Dad was furious.

"I do not want this charlatan hang out near our house," he said. "People start rumors, and rumormongers spread them. That is not good for our reputation."

Dad had told my brother, Sina, all about the "tramp fiddler," as he called Nima. Now, Sina was on the lookout for him, too. Father and son had agreed that Nima was a guy in search of easy money.

"I swear by God, if that fiddler keeps hanging around these parts, I will have someone put a bullet in his head," my father cried. "If I do not, Sina will."

Mom replied that he was making a mountain out of a molehill, but I took what dad said very seriously. It was hard to believe that he was capable of committing such a crime; and yet, I thought of Auntie's story and how in the story they killed the man the princess loved. I had to protect Nima from getting hurt, even if what my father shouted turned out to be just idle words.

# 16

I went to the greenhouse, where Auntie was cutting chives to make Persian pancakes. The colors and smells of the garden enveloped me, and for a moment I forgot why I had gone out there.

Auntie brought me back to reality by asking how I was.

"Auntie dear," I whispered, "I know that it would be too much trouble for you, but I have no one else to ask." I stepped toward her until I was close enough to feel her breath on mine. "I want you to do me a huge favor."

"There's nothing I would not do for you," she answered.

"I am indebted to you forever. I want you to kindly carry a message from me to Nima."

Auntie was clearly disturbed, I could see her clench her teeth. She knotted her eyebrows and said, "Dorna dear, you are asking me to walk through the fire and the flames. Your father's wrath is strong. Last night, my blood stood still when he threatened to make Nima vanish. For your own sake and for Nima's sake, get Nima out of your head. Thinking about him all the time does nothing but drain your energy. Such thoughts are pervasive. Do not let them spiral out of control. They can make your gorgeous face age by years."

Auntie was talking nonstop like a radiobroadcaster.

"Whether you accept it or not," she was saying, "Nima is out of your life permanently. Don't cause bloodshed. We do not want Nima's blood on anybody's hands . . ."

I gently pressed my right hand to her lips.

"Auntie darling, my dear, just listen to me for one minute. I want you to tell Nima that I want to see him one more time. Auntie, just one more time, and then I will go out of his life forever. I swear to God. I need to see him so badly. That would help me to end this relationship with grace and dignity, not the way dad ended it, with humiliation and contempt."

Auntie frowned, but I insisted, and I told her that while at Nima's house, she could also console his mother and apologize to her for dad's behavior. This seemed to convince her. I could tell that she was reluctant, that she was scared that someone would see her in front of Nima's house and report back to her husband or to my father. But she agreed nevertheless.

That afternoon, Auntie got herself into a long conversation with Mashdi and started to gossip about Nima and his mother. She was pumping Mashdi for information about their house and its whereabouts. After figuring out where they lived, she waited until just before sunset and set off.

Auntie told me later that both Nima and his mother had received her with respect and thanked her for apologizing on behalf of my father.

"I blame my own son more than your brother," Nima's mother had said. "If I had known where he was taking me that evening, I would have tried to change his mind. However, your brother could have just said 'no' to us. There was no need for him to smash our pride to smithereens."

Auntie stayed at Nima's house for a total of half an hour, and as she was leaving, while Nima escorted her to the front door, Auntie had told him to meet me at our usual place at the usual time the next day. Auntie had succeeded in her mission, and to this day, no one other than the involved parties has ever found out about her visit to Nima's house.

# 17

When I arrived at our usual place the next day, Nima was already there leaning against the sycamore tree. I was sure that he would be there.

I stood face to face in front of him, and I did what I loved to do—I stared into his eyes. I knew that each moment of that occasion was precious, since that would be my very last chance to enjoy such beauty.

Nima looked at me and recited two lines from Hafez:

> Ever intoxicated keeps me the waft of air of your tress
> Ruins me momently deceit of your eyes of sorcery
> Wretched, I and the morning breeze, two wanderers in distress
> Intoxicated, I, from the sorcery of your eyes; it, by the scent of your tress

He tilted his head in contemplation. Then he addressed me directly:

"My beloved, my darling, my eternal love, my devotion to you is immortal, it will last forever. You know that love is blind, and that lovers cannot see. I swear, by my father's soul, that I had not even once noticed the difference in our social classes. I had seen your house from outside many times. I should have known that you are from an aristocratic family. But I was blind. It did not occur to me even once that our worlds are so different."

"You know that love knows no laws, so it regards no conditions. It is above king or Kaiser. Your father would not be able to understand our love and devotion to each other. He is a businessman. I do not blame him."

I replied that I knew how innocent and genuine our love was. And I told him, too, that I was going to marry Mirza Hadi, a man I had never met. The news turned his face as red as a blacksmith's kiln. He cursed his fate and began to throw punches at the tree. I asked him to stop, but he did not. He continued until his hands bled. I started to cry. But I was sure that he would not loiter around my house anymore. That was what I had wanted—to save him from any possible harm by dad or Sina.

I could have stayed there with him forever. However, the time came when I had to leave.

Right before I left, I did something I could never have imagined I would do. It was as if the courage of the brave women of Persian history had entered my body—it was as if I were Princess Shirin.[8] I held Nima's bloody hands in a tight grip and said to him, "I swear by God, with every fiber of my being, that I have never loved, and will never love again, another man as I love you. You are my only love. You are my first love, and in my dreams, in the wide expanse of imagination, where my thought bird takes flight freely and without fear, I will always be with you, with you alone. Wherever I be and wherever I go, I will carry your heart with me. I will carry it in my heart. You are my kindred spirit."

Nima was in tears as I spoke. I let go of his hands, and without letting him say anything, I left and, walking briskly, soon disappeared.

---

[8] In Persian literature, Shirin was the only relative of the Queen Shamira of Armenia (Armanistan). She was the queen's niece and the crown princess. Khosrow was the only son of King Hormoz of Persia and the crown prince of Iran. When it came to beauty, both Shirin and Khosrow were superior to all their contemporaries. Both were tall and had the most elegant figures.
One day, Shirin sees a painted portrait of Khosrow and falls head over heels in love with him. Love makes Shirin gallop through the mountains and woods unaccompanied until she reaches Mada'in, the capital of Iran, over four hundred miles away from Armenia.

# 18

On my way home, I walked as if I were a victorious hero returning from battle. I was very proud that I had been able to express my emotions to Nima so fully, and I was relieved that his last memory of our fiery but deep love would no longer be my father's outrageous behavior. His last memory would be a passionate expression of love from me to him—that is, from a girl to a man, something which, in my culture, was as rare as a sunflower in the desert.

When I reached home and knocked on the door, instead of Mashdi, Auntie opened. She had been sitting in the Octagonal, restlessly waiting for me.

"I am dying to know how your rendezvous with Nima went," she said, hugging me.

We sat there in the Octagonal, and I told her all the little details of my last date with Nima. After she'd heard everything, she told me, "Dorna dear, what you did was a little short of sheer madness. However, I hope that you got a load off of your mind. I am proud of you. You are fearless, a daring heir to the likes of Shirin and Gordafarid,[9] a brave lioness. But remember that Gordafarid was extremely wise, too. So be wise." She sighed deeply. "God will steer the boat where he wishes. May he have pity on us!"

Auntie had been staying with us for a long time, far longer than she normally would. She missed her daughters, even though they came to visit her now and then, and she had not seen her husband, Hāji Darab, for several months. So, after my relationship with Nima ended and her mind was at ease, she went home, promising my parents that she would return in the summer, after school let out.

"This year, as soon as schools are closed for summer holidays, I will return, help Dorna pack, and she will come stay with my family for a while. Change is good for her," she told my parents.

Dad and mom agreed and thanked her.

Between the day Auntie left and the start of the summer holidays, I had a miserable time. I still could not stop thinking about Nima. We are

---

[9] Gordafarid is a heroine in Persian mythology. She was a daring and wise woman who once disguised herself in knight's armor and challenged the enemy ranks to a fight.

all born once and live only one life, so why was I destined to live mine being deprived of a love that was pure and beyond measure, wider than the vast expanse that encompasses all the galaxies?

At times, I also thought about my future husband, Mirza Hadi. I wondered what he looked like and how it would be to have sex with someone I did not love. Thinking of Nima easily excited me, but I did not have any sexual feelings toward any other men. Imagining that, night after night, I would have to release my naked body into Mirza Hadi's control and bear his tight embrace frightened me. I was afraid that a life of loveless sexual encounters meant that, in reality, I would be denied one of life's most pleasurable gifts.

I hated arranged marriage. In such arrangements, the love between a bride and bridegroom was of no or little importance. Sex should be at the core of any marriage, arranged or not, I thought, and for that, the virginity of a first-time bride was a must. In my culture, the notion of virginity does not even exist for the groom. No one cares what sort of sexual life a man has had before his marriage. As a voracious reader, I had read that, for the divine union between couples, there is an ultimate spiritual significance that the virgin bride shed blood on her wedding night. I wished that this blood might be conditional upon the existence of love between the couple. I could understand such spiritual significance only if there was true love between the newly married. However, I could not see any significance in anything if one of the spouses despised the other.

# 19

Two days after the start of summer holidays, Auntie came over for lunch. While we ate, she asked dad for his permission to take me to her house so that I could spend a few weeks with her and my cousins. Dad agreed.

"These days Sina and Dena are busy with their own affairs," he said. "They do not visit us that often. Poor Dorna is lonely. A change of scenery would be good for her."

After lunch, I packed my clothes and other belongings into a bundle, and around three o'clock in the afternoon, Auntie and I started walking toward her house shoulder to shoulder with Mashdi behind, carrying my bundle. When we arrived at Auntie's house, my cousins, all four of them, received me with one of the heartiest welcomes I'd ever known. Shortly after, they began arguing over me. Every one of them wanted me to stay in her room. Auntie ended the argument by announcing that I would stay in her room. Mashdi brought my bundle to Auntie's room, wished me a great stay, and left.

My Uncle Hāji Darab, Auntie's husband, arrived in the evening. He was very glad to see me.

"Dorna darling," he beamed, "you are like my own daughters, make yourself at home." He asked Auntie and my cousins to make sure that I remained content during my stay. He did not want to see me unhappy even for one second, he told them, which I found a little suspicious. I thought that he knew something about the story of my heavy heart. Perhaps he took pity on me, because he knew that with a broken wing, there was no other flight for my heart.

Auntie's room was adjacent to Hāji Darab's. When I went to bed, I could hear him praying to Almighty God and asking for forgiveness for sins that he had possibly done unknowingly. He thanked God that he and his family were enjoying good health and benefitting from the bounties of nature, and he praised Him for all the blessings in their life.

While listening to Uncle Hāji Darab pray, I began to think of Nima, who, to me, was the second coming of Joseph, the son of Jacob, and an epitome of physical beauty and inner virtue. I couldn't help but draw parallels between Joseph and Nima's lives. Joseph's brothers threw him into a dry well; my father threw Nima into utter despair. In fact, what my father did to Nima was worse than what Joseph's brothers had done to Joseph. My father's contemptuous behavior had been like a burning arrow through my heart; similarly, what Joseph's brothers did to Joseph was like a burning arrow through Jacob's heart. Jacob tore his clothes and mourned Joseph, and nothing could assuage his mountainous grief, nor could anything assuage mine. That night, I cried myself to sleep.

The next day, after breakfast, while I was busy talking with my cousins, Auntie went into her den, brought out a bolt of a spectacular silk fabric that she had hidden in her oak coffer, and asked her daughters to sew a beautiful dress for me. Auntie's daughters were all skillful tailors who spent most of their time cutting up beautiful fabrics and sewing elegant, perfectly fitting dresses. Auntie told us that she had inherited the bolt of fabric from her mother and, until that day, had not known what to do with it.

"Naturally, I should have given it to one of my own daughters, but the fabric is enough only for one dress," she explained. "I cannot possibly choose between my four daughters. Giving it to you, Dorna, makes a lot of sense, since you are also a granddaughter of my mother."

My cousins, who were very kind and generous toward me, agreed with Auntie heartily. I gave Auntie a big hug and I kissed all of my cousins. Auntie was a sun, under whose rays, four virtuous daughters had been raised.

After a few days, Auntie suggested we visit her old friend, Ms. Suesan, who could teach me about tailoring. She thought that, just like my cousins, under Ms. Suesan's training, I myself could become a master tailor. I was not crazy about cutting and sewing, but I knew that Auntie wanted to keep my mind off Nima, so I accepted her offer, and the next morning, Auntie took me to Ms. Suesan's tailor's shop.

Ms. Suesan was a middle-aged lady with a smiling face. As soon as she saw me, her jaw dropped in amazement.

"Glory to God, I have never seen this much beauty in one person," she exclaimed. She touched my shoulder. "God be praised for such an elegant figure and delicate face."

Those compliments immediately reminded me that I was a victim of my beauty. Like a beautiful bird that spends its life in a cage, I was going to spend the rest of my life in the captivity of a rich man who only wanted me because I was a pretty girl from a prominent family. As we say in Farsi, a peacock's real enemy is the beauty of its own feathers.

As Ms. Suesan's pupil, I was as diligent and as serious as I was at school. Nearly every morning that summer, I received private lessons in tailoring, and in the afternoon, under the supervision of my cousins, I practiced what I had learned in the morning. I made quick progress. I learned to measure customers, draw patterns, and work a needle and thread. I even mastered several sewing techniques. I was so busy that I hardly even noticed the passage of time.

I stayed with Auntie and her family for a total of forty-two days. By then, I had grown homesick and was ready to return to my own family. Auntie and my cousins—and even my Uncle Hāji Darab—were all sad to see me go. They helped me pack up my things, and then my cousins walked me home.

Within hours of settling back in, the suppressed fire of my love for Nima flamed up. It was the same story all over again.

## 20

With my parents' permission, I continued taking tailoring lessons from Ms. Suesan. I stayed in her shop longer than before, and most days, after I left the shop, I walked around looking for Nima. Sometimes, I went to our secret rendezvous location, leaned against the sycamore tree, and cried loud until it gave me relief. I also visited Hāji Morad's store frequently and bought stationery that I did not need, hoping I might run into him there. I usually began a long conversation with Hāji Morad to extend my visit and increase my chances of seeing Nima. But it was all hopeless.

Finally, I convinced myself that I was destined never to see Nima again. When, twenty-one years later, in 1960, in Dena and Habib's house, I stood on the ladder and saw him through the window, I believed that a true miracle had taken place.

I believe the day was August 20, 1939. That day, when I arrived at Ms. Suesan's shop, Ms. Suesan was arguing with two women over a bridal dress she had made for them. It was a simple but elegant wedding gown. However, the bride and her mother wanted the dress to be elaborately embellished with fine lace and adorned with sequins and pearls. Ms. Suesan was telling them that such a job was not within her and her tailors' expertise, but the customers were not taking no for an answer.

I still do not know what made me jump into the middle of this conversation and tell them that I could do what they wanted. Ms. Suesan grew agitated and told me that embellishing wedding dresses was beyond my skills: "You need to have months of practice, and it is an irksome task. I will not allow you to ruin a wedding dress so delicately and precisely sewn." I insisted that, in spite of all those concerns, I could do it. So Ms. Suesan gave me a piece of fabric from which the wedding gown had been made and gave me two days to elaborately embellish it the way our customers wanted. She asked the bride and her mother to come back then to see my work. If they liked it, then she would let me embellish the whole gown for them.

I took the piece of fabric, left the shop, went to the biggest bookstore in Tabriz, and purchased a couple of workbooks on dressmaking. Then, I went to a fabric store and purchased lots of lace, sequins, and pearls and some inexpensive fabric. I rushed home to begin reading the books and practicing the techniques detailed within. All that day, I practiced on the cheap fabric I had bought, and the next day, I carefully embellished the piece Ms. Suesan had given me exactly the way our customers wanted. I could see for myself that I had done a superb job.

In the morning of the third day, when I showed my work to Ms. Suesan and the bride and her mother, their faces broke into radiant smiles. They were in awe.

"Dorna darling, this is a feather in your cap," Ms. Suesan said. "I am astounded; you are exceptional in every way." She gave me the rest of the dress and told me that I had three weeks to embellish it all over.

During the next two weeks, I worked every day, twelve hours a day, diligently and carefully decorating the dress. I even invented some techniques myself that made it even more elegant than expected. When the dress was ready, I was too excited to just hand it over to Ms. Suesan. I decided to give a presentation on the techniques I had used and those I had invented myself. Thus far, I had not let anyone see my work. I wanted to surprise everyone.

I also wanted to give a speech about the gown because, psychologically, I needed to. Two years prior, at school, I had been selected to give a speech in a meeting of the members of the parents-teachers association. It had been an honor to be selected, and I had looked forward to giving the speech. But when my father heard about it, he forbade me from attending the meeting. He did not want his daughter to go on stage like an entertainer and have lewd men give her lecherous looks. Ever since, giving a speech had become an obsession for me.

I invited my parents, Sina and his wife, Dena and Habib, Mashdi, our Maid, Aunti, Hāji Darab, my cousins, Ms. Suesan, my best friend, Atoosa, and a few other best friends and classmates to a presentation of the dress, which would be held in the assembly hall of our second courtyard on the evening of September 8. Following the presentation, the guests would be invited to an elaborate dinner in our third courtyard, in the front yard of our residential mansion.

On September 8, before the appointed time, I spread the gown, which was inside a dark garment bag, on the top of the large, old-fashioned podium in front of the assembly hall. I also laid out pieces of fabric and some lace, sequins, pearls, and sewing tools. Dad and mom arrived early and sat in the front row. When the guests were all there, Mashdi locked the front gate and sat in the last row next to our maid. I was in seventh heaven. It was as if I were a normal person, not a fallen lovebird with broken feathers and bloody wings.

I gave a long lecture about the techniques that I had learned and used to embellish the bridal gown. I demonstrated how it worked by making samples in front of the audience, and I explained how I improved some of the standard techniques I had read about in the workbooks. At the end, I unveiled the wedding gown and raised it straight up in the air for all to see. The guests were clearly impressed: they gave me a standing ovation.

My father was the first one to come forward after my presentation. He kissed and hugged me and gave me an eighteen-karat gold fountainpen. He told me that no daughter could impress her parents more than I had. He was followed by my mom and all my relatives and friends, who, one by one, congratulated me and praised my work. Ms. Suesan told me that now it was my turn to teach her tailoring, and we both laughed. Mashdi, who had not understood my lecture at all, said that I was a born dressmaker. I did not like that comment, but I let it go, since I knew that he meant well. In those days, the dress making profession was for uneducated lower-class people, not for educated high-class ones like myself.

The gold fountainpen my dad gave me was the most precious gift I had ever received, because I felt I had earned it. It was not just another gift from my father. Dad gave it to me as an award for a major achievement. So, I decided that I had to use it to write something important and different, and it was right there and then that I promised myself to write with my gold pen the story of my love with Nima and to commit my feelings—passion, love, lust—to paper as frankly and fearlessly as I could. Now, after thirty-six years, I am fulfilling that promise. I am writing all these lines with my gold fountainpen.

That night, after my presentation and dinner party, Ms. Suesan took the bridal gown with her. A few days late, when I went back to Ms. Suesan's tailor shop for new lessons, she gave me an envelope full of money. There was a note inside the envelope from the bride's mother thanking me for my extraordinarily beautiful job. There was a considerable amount of money there, and I immediately divided it equally between the two tailors who were working for Ms. Suesan. They had not expected that. Their eyes twinkled, and they kissed me and gave me tight hugs. They were poor workers, and that much money could probably solve one or two minor financial problems in their lives. From that day on, those tailors became very friendly with me.

That was how I spent the summer before my last year in high school. On the first day of fall, the schools reopened. Twelfth grade went by with no particular events. Even though every day my eyes searched for Nima, I resumed commuting back and forth to school with my friends. I was not looking forward to the next summer, when I would graduate from high school, and Mirza Hadi would return from Paris to marry me. At that point, only God knew what lay in store for me.

# Chapter 3

# Enslaved in an Arranged Marriage

## 1

Mirza Hadi returned from France. Shortly after, I graduated from high school, and as had been agreed between my father and Mirza Hadi's late father, we went through all the formal steps of the traditional Persian marriage process.

The wedding ceremony and the reception were fairytale-like, with all the pomp and dazzle of a royal marriage. All the most prominent citizens of Tabriz were there: the governor of Azerbaijan, the mayor of Tabriz, high-ranking military generals and government officials, and distinguished merchants and businessmen. Also present were some of my friends and teachers, the principal of my high school, and Ms. Suesan. In my wedding dress, I was so gorgeous that Mirza Hadi's mother introduced me to her relatives as the "dream bride" for her son. My wedding ring was a five-carat diamond ring, and the presents I received from everyone formed quite a sumptuous collection of jewelry.

On my wedding night, everyone was happy except me. My father was over the moon. He now had a French-educated son-in-law from an aristocratic family, and the union would surely help him extend his influence around town. My brother, Sina, was happy because he now had a new friend to join him in his debauchery and gambling. My mother was content because she had no doubt that I was starting a new, glamorous life. In particular, she was very impressed with all the pieces of jewelry Mirza Hadi's family had given me. In one evening, they had left me with a lifetime's fortune. Meanwhile, Auntie's happiness was twofold: she was no longer worried that her involvement in my love affair with Nima would be revealed, and she was also convinced that my new life would make me forget all about him.

However, during the ceremony and afterward, my heart yearned for him. He was my kindred spirit and my real love. It was natural for me to think of him on a night that officially ended any hopes, however small, that he and I could share our lives. I would have traded all of those jewels to be with Nima for only five short minutes. And yet, as bitter as I was, I behaved. During the entire celebration, in the words of Hafez, with the bloody heart, I brought forth the laughing lip.

Mirza Hadi was in his late twenties. He had a medium-sized body frame, deep dark eyes, prominent nose, a mustache, and a goatee. He had sideburns and hair that was combed back to reveal a receding hair line. He looked accomplished and distinguished, but there was a cunning look about him, too. Overall, he was a handsome man, and under different circumstances, I could probably grow to love him. But given my feelings for Nima, whom I loved like a wildfire, I was indifferent toward Mirza Hadi. The good thing was that I did not entirely dislike him.

We consummated our marriage on our wedding night. In Iranian culture, the joy of consummation for the bride and groom is compared with the joy of rising to the throne for a prince and his princess. I doubt if our sexual debut was that significant for Mirza Hadi. He was neither in love with me nor new to sexual activity. As a womanizer, he was skillful at sex, and our first sexual encounter was probably only another roll in the hay for him, even though this time, I, his partner, was very young and a virgin. On the other hand, I was curious about sex and quite ready for it. The experience turned out to be quite pleasurable, which I attributed to Mirza Hadi's many years of sexual experiences in Iran and France. However, I would have much preferred a trustworthy husband like Nima to a self-indulgent womanizer who had all the skills to pleasure his woman during sex.

That night, after sex, Mirza Hadi got out of bed to put on his pajamas. I looked at his naked body furtively. It was the first time I saw a grown-up man totally nude. He was perspiring a little, and it was erotic to watch him naked. I was amazed at the complexity of the male and female anatomy. Unlike what I had assumed before, I learned that night that physical pleasure can be achieved from sex without love. I wondered what the difference between sex with love and sex without love was. I imagined that sex with love, or lovemaking, was physical and emotional intimacy together. But that was as far as my thoughts could take me.

Our wedding night set a precedent for all our future sexual encounters. I never became an active, let alone aggressive, partner for Mirza Hadi—I needed to be in love for that, which I was not. And I must add that he did not seem to care about or even pay attention to my role in bed. I was only an object of pleasure for him, that was all.

After the wedding, there was peace and tranquility in my life. I still yearned for Nima, but as a married woman, I was ashamed to fantasize about him too much. There was so much love inside me that I hoped I would soon become pregnant and have a child, so that I could give all that love to my baby. I was sure that by focusing on a child, I would not find much time to concentrate on my ill-fated love and broken heart.

My marriage had pleased no one more than my father. Whenever he could, dad praised Mirza Hadi and bragged about his education in France and his immense wealth. Dad's persistent preoccupation with my new husband was disturbing. He boasted to Habib about Mirza Hadi's riches so often that Dena and Habib stopped visiting dad and mom, and they never came to visit me and Mirza Hadi. Habib was a true gentleman and one of the finest men in Tabriz. He did not deserve to be disparaged, however subtly, because my father's new son-in-law was much wealthier and more educated than he was. As a human being, Habib was superior to Mirza Hadi, and that had always been clear to me.

# 2

Mirza Hadi's house was a beautiful eighteen-room mansion on a large, landscaped plot of land, with gardens, trees, and streams. My mother-in-law had emptied several rooms on the mansion's second floor, so that they could fit in all the gifts my parents had given me and Mirza Hadi as part of my dowry. There were gloriously woven silk and wool Persian carpets with elaborate curvilinear designs; stunning tulip-shaped candlesticks; lustrous 24-percent full lead crystal Georgian candleholders; antique 0.999 silver candlesticks and a candelabra; and precious lamp chimneys. They had also given us three complete sets of the finest china services with rare, elegant designs; a set of antique Victorian 0.999 silver dinnerware, including kitchen utensils, tea sets, and figurines; various sizes of the best copper pots and trays; and all kinds of silver and ivory calumets, pipes, and hookahs.[10]

Also included in my dowry was a king-size mattress and several goose-feather and fowl-feather quilts, pillows, and mattress toppers of varying colors and designs, along with half a dozen sateen bed covers and pillowcases; a dozen beautiful, hand-stitched, pure cashmere tablecloths; velvet curtains; twelve artistically-designed, hand-carved, deep-chocolate-brown antique walnut chairs, with matching dining table; and a breathtaking, three-piece Victorian walnut and burl bedroom set, every piece intricately carved. In particular, the monumental antique king-size bed featured heavy, magnificent carvings.

That was not even all of it. My parents had gone all out for my dowry and had given us everything from A to Z, all top-of-the-line. They were careful not to include anything that did not befit the dignity of Mirza Hadi's family.

In my estimation, Dena's dowry had not been worth even one-fifth of mine. Of course, that was not surprising at all, since my father considered Mirza Hadi's family to be the most eminent and illustrious family in Tabriz. The dazzling wealth of Mirza Hadi had blinded him. I wish dad had lived long enough to see for himself that Mirza Hadi was far from the flawless son-in-law he thought him to be. Not only that, Mirza Hadi was a perfect example of the kind of man described by the great Persian poet Sa'di in 1258:

> He whom I saw like a pistachio, all kernel[11],
> Was actually like an onion, skin on skin.

---

[10] A hookah, also known as a waterpipe, shisha, and hubble-bubble, is a multi-stemmed tobacco smoking device.
[11] *The Gulistan of Sa' di*, translated by W. M. Thackston (Bethesda, Maryland: Ibex Publishers, 2008), Chapter 2, Story 18, p. 55.

# 3

In those days, in Tabriz, it was an important custom that, for the first three days after marriage, the bride stay home without doing a hand's turn. Every morning during my first three days at Mirza Hadi's house, Afra, one of the maids, brought my breakfast into my room. When I was finished eating, she would return with a golden basin and an extravagant ewer full of water. I held my hands over the basin, and she poured water from the ewer over them. After I washed my hands, she gave me a towel to dry them. I did not like this custom, but I had to respect it. I was now the bride of an important master who owned dozens of large and small villages and hundreds of thousands of acres of farms and orchards. I had no choice but to obey the rules.

On the fourth day, early in the morning, I lay in bed, pretending to sleep. Mirza Hadi had already left; he had told me the night before that he planned to make a tour of his villages and farms and would not return for a week, a decision that I found irresponsible. I was a total stranger in Mirza Hadi's house, and I did not expect my husband to leave me for such a long period only three days after our marriage. This was an indication that he did not care about me, which made me worry, especially since, thus far, he had shown no affection for me. He had not uttered a single word about love or about my beauty—no compliments at all. I worried because I knew that coming events cast their shadow before.

Even though I was awake, I kept my eyes shut. I did not want to open them and see myself in Mirza Hadi's bedroom. I imagined that I had not married and that I still lived in my father's house. I started to drift into a daydream. Sina was there, as mischievous as ever. He teased me, while Auntie watched us with joy, dad read a newspaper, mom talked to Mashdi, and our maid cleaned the windows . . .

Suddenly, I heard three hard knocks on the bedroom door. My mother-in-law barged in without waiting for permission. I was startled and embarrassed to be seen in my nightgown.

"Dorna dear, from now on, every morning, you must come down to my dining room for breakfast," she said. Her tone was commanding. "I need to talk with you about some important issues. Hurry up, we are all waiting for you downstairs. Please remember that I do not like to repeat myself." Her previous days' kindness was entirely gone.

I changed right away, brushed my hair, rushed downstairs, and, after exchanging pleasantries, took a seat next to my mother-in-law at the breakfast table. That was where my place setting was. Mirza Hadi had three sisters, one of whom, Jaleh, had married and left the house. The other two, Pegah and Layla, were sitting at the table waiting for breakfast. I was curious to hear what my mother-in-law had to say. However, I had to wait until we were finished eating before she finally began to talk.

She explained that there was a full staff on hand day and night—gardeners, chauffeurs, maids, housemen—and that the lead servants were a husband and wife named Afra and Ali. Afra and Ali had been working for Mirza Hadi's family since they were teenagers.

"You must have noticed that we have built them a beautiful small house at the far corner of our front yard," my mother-in-law said. "We rely on Afra and Ali more than any other servants. They are honest and trustworthy and have our full faith and confidence. When you need something to be done, ask them. They will either do it themselves or ask another servant to do it for you. There are enough workers in this house to enable us to sit still and be idle all day."

"However, as they say, the devil finds work for idle hands to do," she went on. "Dorna darling, thus far, I had three daughters, now I have four, and I do not want to see you or my daughters fool around all day and have no role in the management of this mansion. There are plenty of chores to keep you occupied. You must divide certain tasks amongst yourselves and perform them under my supervision. I am sure that you had some housework responsibilities at your father's house. Here, it is the same."

I had no choice but to nod in agreement. However, the truth was that I'd had no housework responsibilities at my father's house. I had spent most of my time studying, reading books, or painting. To my parents, my siblings, and Auntie, I had been like a beautiful and delicate flower. Without exception, they treated me with love, respect, and kindness. My mother-in-law was the first person in my life to speak to me so roughly. It was not just her tone of voice, it was also her look. Her facial expressions reminded me of Dracula. I felt like the prisoner of some wicked monster.

A lump formed in my throat, and I longed again to be with the love of my life, Nima, who darted like lightning through my life and ignited in my heart the flames of eternal infatuation.

# 4

With all those people who worked at Mirza Hadi's house, I wondered what sorts of tasks my mother-in-law wanted me and her daughters to perform. I soon discovered that she had never hired a chef: either she cooked herself or she asked one of her daughters to cook. Shopping for groceries was also something she did not want her servants do alone. She took them shopping with her, so that they could carry the groceries, and if she was too busy or not in a mood to go shopping, then she asked one of her daughters to go in her stead. (Going to the bakery to buy fresh bread was an exception—that was Ali's duty.) Setting the table for a meal was also a chore assigned to my sisters-in-law. While Afra and the other maids would carry dishes of food from the kitchen, they were not allowed to set the table themselves.

So, my mother-in-law wanted me to learn to cook and help her with groceries and help my sisters-in-law with setting the dining table. That would take a great deal of my time, time that I could have spent reading, painting, or advancing my sewing and tailoring skills.

When Mirza Hadi returned a week later, he did not tell me much about his trip, nor did he ask me how my week had gone. He was indifferent toward me and showed no interest in the social and philosophical topics that I had read about and would have loved to discuss. He was a shallow and uninformed person, and I became convinced that he had not studied while in France: there wasn't a shred of scholarly attainment in the way he talked. I was sure that, in Paris, he had spent a great amount of money and time indulging himself—that was how he had mastered all sorts of sexual techniques. His sexual appetite was ferocious, and he was lucky that I welcomed his advances, even when he woke me in the middle of the night for the second or third time.

A few weeks after Mirza Hadi's return, one morning, my mother-in-law told me that he was hosting a party that evening for his male friends. She said that she needed my help to prepare, and that it was the responsibility of the women to make sure Mirza Hadi's parties were as fun for the participants as possible. I knew nothing about the event and was agitated that Mirza Hadi had not mentioned it to me.

"My son and his friends are a bunch of men who now and then need to enjoy their God-given wealth in pleasurable ways," she told me. "They are not into pornography or after prostitutes. All they want is a good time, with good food, alcohol, and cigarettes, and maybe a bit of gambling, too. And I should mention that some of them also indulge in opium."

My mother-in-law explained that such gatherings had been a favorite activity of her late husband and that, as a child, Mirza Hadi had spent a lot of time sitting next to his father at these parties. "He was only an observer until he turned eighteen," she said. "Today, he is careful not to become an opium addict and smokes only on special occasions. And he gambles only for fun, never compulsively, like your brother."

I must have made a face when she said that, because she paused. She thought she had worried me and tried to reassure me: "Mirza Hadi will never gamble away our money. You do not need to be concerned about our wealth diminishing; it has never happened. It has only ever increased and expanded."

I spent the rest of the day helping my mother-in-law prepare a feast for Mirza Hadi and his guests. Early in the evening, after I set up the huge dining table in the large banquet room for the guests, I had dinner with my in-laws without waiting for Mirza Hadi to come home from wherever he was, and then I went upstairs to my room and began to read.

It was past midnight when I woke up and found myself on the sofa. I had fallen asleep while reading. I was dying to see with my own eyes what Mirza Hadi and his friends were up to, so I snuck downstairs to the front yard.

It was very dark outside, and I could see the light glowing inside the banquet room, which had large, floor-to-ceiling windows that faced the front yard. I stood in front of the side window, which was half covered by a drape, and peeked in at the guests. There were bottles of whiskey and vodka and glasses of drinks all over. Several men were asleep on the floor, fully dressed; others had fallen asleep on chairs and sofas. Mirza Hadi was busy talking with three of his guests, and a group of people sat on the floor cross legged, around a large polygonal brazier that had very short legs and low vertical walls. They were taking turns smoking opium with a pipe made from a hollow tube of mesquite wood that had a small ceramic sphere on one end. The difference between that and a tobacco pipe was that the opium pipe was designed to vaporize the drug, while the tobacco pipe was used to burn the tobacco.

Before that night, I had never seen anyone smoke opium. I watched the smokers very carefully. When it was a guest's turn to smoke, he took a pea-sized piece of opium from a saucer and placed it near a hole in the top of the sphere. Then, using tongs, he grabbed a glowing piece of charcoal from the brazier and set it close to the opium. As the heat from the charcoal melted the drug, the smoker puffed the pipe and inhaled the vapor.

For a long while, I watched the opium smokers. I was so mesmerized by them that I almost missed another fascinating scene. There, in a corner of the banquet room, a group of men were sitting around a table gambling. Unlike the opium smokers, who looked totally lethargic, this group was full of vim and vigor. Suddenly, one of them raised his head toward the ceiling, and I saw his face. It was my brother, Sina. No wonder my mother-in-law had known about his gambling addiction.

I was upset. He had come to my house and yet had not even stopped by to say hello to his own sister. His passion for gambling far exceeded his love for his family. I felt sorry for his wife. His future was grim, and I worried about him. Only God knew whose blood was flowing through his veins. Where Sina had picked up his habit had always been a mystery: my father never gambled, and growing up, we did not even have playing cards in the house.

Standing there in the dark front yard, I felt disgusted by all of these men—men who had drunkenly passed out all over the room; men who smoked nonstop to reach a state of mindlessness, like living-dead zombies; men who tried very hard to win each other's monies, without any regard for their own reputations and finances or those of their families.

Utterly disappointed, I went to bed thinking of Nima, who was like an angel free of any blemish in my mind, and of my brother-in-law, Habib, who was a high-minded, righteous man, and of my uncle, Auntie's husband, Hāji Darab, who was a godly, pious person. Then I imagined my father's face, and I could read the lines of his personal history. Even though he had destroyed my life by making me marry Mirza Hadi, and even though he had rejected Nima in a most shameful way, he was still my hero. He seemed descended from legends of ancient mythology. Men of his stature and courage were an endangered species.

In the morning, at the breakfast table, I told my in-laws everything that I had seen the night before. I spoke harshly of Mirza Hadi's guests, calling them all corrupt, emphasizing that my brother was not an exception. When I finished saying what I had to say, my mother-in-law started to admonish me:

"Dorna dear, never ever again put your nose into Mirza Hadi's affairs," she growled. I could tell she was very unhappy with me. "Mirza Hadi is the only son of Heshmat Mirza, born in affluence. Don't even dare to question the activities that take place at his parties. Only if you aspire to make your life miserable, then pry into the affairs of your husband. Heshmat Mirza used to tell me that pleasure in moderation might be a good idea, but not for our son. He is entitled to pleasure in abundance."

I wanted to reply that, on the contrary, my father used to tell Sina that only a fool is a slave of pleasure, but I held myself in check. I looked at my sisters-in-law, hoping for some reaction to what their mother had said. But as usual, they just acquiesced. They never contradicted their mother, nor did they ever express any opinions about their brother's interests and affairs. Since childhood, they had been led to believe that they were inferior to their brother because of their gender. They obeyed him under all circumstances and were taught never to question him.

When she was finished warning me not to meddle in my rich, spoiled husband's affairs, my mother-in-law announced that she had a doctor's appointment, which meant that I would be in charge of cooking lunch. My sisters-in-law had been invited to spend the day at their uncle's house and would not be there to help me. Up to that day, even though I had occasionally helped my mother-in-law cook, I had never cooked an entire meal on my own, so after all of my in-laws had left for the day, I went to the kitchen and put together a huge pot of ingredients for a rice dish. Then I put the pot on the top of stove to cook, and I went upstairs to my painting room on the second floor to paint a scene that had been in my mind for a few days. I loved to paint—other than reading, it was just about the only activity that brought me tranquility and nourished my soul.

In those days, pre-stretched canvases on wooden frames were not readily available. But I knew an artist who made them for me, and I always had a few of them in my painting room. I used oil paint. I put pigment in the can and mixed it very well with pure linseed oil and pure gum spirits of turpentine.

I set a canvas on my easel, prepared a can of oil paint, and began to work. I soon got so absorbed in painting that I completely lost track of time. Only God knows how long I had been immersed in front of my easel when I was viciously attacked from behind. Someone grabbed my hair and, pulling it, lifted me out of my seat. I let out a scream, loud enough for all the servants to hear. I was scared to death and trembling like a tree during a wind storm.

The attacker began to shout at me. "You imbecile, you have burned food on the stove, and the house is full of smoke." I had yet to see his face, but I recognized his voice. He was my husband, Mirza Hadi. I realized that I had figured that out even before he'd opened his mouth.

While still pulling my hair, he started to kick at the easel until the canvas fell over. Then he started to kick at the canvas and also at my paint palette and the can of oil paint. Paint splattered all over the room and onto one of the fine Persian carpets that my father had given us. I loved the exquisite design of that carpet, which was hand-woven by masters of Esfahan. I am sure that Mirza Hadi did not, and could not, understand that he had destroyed a remarkable piece of art.

He eventually let my hair go and left the room. His mother stepped in a moment later, yelling like crazy.

"Moin-al-Tojjar has not sent a wife for my son, but a toy to play with," she was saying. "Who do you think you are? You must concentrate on homemaking and housewifery. You have not come to Heshmat Mirza's house to practice your damn painting."

I was sitting, curled up, on the floor in a corner of the room. I had a lump in my throat and was ready to cry my heart out, but I stayed quiet. Seeing me suffer gave her pleasure, and I did not want to give her the satisfaction.

I stayed sitting on the floor even after she left. I thought of Mirza Hadi's rage. I refused to believe that burnt food alone had been the cause of it. He had surely lost money gambling the night before; perhaps he had even lost money to my brother. And now he was taking it out on his wife.

As Persians say, I was no longer scared of going to hell—I was already there. For the first time in my life, I felt violated. There had been no violence in my father's house. I was raised in an environment where love and respect were the norm (except, of course, the day my father berated Nima and his mother, which was not typical behavior for him, only an aberration). This new life was foreign to me. I was under the domination of two savage beasts, and I had to learn to defend myself.

When Mirza Hadi pulled my hair so relentlessly, I should have smacked hard elbow-strikes into his gut or, better yet, into his testicles. Then I should have escaped to my father's house and explained everything to my parents. I would have even insisted on divorcing Mirza Hadi, even though divorce was taboo.

But I knew that I could never bring myself to do any of that. I would be afraid to disappoint my father. He had been so proud that my marriage with Mirza Hadi had occasioned the union of his family with that of Heshmat Mirza's.

I was still on the floor when the lead servant, Afra, came in. She told me that after she and her husband, Ali, had heard me scream, they had rushed to the painting room to help. But when they saw Mirza Hadi pulling my hair, they had not dared to interfere.

"One must have eaten the brain of a donkey to torture such a gorgeous and innocent bride," she said trusting me with her life.

That night, in bed, I ignored Mirza Hadi's sexual advances, and every time he approached me, I moved away from him. He grew frustrated. Suddenly, he grabbed me, pushed my back flat onto the bed, and held me tight around my legs and back. He undressed me forcefully and raped me.

When, in the middle of the night, he woke me up for another round of sex, I did not resist. It would be many years before I learned that what happened that night had been rape. In those days, when it came to sex, whatever men did to their wives was of no concern to the law, let alone human rights. "Marital rape" was an oxymoron. In many countries, including mine, it is still like that. But, thanks to courageous feminists all over the world, we have come to understand and talk about marital rape, even if there is still much progress to be made.

# 5

At first, I'd had no desire to learn how to cook, which didn't stop my mother-in-law from spending several hours each day teaching me to prepare a variety of Persian foods. But I eventually developed interest in the recipes she showed me and gradually became a creative, confident cook. Even Mirza Hadi began teasing his sisters about how much better my cooking was than theirs, to which I would reply, "They are master cooks, and I am only a novice." Such statements made my in-laws happy and helped keep the peace around the house.

Eventually, I learned to coexist with Mirza Hadi and his family by following my own three self-made rules. First, I kept my readings and my thoughts to myself. I never brought up serious social, psychological, historical, or political topics for discussions. I had learned that intellectually stimulating issues intimidated them and could only lead to hostility. Second, I took cooking and grocery shopping seriously; and third, I continued to accommodate Mirza Hadi's insatiable sexual appetite. Observing these three rules made my life as Mirza Hadi's wife much easier.

Mirza Hadi made periodic tours of his father's beautiful villages, vast lands, farms, and orchards. I badly needed a change of scenery and started asking him to take me with him on some of those trips. He was reluctant at first, but I did not take no for an answer, and finally he agreed to let me join him on one of his inspection tours.

Although, in his will, Heshmat Mirza had divided two-thirds of his wealth among his wife and his three daughters equally (leaving the remaining one-third to Mirza Hadi), my mother-in-law and sisters-in-law had yet to see even a penny of their inheritance. This was because, before his death, Heshmat Mirza had transferred all that he owned to his son. Mirza Hadi's was the sole name on each and every deed, and with no assets or property under Heshmat Mirza's name, there was nothing left to be divided when he died.

My eldest sister-in-law, Jaleh, who was married and did not live with us, had explained to me once that her father's greatest fear had been that, after him, his properties not be kept together and be divided and later subdivided among his children and his children's heirs. For that reason, he had wanted Mirza Hadi to be in full control of all his riches. He believed that a master with numerous villages, farms, lands, orchards, houses, and mansions would be a more powerful and effective master than someone without as much property. Jaleh also told me that her father unequivocally stated, more than once, that, each year, Mirza Hadi should divide the total proceeds from his entire estate based on the proportionate shares outlined in his will. Furthermore, he had emphasized that Mirza Hadi was not entitled to any compensation for his management responsibilities, as he considered that beneath the dignity of a major landowner.

But these had been verbal instructions, and without a strict contract in writing, my in-laws were at the mercy of my husband for their share of Heshmat Mirza's wealth. Whether or not Mirza Hadi intended to pocket his mother's and his sisters' shares of their inheritance was not clear to me, but I feared it was possible. I did not want for me or my future children to live off stolen wealth.

The day arrived when I was going to accompany Mirza Hadi on his tour of his villages. We left when it was still dark and arrived at his largest village as the first glimmer of dawn lit the horizon. The sun rose behind a range of mountains that reached up to the sky, shedding light into the lingering darkness and painting the sky with brilliant shades of pink. The dawn light over the densely clustered adobe houses of the village created a glorious scene.

We went directly to our own mansion in the village, which was surrounded by beautiful Lombardy poplars in the middle of a thousand-acre orchard. While the servants prepared breakfast, I took a walk through the orchard, taking in every tree and every garden. It was a slice of heaven. There were natural springs all over the orchard, and I saw how the stream that flowed from one of them turned into a watercourse and how the gardeners had directed the watercourse toward the almond trees. It was spectacular to see all those walnut, apple, cherry, sour cherry, and apricot trees, all the poplars and willows, and gardens of transplanted petunias. It was refreshing to smell fragrances of mint and tarragon all over. I was curious why my in-laws did not spend much time in this village. And yet, I remembered that my own family did not spend much time in my father's villages, either.

That morning, we had a heavenly breakfast of sesame bread just out of the oven, tasteful honey spun out of the natural beeswax honeycomb, goat-milk butter, fried fresh-laid eggs, authentic barrel-aged Persian feta cheese, and fresh walnuts just out of the shell.

After breakfast, we took a tour of the farms that Mirza Hadi owned in the vicinity of his village. First, we went to his lush green-wheat farm, then to his highly profitable barley plant, and afterward to his award-winning grain farm. Before returning to the mansion, we also paid visits to Mirza Hadi's beet, potato, and tobacco farms. At each farm, while Mirza Hadi spoke with the farmers, I walked around and took pictures of the landscapes, villagers, and animals—later, I would use those pictures as inspiration for paintings.

When we returned to the mansion, it was nearly two o'clock in the afternoon, and we were quite hungry. The village headman and a few prominent villagers and their wives were invited to have lunch with us. They were already there waiting for us. Each couple had brought us, as a gift, a small carpet woven by the village girls.

Even though at home we had no cook, at our mansion in the village, we had an excellent chef, who had prepared for lunch a huge tray of a pilaf of herbed basmati rice, mixed with tender lima beans and seasoned with dill weed. On the top of the rice were quite a few braised whole lamb shanks served with onions, garlic, and tomatoes that had been sautéed in butter with a variety of Persian spices.

After lunch, it was time for nap. Mirza Hadi and I slept for a couple of hours, and when we woke up, we had intense sex. Even though the sex was still loveless and only physical, I hit a new height of pleasure. That was the first time I had sex in broad daylight, and I greatly enjoyed it.

In the early evening, we had an open house. All the villagers were invited to come and discuss their problems and achievements with Mirza Hadi. Our mansion had a huge terrace, which our servants had covered with carpets, and Mirza Hadi sat in the middle of it. As guests arrived, they sat around the terrace, the richer ones sitting closest to Mirza Hadi.

Meanwhile, the women came to see me in our spacious reception room. I felt that the female visitors liked me. I had a very sincere dialog with them, and for the most part, I was sympathetic to their difficulties. Most of the guests had brought us modest presents, whatever they could afford. Some gave us one or two chickens or roosters, others brought us baskets full of eggs or sweet bread, small bags of almonds, walnuts, crushed wheat, barley, and boxes of sour plum rolls.

At one point, an old woman with a bent back and cracked lips left her seat in the reception room and came to sit next to me. Her face was completely lined with deep wrinkles. She stared at me with her cloudy eyes and began to speak in a low voice.

"My dear," she said, "I could not afford to bring you a present. Instead I want to give you two pieces of advice." Confidently, the old woman went on to tell me that it was clear to her that I was not of the same ilk as Mirza Hadi. Even though I was beautiful, so were some of the young village girls, and not all of them were shy. There were flirtatious beauties among them, who could easily steal Mirza Hadi from me. "I apologize for being blunt," she said, "but he is known to be a womanizer. So, watch him. Do not let him travel without you. Go with him everywhere."

"My second piece of advice, you might not be able to do anything about, but you should know that the villagers, especially the farmers, are unhappy with your husband. He does not have the skill his father had to manage all these villages and farms. He is not an effective master. His amateurish orders frustrate the farmers. He simply does not know enough about trees, plants, or crops. In addition, he is greedy and wants everything for himself. He does not understand that others must make a living from these farms, too."

The old woman paused. I was in awe of her honesty. The last thing she told me was this: "Heshmat Mirza, may God bless his soul, was concerned about the quality of life of his farmers and other workers. Mirza Hadi does not give a damn about them."

Even though more than thirty-five years has passed since the old woman told me all of this, I remember every word she said as if it were only yesterday.

The next morning, Mirza Hadi and his steward sat on horses and went out to inspect the other nearby villages and farms. I had all day to myself with nothing special to do. So, I went for a long walk along the dusty alleys of the village. As I passed the houses, the villagers stopped me and invited me inside. They were very kind to me. It was not only their doors that were open to me; I felt that their hearts were, as well. In some houses that I visited, young girls were looming carpets, and as they knotted with their little fingers, they sang sad country songs about hard youth and hard lives.

Around some houses, the sweet, warm scent of baked bread filled the air and whetted my appetite. As I passed by a water spring, I had a sudden sinking feeling in the pit of my stomach. I felt an intense craving for Nima. I cannot explain how watching the spring triggered that. All I can say is that the water was amazingly clear, so clear that I could see my own reflection in it. It was like a perfectly smooth mirror. And wouldn't that be a description of Nima's heart, as well?

I wished that I had married Nima—Nima, who was a personification of goodness, who was of a most beautiful countenance, a perfect human being. In my eyes, God had made him so that we can see and understand who Joseph, son of Jacob, had been. I imagined that Nima and I lived in one of those adobe village houses and that, every day, I went to that spring, filled my large earthen pot with water, and carried it home on my shoulder. I wished I was a village girl with a simple and earthy life, sharing each of its moments with Nima. That day, I realized that when it came to love, the proverb "Out of sight, out of mind" was not applicable at all. Nima was in my mind night and day.

We stayed in the village a few more days. The days that Mirza Hadi traveled to other villages by car, I went with him. On the days that he traveled by horse, I stayed at our mansion. On our last day in the village, as I was walking down an alley, a middle-aged gypsy stopped me, grabbed my right hand, and began to read my palm. She did not give me a chance to tell her that I did not believe in palmistry. She said, nodding her head gravely, "Oh, my lady, your life's path is constricted, narrow, and dark." I gave her a coin and quickly walked away from her.

What she uttered made me very anxious. To avoid a panic attack, I pumped myself up by repeating phrases like "I am not a superstitious person" and "I do not give a damn about palmists." Was that gypsy sadistic? It was unusual for a palmist to say something so gloomy.

The rest of that day, I had a Hafez poem stuck in my head. I recited it repeatedly to myself:

> The dark night, and the fear of the wave, and the whirlpool so fearful[12]
> The light-burden ones of the shore— how know they our state?

---

[12] *The Divan-i Hafiz,* translated by H. Wilberforce Clarke, p. 3.

# CHAPTER 4

## LIFE UNDER OCCUPATION

### 1

It was before dawn on August 25, 1941, when we were awakened by the deafening sound of bombs.

Mirza Hadi and I put on our robes and climbed onto the roof. Ali and Afra were already there, and my in-laws and those servants who were living in the mansion joined us one by one. The roofs in Tabriz are all flat, and because of the size of our mansion, our roof was higher than those of other buildings in the town. We had a perfect view of what was happening: bombs were raining on government office buildings, military bases, and also on residential areas and commercial buildings, enveloping Tabriz in a shroud of smoke.

The explosions shook our mansion to shake again and again. My heart was in my mouth, and I badly needed to be held and comforted, but Mirza Hadi was indifferent. He saw me trembling, but he ignored me. If I had had an intimate relation with my in-laws, I would have hugged them tightly. But I was not close to any of them.

We should have sought shelter, but foolishly, we stayed on the roof until the bombardment ended and the planes instead began to drop leaflets.

We went down to our room, where Mirza Hadi sat in front of the radio and tuned the dial. The radio dial had to be on the exact frequency to receive the signal of the broadcast; if there was the slightest deviation, he lost the channel. At last, he found a station reporting that the Soviet Union had invaded Iran.

When he found a station talking about the invasion, we listened until it changed the subject. Then Mirza Hadi searched for another frequency that was covering the raid and offensive, and he continued doing so until the stations available to us all signed off of broadcasting. In those days, radio stations operated only a few hours a day.

Listening to the radio, we learned that while the Soviet Union was bombarding Tabriz, Ardbil, and Rasht, the British Royal Air Force was dropping bombs on military and government targets in Tehran, Qazvin, and other cities in central and southern Iran. The British forces had also bombed civilian and residential areas.

In the early phase of World War II, Iran had officially declared itself neutral. However, the Allied Powers were skeptical about Iran's neutrality, because Iran had a very close relationship with Germany. Unlike Russia and the United Kingdom, Germany had no imperial history in the Middle East, and Iranians were convinced that Germans had no intentions to invade their country. The radio reporter recapitulated these facts and discussed how, in a broadcast to the Persians, the Nazis had emphasized that Iran and Germany, as two Aryan nations, were natural allies, and how the Shah of Iran, who was very proud of his Aryan heritage, had joined the Hitler camp. The reporter stated that the Allied forces estimated that there were a thousand Nazi advisors in Iran, while the official number quoted by the Iranian government was 690. Persians did not think of these Germans as Nazi advisors but as German engineers and technical consultants who were helping Iranians in the development of infrastructure projects.

That day, I went on to read in the newspapers that there were 4,630 foreign nationals working in Iran, of which 2,590 were British. That is, there were almost four times as many British citizens as there were Germans living in Iran. The papers claimed that the presence of German engineers in Iran was merely an excuse for the Allied forces to occupy Iran. The actual reason for the occupation and raid was that approximately four million soldiers from the Axis Powers, the coalition of the countries that opposed the Allies, had invaded the Soviet Union. The Allies needed full control of Iran, which they called the "The Persian Corridor," to transfer supplies that the Soviets desperately needed. The United States shipped goods to the Persian Gulf, and the Allied Powers, through the Persian Corridor supply route, got them to the Soviet Union. Later on, in my readings about the Soviet and British invasion of Iran, I learned that the Shah of Iran had made offers to these countries to expel all Germans if they promised not to attack Iran. The offers had been refused.

Later, at the breakfast table, my mother-in-law, who had never shown any interest in or taste for politics and history, suddenly began to explain what she had learned from her late husband about Russia's wars with Iran. She spoke of how the Russians had long sought access to the "warm waters" of the Persian Gulf and how they had captured the Arran territories in 1812, which the Bolsheviks renamed the "Soviet Socialist Republic of Azerbaijan" in 1920. The use of the name of "Azerbaijan" for Arran was a mere sham to claim later that the Iranian state of Azerbaijan and the newly renamed Republic of Azerbaijan were one state divided in two, which the Soviets had a moral obligation to reunite. My mother-in-law expressed concern that perhaps the Soviets had come back to conquer and annex our land to their country, as they had conquered and annexed so many of our states in the nineteenth century. Mirza Hadi assured us that the times had changed for those sorts of actions. The new world power, the United States of America, would not allow the Soviets to compromise Iranian territorial integrity, he said. I concurred. History would prove us right.

We had just finished our breakfast when Afra entered the dining room and informed us that Mashdi had dropped in to make sure that we were all safe. I rushed out to the front yard, where Mashdi was sitting on the edge of a fountain with his hand running through the water. In his other hand, he held a bunch of leaflets.

As soon as he saw me, he stood up. I greeted him affectionately and told him how much I had missed him. I asked him about my parents and family members one by one, and he assured me that they were safe and sound, even though he had no news yet from Dena and Auntie. He had first gone to check on Sina and next had come to our house to make sure that Mirza Hadi and I were doing well. His next stop was Dena's and then Auntie's residences.

I invited Mashdi inside to have breakfast, but he had already eaten and told me had to go. He smiled.

"After all this time, some days around 4:30 P.M., I still go to the Octagonal unconsciously and wait for you to return from school," he said. "Now and then, I even hear your footsteps inside the house!"

Mashdi gave me one of the leaflets he had picked up from the street. I accompanied him to the exit door. He said, "So long, the angel of Moin-al-Tojjars," and left. In tears, I watched him as he walked away. Only God knew how much I missed my life before marriage. As I was watching Mashdi move away, I heaved a deep sigh and wished there was a way I could make sure that Nima was unharmed.

The leaflet Mashdi had given me had been dropped from Soviet aircraft after the bombardment. It contained the following message:

> "Iranians, there are thousands of Germans in your country, who work as advisors, but, in fact, they are Hitler's agents in disguise. They have taken control of your industry and agriculture. The German embassy is a well-integrated, cohesive organization, and each German in your country has a specific mission. These agents are on the alert for orders from Hitler in due time to destroy your agriculture and industry. You know how the intrigues of German agents in Iraq turned that country into a riot-torn chaotic land with Iraqi people trapped by violence and fear, and by unfathomable brutality. We have no doubt that Germany's plan for Iran is identical to what they planned for Iraq. Iran today is like the Netherlands and Belgium shortly before the Germans occupied those countries. As your friends, we wish for the welfare of Iran, and we want an independent Persia. Since your country took no action to expel the German spies, the British and we have occupied your country to remove the Germans from the Persian territories. The Soviet Union's army is one of the world's most powerful armies. Any impulse toward resistance will immediately be stifled. When Iran is free of the Germans, we will leave your country. In these difficult situations, if you cooperate with us, we will also cooperate with you, to any reasonable extent, now and in the future."

The message was signed by the commander of the Red Army.

The Red Army destroyed Iranian airbases and quickly occupied Tabriz, Ardabil, and a great part of Northwest Iran and the Iranian heartland. In those days, the population of Persia was under fifteen million, and the Iranian military had a standing force of no more than

200,000 men, perhaps as little as 130,000; meanwhile, the Red Army's invading force was made up of 120,000 soldiers and more than a thousand tanks and motorized infantry. Reza Pahlavi, the Shah of Iran, was in the midst of modernizing his army when the undeclared attacks caught him by surprise. His army was not ready to resist external invasion by two major powers. He fought hard, but four days into the invasion, after massive defeats, he proclaimed unconditional surrender to the Soviet and British forces. Eighteen days later, on September 16, 1941, Reza Shah was forced to abdicate at the hands of the Allied powers, and his twenty-three-year-old son ascended to the throne.

In the early days of the occupation, none of us left the house. Only male servants went out grocery shopping or on other errands. Ali informed us of all that was happening beyond our walls. He told us that the Soviets had taken control of the government offices, hospitals, and barracks. They had installed their flag on the highest point of Tabriz and had erected gallows all over the town. They were hanging or executing, by firing squads, non-obedient government employees, hospital staff, and officers.

Mirza Hadi reacted very harshly to erection of gallows.

"These ruthless murderers could fulfill their diabolical needs by just shooting innocent people," he thundered. "They have intentionally erected gallows, and they hang people to create an even more frightful environment."

One day, Ali came in to give us his report. "I have never been as infuriated as I was today," he said. "I was seeing red. I had to use all my might to stop myself, otherwise those Russian bastards would have shot me right there."

Mirza Hadi asked Ali to back up his story and explain.

"I saw a Soviet soldier dragging a girl on the ground," Ali said. "He was taking her to a back alley to rape her. Other soldiers carrying machine guns had blocked the alley, and the girl was screaming and cursing the soldier. She called him baseborn, godless, bastard, faithless, villain, devil, beast, and she yelled that she will pray to God, day and night, for a car to smash into him and crush his head under its wheels. It was one of those moments that if I could, I would have started a bloodbath and slaughtered all those savages."

I clenched my teeth in anger as I listened to Ali's story. Mirza Hadi's face had turned all red; he was enraged, but he said nothing. I recited a line from Hafez, "Like that remained not; like this shall not remain." Then I recited another line: "The imprints of violence and the mark of tyranny shall not remain." But I knew that sometimes such imprints and marks did remain.

The Soviet Union did not supply its occupying army with food. The Iranian people had to feed 120,000 aggressors three meals a day. As a result, it did not take long before we faced a shortage. Two months into the occupation, the government was forced to impose food rationing by issuing coupon stamps. Soon radio stations were reporting that, every day, hundreds of poor people were dying of starvation and hundreds of others were dying because they had been denied access to health services. Along with the thousands of men who had been shot and hanged, these deaths added to the toll. The Soviet massacre continued.

We were all outraged when we read in the newspaper that, in the eyes of Joseph Stalin, raping young girls and women of all ages indiscriminatingly, killing and hanging innocent people daily, taking food from women and children—not to mention all sorts of other atrocities—were problems that bourgeois society brought upon itself. Witnessing the Soviet occupation made me understand why the women of Azerbaijan had always panicked at the thought of a Russian invasion. They considered it worse than typhoid.

In those days, at times, I remembered the lessons of my high school history teacher concerning the Persian wars with Russian. Her voice reverberated in my head: In its very long history, the mighty Persian Empire, was weakened many times. For example, when it was defeated by Alexander of Macedon in 331 B.C., and again when it was occupied by the Arabs in 651 A.D., and later in history, when the Mongols and then Tartars attacked and occupied Iran. However, never did Persia plummet to the depth of wretchedness as it did during the Qajar dynasty. Throughout the reigns of Qajar kings, the Russians attacked Iran repeatedly. They began a war in 1812, and in 1813, they subjected us to a miserable defeat. As a result, they officially annexed the Iranian territories of Arran, Daghestan, Eastern Georgia, and Northern Armenia to their empire. After a 13-year truce, the Russians attacked Iran again in 1826, and after two years of fierce fight, once again they defeated us decisively, and this time, in 1828, they annexed the modern-day Armenia, Nakhchivan, and all parts of Iran's Caucasian territories.

# 2

Several months into the occupation, as a result of serious negotiations with Iranian officials, the Soviets removed all the gallows from the streets and agreed to stop their troops from raping girls and women. (It was quite ironic that an army of murderers and rapists had occupied our land to save us from German engineers, who were not Nazis and had done nothing but help us with infrastructure and development projects.)

Little by little, people dared go outside, schools reopened, and girls and women reappeared in the streets. But even under such newly relaxed circumstances, my in-laws and I took extra precautions when we left the house, making sure that we were accompanied by at least two male servants.

As a devoted patriot, my father started a resistance movement whose members were mostly major food merchants. These merchants hid most of their rice, flour, grains, and sugar in secret rooms in their warehouses. Safeguarded from the Soviets, these food items could be reserved for the people, and eventually my father and his activist partners developed a clandestine distribution scheme that fed the whole town. The Soviets knew that there was a great deal more food than the merchants claimed, but they could not find it, even when they raided the warehouses.

Mirza Hadi learned that the Soviets were planning to arrest all the food merchants of Tabriz and beat the soles of their bare feet in public. For inflicting the maximum pain on the person beaten, they were gathering pomegranate tree branches, stripping them of leaves, and storing them in basins of ice-cold water, to be used as bastinados in the beatings. Mirza Hadi was concerned that the merchants might expose the hiding places in their warehouses for fear of the bastinado and the subsequent humiliation. I shared his concern, and I thought of a line from Shakespeare: "Our fears do make us traitors."

The Soviets were aware that my father was leading one of the anti-occupation movements. They sent an envoy to tell him that if the merchants continued to hide food, then they would have no choice but to punish them. They emphasized that giving each merchant one hundred strokes of the bastinado was only the first step. A lot more would follow if they did not cooperate.

The Soviets' message enraged my father.

He arranged a meeting and invited all the merchants and other influential citizens of Tabriz to gather at his home on the last Friday of February. The meeting could not possibly remain secret: too many people were invited, and it was impossible for the news of the assembly not to reach the Soviets.

On that Friday, when Mirza Hadi, my mother-in-law, and I arrived at my parents' house, Dena and Habib, Auntie and her husband, my Uncle Hāji Darab, and Sina and his wife were already there. The other guests began to arrive, and by mid-afternoon, the assembly hall in the second courtyard was packed with people. Shortly after three o'clock, four unusually dressed people entered. They wore robe-like black dresses covering their entire bodies and veils that shrouded their faces, leaving only an opening for the eyes. Wearing such a *burqa* was not common anywhere in Iran, especially not in Tabriz. I was sure they were men disguised in women's clothing.

Following these unusually dressed people was a famous street thug and six of his boys. After the occupation, these hoodlums had been at the service of the Soviets and often stormed political gatherings. Their leader also led mobs of street prostitutes. Their presence at my father's house made me extremely nervous. I wished Mashdi had bolted the entrance door before all these people had shown up.

Others shared my concern. Mirza Hadi whispered in my ear, "May God save us all. These thugs are the Soviets' attack dogs. Those black-robed ruffians are not women." Hāji Darab took my father aside and suggested that he cancel the meeting and dismiss the audience.

"Let them storm our meeting," he replied. "Roughness breeds hatred, and those whom people hate, they wish dead. We have no choice but to bear these thugs' presence. They are professional criminals, and my workers are not strong enough or equipped to be rid of them."

Then, my father turned to the audience and began his speech:

"My compatriots, my fellow Azerbaijanis, as you know, ever since 1812, the Russians keep attacking Iran. First, they occupy our land, and then they remember that their troops need to be fed and that their horses and mules live off grass and grains and hay. Our farmers can produce only enough for our own consumption and for our livestock. We cannot produce for 120,000 Soviet troops and God knows how many horses and mules on a daily basis."

My father went on to condemn the Soviets' barbaric threats to give our reputable and honorable merchants each one hundred strokes of the bastinado in public. He then expressed outrage that they had occupied the telegraph offices of Tabriz, Ardabil, and other major cities and had cut off our lines of communication with the rest of our country.

"What did German engineers ever do to endanger our independence and freedom? They helped us build bridges, railways and dams. They are not Nazis. Not all Germans are Nazis. Soviets claim that they have occupied our country to save us from Nazis. Ask yourselves, how many Nazis have they captured? None! Does it look like they are after Nazis? Definitely not! They have come here to make our lives miserable and to capture our land. They rape our daughters and sisters, hang our brothers, torture our heroes, and pluck the morsels from the mouths of our children."

The audience was riveted. My father was emotional as he talked about Iran's independence and the necessity that all parties put aside their differences and unite against the Soviets. Suddenly, one of the black-robed people stood up, reached under his robe, pulled out a small caliber pistol, pointed it at my father, and fired three shots. It all happened so quickly. I watched as my father collapsed to the ground in a pool of his own blood. He was dead.

Auntie reached him first. She sat down, lifted his head off the floor, and put it on her lap. She sprinkled a rain of kisses over his face and forehead. My mom, Dena, and I rushed to join her. I sat next to my father's body, held his hand, and kissed it with all the love inside me. Dena did the same with his other hand. We wailed and wept like a rain-cloud. Others tried to lift us off the floor and comfort us, but it was no use. Sina held our mother close to his chest, and Habib and Hāji Darab tried to control the audience. Meanwhile, Mirza Hadi stood dumbstruck in a corner, staring at my father's slain body.

Protected by the street thugs, the black-robed ruffians fled. Some members of the crowd tried to chase them, but they were stopped at the front door by Soviet soldiers, who carried machine guns. The soldiers started to allow the crowd to leave my father's house only after the ruffians and thugs had completely disappeared.

The next day, the Soviets summoned Sina, Hāji Darab, Habib, and Mirza Hadi to their headquarters. They said that any funeral for my dad would have to be held in private. However, Hāji Darab convinced them that it was impossible for us to bury my dad without people's knowledge. He argued that the news would inevitably leak and thousands, if not hundreds of thousands, of gallant Azerbaijanis would pour into the streets. There would be a riot, and another tragedy would be inevitable.

Hāji Darab and the Soviets agreed to an orderly, controlled funeral for my dad. If anything got out of hand, the Soviets said, they would direct their troops to crush the crowd.

# 3

My father's funeral was set for Sunday, February 29, 1942. Starting at six in the morning, people began to fill Tabriz's magnificent historical Jameh Mosque. By the time the family arrived, there were already thousands of teary-eyed mourners gathered at the mosque and in the surrounding streets. Many of them had black armbands.

As agreed upon, Habib and Hāji Darab made sure the affair remained orderly and organized. No one wanted any confrontation with the heavily armed Soviet soldiers. It was estimated that a hundred thousand of my father's admirers had attended that day to join the funeral procession. The Soviet soldiers kept a considerable distance from the mourners. The large turnout made quite a statement, and I am sure that it shook the Soviets.

At 8:30 A.M., a group of townsmen lifted my father's coffin and put it on their shoulders. The crowd began to chant: "There is no God but God." I felt like their voices were shaking the earth.

As difficult as it was, the crowd parted and kept space enough for the procession to pass. Family, close relatives, friends, and dignitaries were allowed to walk behind the coffin.

The chanting continued until we reached outside of the mosque. There, the tone was less religious. People waved clenched fists and shouted anti-Soviet messages:

> Soviets, Soviets, blood dripping off your hands, leave us alone, leave our lands!

After repeating this over and over, they began a new slogan in a new tone:

> Martyr Moin-al-Tojjar, you a lion of Iran, your legacy will live on!

And yet another slogan with another tone:

> Righteous man, righteous man, we will avenge your blood and create red flood!

And the last slogan I still remember was:

> What a loss today, let us mourn, for Soviets feel scorn!

It was a long way from the mosque to our private mausoleum at the Tabriz cemetery. There were people all around us, as far as the eye could see. Many were angry, and they yelled their wrath at the Soviet occupation. And yet, the procession made its way peacefully. Mourners offered to help carry the coffin for some distance, and one at a time, the pallbearers gave their spots to others. This went on all the way until we reached the cemetery.

While tracking slowly across the town toward the cemetery, my heart was heavy. The wind was wailing in the trees, the way I wailed for my father's death. Perhaps between me and the wind there existed a harmony of feeling, and the wind was also grieving.

It felt like Tabriz had turned into a pit of quicksand that was sucking me in. Alongside my grief there was rage: the Soviets had kindled my wrath, and I had an urge to pull myself out of the mire by destroying our oppressors. Every cell in my body yearned for bloody revenge, a revenge that I knew I would never have. Not then and not ever after. Not in this world and not in the next. I only hoped that the slayer would soon follow the slain.

My father's murder had struck a crushing blow to my psyche. Not only had he been my hero, he was also the person I relied on for unconditional support. His mere existence had given me enormous self-confidence. With my father gone, I dreaded what was to come. I did not trust Mirza Hadi, and I knew that with him and Sina controlling all aspects of my life, my future would not be smooth sailing. So, contrary to the famous Turkish maxim, I *did* fear tomorrow's mischance.

As I walked behind my father's coffin, shoulder to shoulder with Mirza Hadi, I suddenly recalled the gypsy whom I had met on the last day of my trip to Mirza Hadi's villages. She had told me that my life's path was going to be constricted, narrow, and dark. Such a prediction no longer seemed baseless.

I had been a daughter of the Honorable Moin-al-Tojjar. His very being was necessary for my existence; he was the source of my identity, the foundation of the person I am.

He should have lived long and died of natural causes. Yes, he had died the death of the righteous, and as friends kept telling us, "Whom God loveth best, those he taketh soonest."[13] But these were only words. I am not sure that any logical person could be convinced they were true.

And yet, in the midst of all these persisting thoughts, what gave me satisfaction was that, for all of my life, I had measured up to my father's expectations. He was always proud of me. I had done everything he wanted me to do: I studied hard, read as much as I could, became an intellectual and an artist, and got married to Mirza Hadi—my greatest sacrifice in life. Thinking of that sacrifice put me in mind of my Romeo, for whom my love had never diminished. I wished that, instead of Mirza Hadi, Nima walked beside me. He would have lifted my chin, and while gazing deep into my eyes, with his beautiful fingers, he would have wiped the tears that fell down my cheeks.

I scanned the crowd. There were thousands of men around me. Was Nima one of them? My father had been very mean to him, but Nima was not hardhearted. Now that my father had given his life for his country, I had no doubt that Nima forgave him.

In the cemetery, when my father was laid in the grave, I bade farewell to my soul's moon and sun, to the essence of my being. I

---

[13] Old Testament

whispered to myself, "Dad, joy and pain will not be ours in common anymore. Your presence and aura will be forever remembered, since you died the death of the people's martyr. You gave your life for our homeland and for freedom, for the eminence of all Persians." Then I let my sorrow fill me, and I wept. The flow of my tears washed away the lump in my throat and released me from the extreme feeling of tightness and pressure there. Looking at me, Mirza Hadi said that it was as if they had put a grieving mask over my face. I was the personification of sorrow.

# 4

Unlike Heshmat Mirza, who had legally transferred all that he owned to his only son, Mirza Hadi, my father had not transferred any of what he owned to any of us. On the deeds of his properties, there was no other name but his own. However, dad's will was similar to Heshmat Mirza's. He had given two-fifths of his wealth to Sina and had divided the remaining three-fifths equally among Dena, my mom, and me. Furthermore, in his will, my father had urged the three of us to give Sina a general power of attorney, the type that gave him the authority to do anything he wanted in our stead. Dad wanted his properties to be kept together and not be divided after he was gone. So, it was his will that Sina be given full power for independent action on our behalf.

Mirza Hadi said I should give Sina no such power. He did not trust Sina with my father's wealth. He knew my brother well, and he was sure that he would throw it all away in gambling. He explained that Sina's gambling partners were swindlers who sometimes let Sina win so that he would continue to play.

"They are scoundrels," he told me. "Every time they play, they get together ahead of time to plan on how to empty Sina's pockets. They'll call each other's bets just to raise the stakes higher and higher. Sina can't help himself. He plays right into their hands and loses great amounts of money."

Mirza Hadi said that I could not imagine how stupid my brother was: Sina was the kind of man who lit his cigarettes with the burning bills, he told me.

Calling my brother stupid did not offend me; in fact, I believed all that Mirza Hadi had to say. Sina considered himself to be a mastermind, but he was irresponsible and thoughtless, and he had no clue of his follies.

I discussed Mirza Hadi's concerns with my mom and Dena, but my mother refused to listen and forbade us from disrespecting our father's will. It took Dena and I several weeks until, reluctantly, we bowed to mom's pleas and did what we should have never done—we gave Sina power of attorney.

It had taken decades of hard work for my grandfather and my father to earn and accumulate all that wealth. But it took Sina less than six months to blow it all at the betting table—all of our riches, our vast holdings of orchards and farms, villages and houses, lands, horses, sheep and goats, shorthorn cattle, and God only knows what else.

They say that gamblers and racehorses never last long. The day after Sina lost my father's house, he was found dead, hanging from our eucalyptus tree. The house was the very last piece of my father's tremendous wealth. There was not a penny left. "Shirtsleeves to shirtsleeves in three generations," as the proverb goes.

Sina's suicide devastated all of us, especially my mother, but he had left no path for himself, none except the one that led beneath the ground. I would have done exactly the same. And yet, thirty-three years has passed since those days, and I still get chills whenever I imagine my beloved brother's body hanging from that tree, the one where he and I had played in our childhood years.

I find it bewildering that I do not have much to write about how my father's glorious riches vanished in the blink of an eye. How true is the saying that high winds blow on high hills!

> Ah, make the most of what we yet may spend[14],
> Before we too into the Dust descend;
> Dust into Dust, and under Dust to lie,
> Sans Wine, sans Song, sans Singer, and—sans End!

Mom went to live with Dena and Habib. Given Mirza Hadi's and his mother's attitudes toward me, it was not possible for me to ask my mother to come live with me, and she understood that. Besides, Habib was like a son to my mother, and she felt more comfortable living with him and

---

[14] *Letters and Literary Remains of Edward Fitzgerald*, edited by William Aldis Wright (London and New York: MacMillan and Co., 1889).

Dena. They also invited Mashdi to live with them. All his life, Mashdi had lived in my grandfather's and my father's houses, and his love for our family was boundless. We loved him dearly, too. For Mashdi, Sina, Dena, and I were like his own children. In the end, the demise of the Moin-al-Tojjar family dynasty was too much for him to bear. Dena and Habib took care of him until he died of severe depression.

Italians say, what will be, will be, and I do not dispute that. Greeks, however, say that the destiny assigned to people is suited to them, and I do not agree with that. I never deserved the life my destiny condemned me to live. After my father was gone and his wealth squandered, I had to go on suffering the cruelties of a sadistic mother-in-law and a psychopath husband, who, other than sex, had no use for me. Mirza Hadi disparaged me for being completely destitute, and he pulled my hair and beat me. Sometimes, while beating me, he scolded me for not having listened to him and for having given my "good-for-nothing brother" power of attorney to destroy "our wealth." He always said "*our* wealth" rather than "your wealth," implying that my inheritance had been his, as well. All this while he punched me in the head and slapped me across the face. It was obvious that, just as he had pocketed his mother's and his sisters' shares of their inheritance, he had pinned his hopes on attaining a share of my father's fortune, too.

There was no limit to Mirza Hadi's greed. Other than sex and money, nothing else mattered to him. And there I was, the pampered daughter of Moin-al-Tojjar, raised in a loving and affluent home in the lap of luxury, desperate and hopeless, under the domination of a barbarous, pathological narcissist. I was only twenty-one years old. How long, I wondered, could such behavior continue.

# CHAPTER 5

## TRAUMATIC REPETITIVE BETRAYAL

### 1

Mirza Hadi did not have his father's leadership skills. He lacked decision-making abilities and had serious trouble managing the family properties. Like most other masters, he was burdensome, unjustly harsh, and brutal. But unlike some of them, he showed no compassion for others and did not empathize with his workers and other people around him. He did not have a conscience. He might have been a sociopath; I cannot be sure. But I am certain that he was a narcissist. He could not bear any thoughts, ideas, and suggestions that conflicted with his own. He was chronically self-centered and was in no position to seek or welcome unsolicited advice. Those who questioned him suffered consequences. And yet, given all of this, I think that he was well aware of his shortcomings—that is, his inability to manage all those properties that he, his mother, and his sisters had inherited. That is why, one day, he decided to sell them all and deposit the cash in Iranian and French banks.

It was in the morning, a few weeks after Sina's suicide, that a heated exchange erupted between Mirza Hadi and his mother. I had just come down to join them for breakfast. I stopped right there in the doorway of the dining room and watched them. They were too busy yelling at each other to notice me.

"What the hell did you just say? Did I hear it right?"

"Yes, mother, you know Divan Salar, the landowner tycoon who is rolling in money. He has offered me an exorbitant amount of cash for everything that I own except, of course, the mansion, which I will not sell."

"Stop all this nonsense—'everything that I own!' Four-sixths—that is, two-thirds—of all that we have belongs to me and your three sisters. Who the hell do you think you are? You are dead wrong if you think that you can pocket our money and then skedaddle away from Iran."

"Don't worry, mother. I will give you and my sisters hefty monthly stipends so that you can continue your aristocratic lifestyles."

"We'll see about that! You, the wayward son of Heshmat Mirza, do you think that the noble title that the Qajar king gave your grandfather was merely a piece of paper? No, you delinquent! The real certificate of nobility was the collection of villages, lands, farms, and orchards. The title deed to our nobility is all that we own, and I will not let you burn it. I will disown you."

"Oh, mother, nothing is more useless than such titles. They are all meaningless. All that matters is what you are, not what you are thought to be. The only real noble person in our town was my father-in-law. Not because of a king's decree and not because of his wealth. He was noble because of his character and his deeds. And yet, take a look at what happened to him and to all that he had worked so hard to build: naught in naught! In this world, which is an unending movie, he was a player; we are extras."

Mirza Hadi continued, "I am not going to waste the rest of my life dealing with peasants in villages. I would rather the ground open and swallow me. I am determined to enjoy every second of my life. Like Hafez, 'I am free from whatever taketh color of attachment.' I need to be free from any responsibilities. Let us face it, I cannot be tied down to family life, either. I want to travel often, like a bird, as much as my heart desires. And that's why, this week, I will sell everything that I own." Mirza Hadi smirked. "Put that in your pipe, mother, and smoke it."

When he was finished, my mother-in-law shouted at him, "You wimp, inept, incompetent! You imbecile, do you want to join the societal parasites? Is that what you want to do?" Then she got up from her chair and headed toward the doorway. She was surprised to see me standing there watching them. She shot a furious glance at me and left. I immediately rushed inside the room and sat at the dining table in front of Mirza Hadi, who, as usual, took his anger out on me, screaming that, if I ever again stopped and watched him and his mother quarrel, he would first fracture my ribs and then beat me to death. Without having a bite, I got up and left.

I went upstairs to my arts room and began to paint. I had known that Mirza Hadi was a pervert, narcissist, wife-beater, wife-abuser, womanizer, and an incompetent farm and village owner, that he was spoiled, selfish, rotten, corrupt, and a miserably tight-fisted multimillionaire. But that day, I learned that his wickedness was not inadvertent. By praising my father and showing so much respect for him, Mirza Hadi proved that he could tell between good and evil. Therefore, his behavior and actions were all intentionally and knowingly vicious.

These new observations made me despise him even more than before, and I was ashamed of the purely physical sexual encounters that I regularly had with this man. I hated that, almost every night, I was in bed with this odious person. I knew that I had no choice, that I had to submit myself to him, even though having sex with him was a burden. And yet, after all these years, I still puzzle over the way that my mind was able to block these thoughts out so that sex could still bring me physical gratification.

Mirza Hadi's decision to sell all that his family owned brought me great glee. It was the very thing I wanted. The strength and power of my husband's family stemmed from that wealth, and now it was vanishing. My mother-in-law, with all that lust for power and with her insatiable appetite for influence and prominence, was taking crushing punches from her own spoiled and useless son. I rejoiced that, soon, she would no longer be able to flaunt her landlordship. It did not matter how much money there would be in her son's bank accounts; that did not give her anything like the social status associated with feudal lordship. There would not be even one peasant's wife to kneel and kiss her hands!

Within a couple of weeks, Mirza Hadi sold all that his grandfather and his father had worked so hard to acquire, build, and accumulate. All that he kept were his family's residential mansion and cars. To calm his mother down, Mirza Hadi lectured to her about industrialization. He argued that times had changed and the era for building manufacturing plants was upon us. He promised that, by becoming the leading factory owner of Azerbaijan, he would take his family's prominence to new heights. However, none of us took him seriously. Everyone in the family knew that he was not capable of performing such a feat of engineering. He was just a loud, empty drum.

My sisters-in-law were unbelievably cowardly. Their brother had swindled them out of their inherited monies, and they did not dare to fight him to get their rightful shares of that hefty cash. My mother-in-law, on the other hand, spent the rest of her life trying to get her portion of the tens of millions of dollars that Mirza Hadi had received from the sale of the properties. But all of her desperate pleas, her entreaties, threats to sue and to shame him by telling people that he stole his mother's and sisters' monies—fell on deaf ears. On such occasions, no one was deafer than Mirza Hadi.

# 2

Now, with his French accounts loaded with cash, it was more convenient than ever for Mirza Hadi to travel to Paris and stay there as long as he wished. In Paris, far from his mother's incessant grumbling and scolding, he was free to indulge himself. There, he could consort with promiscuous women without being recognized. He was not a marked person there as he was in Tabriz. He could behave as irresponsibly as he wanted, be sworn to a life of debauchery, wine and dine, seduce women, and fornicate.

I was sick and tired of being left alone with my sadistic mother-in-law and useless, good-for-nothing sisters-in-law while Mirza Hadi lived it up in Paris. We never knew how long he planned to stay there. He just said goodbye and disappeared, without hugs or kisses and without affection. He did not care about his family, and he no longer owned all those villages, orchards, and farms to worry about them. He knew that, in his absence, no one could touch his bank accounts. With peace of mind, he could stay abroad for as long as he liked.

There was a young girl living in our neighborhood. Her name was Anvar, and she was not married. My mother-in-law had a very close friendship with her. She visited my in-laws often, which is how we became acquainted. Over time, we developed a friendship of our own, then we became good friends, and eventually we were best friends. And all that was fine with my mother-in-law. Our fantastic friendship met her approval, and in fact, she encouraged it. Anvar was a stunning beauty with a flawless complexion and big green eyes that resembled pure topaz. She was mesmerizing. You could not help but wonder what was behind those eyes. She was tall with a very elegant figure. She was contemplative, a little reserved, watchful and attentive, introspective but yet an extrovert, and impressively intelligent. On top of all that, she did not care about how others perceived her. Auntie and most other relatives and friends considered me to be the most beautiful woman in Tabriz. I wondered if they saw Anvar, whether they might change their minds.

It did not take long for my friendship with Anvar to reach a stage where I could completely trust her, and I soon told her all about my life from A to Z. I gave her a detailed account of my relationship with Nima, and with that, I unfolded the biggest secret of my life. In exchange, Anvar revealed to me why she was still single. Although she had as many suitors as there are leaves on trees, she had been madly in love with one person, a man named Kasra, who had left her and married the daughter of a very rich landowner. She regretted that she did not belong to an aristocratic family, that she was only an upper-middle-class girl. Before Kasra got married, he and Anvar had a very close relationship. She often went to his house after dark, where they would sneak into the woods on Kasra's property and explore physical intimacy without intercourse. I was astonished how far Anvar and Kasra had managed to advance in their physical relationship. I could not imagine a boy and girl in Tabriz having that sort of intimacy before marriage. I would not have even dared to kiss Nima without marrying him.

Anvar told me that still, even after Kasra had married, she was fixated on him and gathered as much information as she could about his life. Kasra was in her mind all the time everywhere, and she often had imaginary conversations with him—and, of course, fantasies. Once, Anvar told me that she could easily have had an affair with Kasra, but that was not what she wanted. She wanted Kasra to herself. "I live only once, and I am determined to get him back at any price," she said. "He is mine."

Anvar had no sisters, only a brother, and her father had passed away. Her mother had no power or control over her. Anvar did whatever she wanted to do. But she was obsessed with Kasra, dangerously so. She was angry that she had lost him and came up with schemes to manipulate him, ruin his marriage, and win him back. Anvar was clearly a homewrecker, and I was concerned for her. But there was nothing I could do to change her mind.

# 3

In the two years since I had married Mirza Hadi, I had lost my father and my brother, we had come under a brutal occupation by the Soviet Union, my family had lost everything that we had, and my mother was destitute and living with my sister. What were the chances that a person went through so many mishaps in such a short time?

At that point in my life, my only wish was to become pregnant and bear a child. I spent almost all of my time in Mirza Hadi's house, where I badly needed to love and be loved. No one could do that for me but a child of my own. Plus, having a child might strengthen my relationship with Mirza Hadi. Our marriage was hanging by a thread, and my mother-in-law threatened me with a divorce several times a week. Strangely enough, she did not reproach me for not yet having given her a grandchild. For a woman with my mother-in-law's character, this was highly unusual. It was difficult to know what she was up to. Something was fishy, and there were definitely wheels within wheels.

Since becoming destitute, I feared that Mirza Hadi lacked motivation to stay married to me. I was scared to death when I thought about my future. Mirza Hadi and his mother had worn me out. What had the fates done to me? Where was that liberated woman who, in Auntie's words, was a daring heir to the likes of the brave women of Persian history? I was ashamed of myself, even though I had no reason to be. I saw myself as the eagle in the famous poem by Khanlari,[15] whose flight domain was the firmament: "Viewing the clouds majestically below and the world in her mighty grip. But fallen so deeply into disgrace that filthy crow was setting the pace for her."[16]

Although the inner city was safe, the Soviet occupiers still held onto Tabriz's outskirts. My sisters-in-law were free to go out whenever they wished, but I had to get permission from my mother-in-law to leave the house. I had to tell her exactly where I was going and when I planned to return. She rarely permitted me to go and visit Auntie and her family. Only once, sometimes twice, a week, she allowed me to go and see my mom, but only for a maximum of two hours. If I had to go shopping,

---

[15] Parviz Natel Khanlari (1914-1999), an Iranian literary scholar, poet, and linguist.
[16] Lines from "The Eagle," by Parviz Natel Khanlari, translated by Iraj Bashiri.

either Afra or Ali had to escort me. If I ever returned home later than the time I was supposed to, she became my worst nightmare.

On one of my visits, I bit the bullet and told my mother and Dena everything that was happening to me at Mirza Hadi's house. My mother cried the whole time, and as her tears fell, she reminded me that, just as a girl moves to her husband's house in a *white* wedding dress, in our tradition, she must leave her husband's house only in a *white* death shroud. She advised me to suffer and endure.

"Your mother-in-law is not going to last forever and, sooner or later, Mirza Hadi will get tired of a life of debauchery," she said. "He is just an animal in a savage state. He will be domesticated. That will happen." Then she recited a line from Hafez:

> If, for a space of two days, to our desire, the sphere's revolution turned not,[17]
> Ever, in one way, the state of revolution is not: suffer not grief.

It was easy for mom to give such advice. It was not easy for me to bide my time until the day when my fifty-eight-year-old mother-in-law was damned to hell and until a time when my brute and shamelessly dissolute husband was domesticated. That time, I was sure, would never come.

As I left Dena's house, she walked with me to the gate and told me, with utmost sincerity and with passion and love, that I should not be scared of divorce. "You are still a Moin-al-Tojjar, and a Moin-al-Tojjar must live a glorious life," Dena said. "If Mirza Hadi divorces you or if you decide to divorce him, that is perfectly fine. Neda, Habib, and I would be thrilled to have you live with us. We have a huge house, half of it unoccupied. You can choose whichever room or rooms that you want and live there, in peace and grace, a life that a noble woman such as yourself deserves to live."

In tears, I hugged and kissed my sister. Then I left. Deep down inside, I always knew that if I were thrown out of Heshmat Mirza's mansion, Dena and Habib would take care of me. I could count on Auntie and Hāji Darab, as well. However, it was great to be reminded that my situation was not as desperate as my mother-in-law and Mirza Hadi would have me believe.

---

[17] *The Divan-i Hafiz*, translated by H. Wilberforce Clarke, p. 499.

After I had told mom and Dena the stories of my daily harassments in Mirza Hadi's house, Dena said something that has stuck with me all these years. "I think now I know why you never refer to your in-laws by their names," she said. "They don't merit their names, do they?" It was true. My mother-in-law was not worthy of her given name, Afsar Banoo. Banoo means lady, which clearly, she was not, and Afsar means crown, implying high status—but obviously, she was even lower than a parasite. And my sisters-in-law deserved no names at all, since they were so inconsequential that I often wondered why our galaxy needed their existence.

That is how I saw my in-laws, and I believed that was how they were. However, if you asked Anvar, she would have told you that my mother-in-law was superior to any other woman she had known, a cut above the rest, a true "afsar." That was why I was very cautious never to say anything negative or inflammatory about my husband's family in front of Anvar. Once, I almost lost my cool: I wanted to say to her that naming my mother-in-law Afsar Banoo was like naming a bald person Ringlet or a blind man Spectator. But I came to my senses and stopped myself.

# 4

One afternoon, while I was in my room painting, Dena's servant, Uncle Verdi, brought me a very sad message saying that my mother was on her deathbed and that she wanted to see me right away. I told Uncle Verdi not to wait for me; I would be along shortly.

I put on some decent clothes, picked up my shoes, and tiptoed down the stairs. I did not know where my mother-in-law was, so I tried to remain stealthy. However, as I approached the mansion's front gate, she appeared like a bolt out of the blue. My heart nearly stopped. I dropped my shoes on the ground reflexively. Then I bent over, picked them up, and put them on. With her hand on her hip, she began sarcastically berating me.

"Sneaking out of the house on tiptoes? Shall I prepare your golden carriage, your highness, your majesty the queen, the world's warming sun? Alert your entourage that they be ready to escort you?"

"Please, let me go," I said. "My mother is on her deathbed. I want to see her one more time. I must say goodbye to her."

"You cannot go. While your husband is away, I am the one who controls you. You are not free to do anything on your own. Since you were trying to sneak out without my permission, it is now your punishment to stay home. From now until your body, wrapped in a smelly shroud, is put into a grave, you will regret the day you ignored my authority."

"I am so sorry. I apologize from the bottom of my heart. I beg you not to be ruthless. Have mercy." I began to cry.

My pleas must have worked, because my mother-in-law decided to let me go. She would come with me and wait outside of Dena's house for half an hour only. If I did not return on time, that would be the end of my marriage to Mirza Hadi. "I will throw you out like yesterday's trash," she warned, and with that, we began walking toward my sister's house.

On the way, we did not say a word to each other. She watched me the whole time as if I was about to escape from her hands. When we reached Dena's house, I asked her to come in with me and see my mother one last time, but she responded that she had no interest in seeing "that piss-poor woman."

After all these years, I still cannot understand how I tolerated this behavior. I regret that I put up with so many cruel remarks and with such verbal and physical abuse. Auntie was wrong about me being a lioness of the caliber of mythical Persian heroines. I was insecure and had been ever since my father was killed and my family became utterly destitute. I had fallen from the zenith of glory to the depth of abjection. What a shame that, when my mother-in-law caught me sneaking out of the house and decided to humiliate me, I did not slap her as hard as I could. I should have done that and then fled to Dena and Habib's house. Or afterward, when she called my mother a "piss-poor woman," I should have punched her in the face and knocked out as many of her front teeth as I could. What a shame that I was so passive! Now I have to live with such regrets forever. A thousand pities that, in youth, we do not have the wisdom of an aged oracle—that's when we need it the most. Then again, when I think back on those days, I try to remember that I was only twenty-one years old, a naïve and immature young woman scared to death of being abandoned and becoming a burden to Dena and Habib or Auntie and my Uncle Hāji Darab.

Sociologists warn us not to mistake an arranged marriage for a forced marriage. That may be so. However, in a case like mine, where I was madly in love with someone else and I had no say about my future husband, I cannot agree that an arranged marriage is much different from a forced marriage. In arranging my marriage with Mirza Hadi, my father's goal was primarily the union of his and Heshmat Mirza's families. My marriage was merely a means to an end. My father had meant well: he honestly thought that I would live a blissful life in Heshmat Mirza's mansion. He could never have imagined that that mansion would turn out to be a jail cell.

At my mother's bedside, I told her that I was a prisoner in Mirza Hadi's home and that the prison guard, my mother-in-law, was waiting outside. We both cried, and I showered kisses on her. In no time, my allotted thirty minutes were up. I said goodbye to my mom, and I left. Soon, part of me would die with her. Sooner than I thought: that night my mother's body and soul separated, and she fell into a deep sleep, "That sweet sleep which medicines all pain."[18]

Outside, my mother-in-law was shocked. She told me that, under the circumstances, she was certain that I would not have parted from my mother after so short a visit. It was as if her words came out of a cold iron rod, not out of the mouth of a human being. I guess she had been planning on getting rid of me that day forever.

I do not know why I wanted Mirza Hadi to come back from Paris. In his absence, I did not have to worry about being physically abused. However, I was sick and tired of spending all that time with my mother-in-law. Jaleh, the sister-in-law who was married, rarely came to see us, and I and my other two sisters-in-law had very little in common and did not spend much time together. I was happy only when I was reading or painting or when I was with Anvar. Most of the time, inside the golden cage, I was living a life full of blisters and grievous afflictions with a woman who masterfully walked and danced on the devil's ice.

But things did not change when Mirza Hadi returned. After six months away, he did not greet any of us with warmth. He had brought a suitcase full of presents for his mom and a couple of dresses for each of his three sisters and for me, but he did not kiss or hug me. The only thing he said to me was that he was sorry that my mother had passed

---

[18] *The Complete Poetical Works of Percy Bysshe Shelley, The Cambridge Edition* (Boston and New York: Houghton Mifflin Company, 1901), p. 159.

away. He thought that, after death, she was in a better place. That was something that always puzzled me about Mirza Hadi: he seemed to have more respect for my parents than for his own. He always talked about them with admiration. It was bizarre that he did not extend to me even a small fraction of the respect he showed my parents.

My twenty-second birthday came and went. Nobody seemed to care. I meant nothing to that family, and I was very sad that I had allowed myself to gradually turn into my husband's and mother-in-law's slave. "That calm submission was dishonorable and vile."[19] I would love to forget that part of my life altogether, but it is not possible. It haunts me still.

Several weeks after Mirza Hadi returned from Paris, I found out that I was pregnant. Overjoyed, I announced the news to Mirza Hadi and his family. I was surprised when they did not react with squeals, kisses, or hugs. I expected them to be ecstatic, but they could not even feign excitement. Cold and indifferent, Mirza Hadi just murmured, "How nice!" Meanwhile, my mother-in-law took the opportunity to be vicious to me yet again. "Good thing that I am still young enough to raise that baby for you," she said. "I am happy for you, my child, you really needed a playmate."

I was disappointed, but I tried not to be bothered by their reactions. The important thing was that, in that mansion, there would soon be someone I loved and who loved me, someone I would raise to be not like his or her father but like a real Moin-al-Tojjar.

Fearing abuse, I submitted myself entirely to the will of Mirza Hadi and his mother. As a result, almost every day, my mother-in-law came, sat next to me, and told me long stories from her youth. I had no choice but to sit and listen to her. One day, she cornered me and started telling me all about her husband's proposal ceremony and about how her all-powerful handlebar-mustachioed father had negotiated her dowry with Heshmat Mirza's father when suddenly Ali entered the room and interrupted her.

"What do you want, you, the rooster that crows at odd hours?" she growled.

Ali apologized for interrupting and said that he had no choice because the mailman was at the gate and had registered mail for us. He was illiterate

---

[19] Paraphrasing Shakespeare, *Romeo and Juliet*, Act 3, Scene 1.

and could not sign the delivery receipt himself. My mother-in-law asked me to go sign the receipt for the mailman and bring the letter to her. She was also illiterate, but she always pretended that she was not.

The letter was addressed to Mirza Hadi, and it was in English, sent from Paris by someone called Iris Coughlin. My mother-in-law's first reaction was to ask whether Iris was a male or a female name. When I told her that it was a female name, she asked me to open the envelope and read the letter. Even though I was equally curious, I was reluctant to do so, since the letter belonged to Mirza Hadi. But she ordered me to open it at once.

It was a love letter. Ms. Coughlin was wondering why she had not heard from Mirza Hadi, whom she loved with all her heart, who was the air she breathed, the breeze that flowed through her soul, and the bird that flew her up over the clouds and beyond the stars. While in tears, I translated the letter for my mother-in-law. She listened and grinned.

"Fair feathers make fair fowl. I am not surprised that Mirza Hadi has lovelorn European lovers. He is my son, after all." Then she called Ali in and ordered both of us not to say anything about the letter to Mirza Hadi. Obviously, she feared to lose her son to a foreigner. So she took the letter, put it in its envelope, and left the room to go hide it somewhere.

Everyone knew that Mirza Hadi was a womanizer. His unfaithfulness to me was not a secret. As Persians say, the only person unaware of it was Hafez of Shiraz.[20] However, I always thought that, on his trips to Paris and elsewhere, he spent his time with prostitutes and hustlers. But a romantic love letter from a woman who sounded like a decent person? That hit me like a ton of bricks. I was hurt and humiliated. Nevertheless, with a baby in my tummy, I had no choice but to tolerate my miserable life even more than before. I had to control my emotions, diffuse my anger, and concentrate on my pregnancy. I was scared that dwelling on Mirza Hadi's lustful and animalistic tendencies, which always resulted in crushing psychological blows, might harm my baby. So, I tried not to think about him and his deeds. But I was only partially successful.

---

[20] A proverb. He was unaware because he was dead.

# 5

For the next month, almost every day, we received a love letter from Iris Coughlin. The letters were all full of beautifully wrought phrases. In one, she wrote that in Mirza Hadi's absence, the roaring waves of her love hurled themselves madly at the boats that sailed toward the Persian Gulf. In others, she talked about how she longed to be with him and reminded him how often they explored the heights of sexual pleasure together. Sometimes she was explicit. I was reluctant to translate all those sexual fantasies for my mother-in-law, but I did so anyway, and she cursed Mirza Hadi for wasting his life with such "brazen hussies," such "shameless rascal whores." To my mind, Iris Coughlin was a naïve woman, innocent and deceived; the shameless rascal was her own son, Mirza Hadi! But I did not correct her.

The letters kept arriving, and we kept them from Mirza Hadi. However, one day, while my mother-in-law prattled on about her youth, Afra came in and informed us that a horse-drawn carriage was at the gate with a beautiful lady of diminutive height and two suitcases inside the carriage. She said in amazement that the lady wore shoes with six-inch stiletto heels and could not speak Farsi or Turkish.

My mother-in-law and I rushed to the gate at once. There she was, an elegant, pretty woman in a carriage. Neighborhood kids had come out to look on. They had never seen such a sight. Afra asked the crowd to disperse, and the visitor got out of the carriage. She was a very attractive lady with large, doe-like eyes, a strong jawline, high cheek bones, wavy brown hair, and a beautiful smile. She greeted me, shaking my hand—She thought that I was Mirza Hadi's sister. Then she went toward my mother-in-law to greet her, but my mother-in-law gave her an angry look and, without shaking her hand, left. The woman told me that her name was Iris Coughlin, that she was from Ireland, and that she and "my brother" had met and fallen in love in Paris. In fact, they had even gotten engaged, but Mirza Hadi had returned to Iran and she'd had no word from him. Worried, she had come to Tabriz to find out what was wrong.

She paid the carriage driver such a big note that his eyes shone like diamonds, and I told Afra to call Ali to bring Ms. Coughlin's suitcases inside. What else could I do? She was from a foreign country and had nowhere to go.

I escorted her to the living room. She was very impressed with Mirza Hadi's mansion and was somewhat overwhelmed by its size and the elegance of its interior decoration. She sat down and I sat next to her. I was mesmerized by her beauty, her devilish eyes, graceful neck and hands, and long slender arms. She was cat-like, smoky, and seductive. Nowadays, whenever I see Natalie Wood's movies or pictures, she reminds me of Ms. Coughlin. The resemblance is uncanny.

I had taken six years of English classes in school, and for years, I had a private British tutor who taught me at home. I was proficient in English, could talk fluently, and I regularly read English novels without difficulty. Mirza Hadi was not aware of my excellent English skills, and I was not aware of his until Iris Coughlin showed up. I always thought that he only knew French, since he had lived in France for years and supposedly studied there. This showed how little we knew about each other. Ms. Coughlin told me all about her trip. After arriving in Tehran, she had taken a 393-mile bus ride to get to Tabriz. The bus was stopped twice by British soldiers and, later on, three times by Soviet occupiers. At each control station, she was the only passenger who was asked for her travel documents. Each time, she explained that she was going to join her fiancé in Tabriz. The British did not give her a hard time, but the Soviets did. They bombarded her with unfriendly questions. I told her that, as beautiful as she was, she was extremely lucky that the Soviet soldiers had not dragged her off the bus and brutally raped her. That was what Soviet soldiers did in those days in Iran. However, in Iris Coughlin's case, maybe they were afraid to rape her, since she was Irish.

She was recounting these details when Mirza Hadi entered the room. He was shocked to see Iris Coughlin sitting there. No one had told him of her arrival. His jaw dropped, his eyebrows curved upward, and deep horizontal wrinkles appeared on his forehead.

"Oh, my Iris, I had missed you so dearly," he said. "What a splendid surprise! How could I allow my life to unfold without you? I cannot believe that you are here." He walked toward her and, before my eyes, kissed her with a lengthy, sensuous French kiss. When they were done, Mirza Hadi turned to me and said, "Dorna, on my way in, my mother told me to ask you to go see her."

He was sending me on a wild goose chase. However, as I was leaving the room, I heard Iris Coughlin tell Mirza Hadi, "Your sister is dazzlingly gorgeous. She could easily be a movie star."

I could not hold out any longer. I turned around and said, "For your information, I am not his sister. I am his wife, and I am carrying his baby."

Mirza Hadi turned red. If Coughlin had not been there, he would have punched me to death. It was the first time that I had spoken English in front of him. I am sure that he could not believe that I could speak English that well with almost no accent.

Coughlin began to tremble and clench her jaw. I could see the hurt in her eyes. She remained silent for a few minutes, then she suddenly began shouting at Mirza Hadi: "You cheated me, you have been lying to me all along. You pretended to love me only to get into my pants. You have been playing with my feelings. No wonder you did not respond to my letters." Then she began to cry uncontrollably.

Mirza Hadi embraced her, put her head on his shoulder, stroked her hair, caressed her cheek with his fingers, and tried to comfort her. I stood there and watched them. Mirza Hadi told Iris that he had not received even one letter from her and that his marriage to me was an arranged one. There was no love between us, and he planned to divorce me immediately after our child was born and marry her, Iris, instead. He added that, in Iran, child custody always goes to the father, and he wanted his child. Otherwise, he would have divorced me by now.

I had heard enough. I left the room. In the hallway, I found my mother-in-law eavesdropping. She took me aside and asked me what was going on. I told her everything, and she assured me that Mirza Hadi would never marry Iris Coughlin. Then she shamelessly added that if he divorced me, he would marry another girl from Tabriz, someone that she had already had in mind well before I came along. "That was a mistake," she said of Heshmat Mirza's arrangement with my father. "I was strongly opposed to their agreement. I lost that one, but I have not given up, and I will seize the opportunity as soon as it comes along. I want you to be prepared." She added that the girl she had in mind had the charisma and magnetism of Heshmat Mirza's wife—meaning, herself.

After venting her venom at me, she called Afra and told her to go and tell Mirza Hadi that that European whore was not allowed to stay in their house. "Tell him to let that slut go to hell, go to blazes." I never asked Afra how she conveyed my mother-in-law's message to Mirza Hadi, but shortly after, Ali carried Ms. Coughlin's luggage to Mirza Hadi's car, and the "lovebirds" left. My mother-in-law was like a barrel of gunpowder ready to explode. All she needed was one wrong word or wrong move from me or Afra to ignite.

That day, the nature of Mirza Hadi's character revealed its most despicable face. Until then, I had not known how badly my mother-in-law wanted Mirza Hadi to divorce me. Although I would have welcomed a divorce, I was horrified at the prospect of being separated from my child. I was utterly helpless, and I clung to a dim hope that everything Mirza Hadi told Iris Coughlin was only to calm her down and that he would resist his mother's demands to divorce me. After all, with all that respect for my parents, perhaps he had some interest in remaining their son-in-law.

These were the sticks I grabbed hold of while drowning in a sea of despair.

# 6

That night, I could not sleep. I sat on a chair that was placed in front of a window, and in the silence of night, I fixed my eyes outside to the path that led to the main gate of the mansion. That was the path Mirza Hadi usually walked along after parking his car. But it was one in the morning, and he had not come home yet.

On nights that Mirza Hadi was not home, Ali kept the front yard lit. I could see outside clearly. While I watched the path, I thought about Mirza Hadi's despicable character. For hundreds, perhaps thousands of years, the feudal lords cared immensely about their images, their aggregate of features and traits. Whether or not they possessed moral and ethical virtues, they made great efforts to be identified with fine qualities. They behaved as honorable masters. And yet, my husband, Mirza Hadi, was totally oblivious to these codes of behavior and manners, to the people around him and what they thought about him, and to the traditions and rules of etiquette. I asked myself how could it be that he had not inherited his parents' and grandparents' passion for maintaining their status as feudal lords. Why did he not share in their enjoyment of all the power, influence, and glory associated with his class?

That night, I think I found the answer to my questions. The reason was simple. Forever and ever, feudal lords basically lived in the villages they owned. Even though some of them had properties and connections in the cities, their cultures were rooted in the traditional, rural values of villages, where the economy was based on animal husbandry, agriculture, and country crafts. However, Mirza Hadi had not been raised in such a culture. He was basically a city boy, a product of the decadence and extravagance of city life, whether in Tabriz, Tehran, or any of the European cities.

Mirza Hadi, just like my brother, Sina, lacked the conscious awareness that big cities were vibrant, thriving centers of culture, where the best schools and universities were located and where learned people such as scientists, poets, literary figures, and historians lived. To the extent that I had witnessed, Mirza Hadi had no interest in bookstores or libraries, concerts or art exhibitions. He never talked about the great museums or art galleries of Paris. I doubt he ever visited them. He had no learned or intellectual friends, knew no painters, calligraphers, or musicians. His friends were a bunch of dissolute men who attended his regular all-male parties and nourished themselves with alcohol, opium, and gambling. In a nutshell, Mirza Hadi was neither a product of a rural culture nor a product of the virtuous aspects of a city culture. He was simply the culmination of those aspects of an urban society that fostered corruption and moral decay.

This was my thinking in 1943, when I was twenty-two years old. I am now fifty-four, and I still believe that I was not too far off the mark.

I began to dose, until suddenly, there was a noise from outside. There he was, Mirza Hadi, walking up the path toward our bedroom. I looked at my watch. It was 4:45 in the morning.

He entered the room and noticed I was awake.

"How come you are still awake?"

"Did you really expect me to sleep after you caused such a shameful scandal?" I replied.

He ignored me, took off his jacket, and began to untie his tie. I continued: "Where were you all night? Have you noticed what time it is now?"

"I was looking for a hotel."

"Oh, yes? How many hotels does Tabriz have? Under the Soviet occupation and in the midst of the war, how busy are those hotels? Do you think I'm a fool? Well, if you have not figured it out yet, I am ten times more intelligent than you and your family members combined."

"Hey, watch your mouth!" he said sternly. "You have forgotten that if I throw you out of this house, you have no option but to hold out your begging bowl."

This sent me into a fit of rage. Words came flying out of my mouth.

"Fornication with sluts, prostitutes, and hookers in Paris and Tehran was not enough! Now you bring your mistress home and, before the eyes of your pregnant wife, kiss her! You shameful, shameless whoremonger! Reprobate! Thief!"

Mirza Hadi reached for me, grabbed my shirt, and slapped me across my face so hard that I lost my balance and fell onto the floor. He grabbed hold of my hair from behind and began to pull it hard to raise me to my feet. I was scared he was going to remove my scalp from my skull. I hurried and reached to the handle of a chair that was near me, grabbed it and raised myself. When I was back on my feet, he slapped the back of my neck with God knows how many newtons of force. I was seeing stars. I staggered miserably for a few steps then threw myself in the chair. Mirza Hadi left me there, and when I was sure I could walk, I stood up and dragged myself out of the bedroom to my painting room and lay down on the sofa. I eventually fell asleep.

# 7

From that day forward, Mirza Hadi became cold and distant. I was cold toward him, as well. We ignored each other. Not only did he evade eye contact but he tried hard not to look at me. On the contrary, I kept him in my line of sight most of the time. He left the house in the morning and returned after midnight. Some nights, he did not come home at all. When he did come home, he slept next to me in bed but did not touch me at all. That was a sign that, with Iris Coughlin in his life, he had already immersed himself in so much sexual pleasure that he could resist having more sex with me.

Meanwhile, Mirza Hadi's open relationship with Iris had inflamed my mother-in-law. Naturally, she blamed me. She would say to me, "A capable wife with courage and fortitude ties down her husband to family life. There is a reason when a man seeks pleasure outside his marriage." And, of course, by pleasure, she meant sexual pleasure, as if she did not know that her son was a satyromaniac.

With Iris in Tabriz, Mirza Hadi started acting differently. He spent a long time staring at himself in the mirror. He looked straight at his own face, then at its left side, and finally at its right side. He fiddled with his mustache, which he now trimmed daily, and after taking care of his mustache, he styled his hair in a type of crew cut, which is nowadays referred to as an Ivy League or a James Bond hairstyle, a style that was quite attractive.

He wore expensive French fragrance and applied perfume in his hair, around his neck, behind his knees, and, interestingly enough, in his belly button. His body smelled great all the time, but I could never ignore the stench of his vile character. I felt sorry for Iris, who was probably entranced by the aroma of all that French perfume that Mirza Hadi wore but was unable to detect any of that other pungency.

# 8

I badly needed to vent—I was not the type of person to suppress her emotions. But I was afraid to reveal to Dena, Habib, and Auntie all the mental and physical abuse I had suffered at the hands of Mirza Hadi and my toxic, soul-sucking mother-in-law. If they knew the extent of it, they would confront them, causing my relationship with Mirza Hadi and my mother-in-law to further deteriorate and the abuses to intensify.

In those days in Iran, after a divorce, the father automatically had full custody of a child and had legal authority to exercise that right without a court order. Furthermore, he had the power not to grant any visitation time to the mother. In the male chauvinistic patriarchy of those times, such a cruel and inhumane law was carte blanche for unconscientious fathers to mistreat their wives. In my case, that carte blanche was the trump card Mirza Hadi would have played if he was challenged in any way or manner by me, my sister, Habib, or Auntie. So, to vent, my only choice was to confide in my best friend, Anvar.

To get permission from my mother-in-law to go see Anvar, I made up a story that I'd had a dream that Anvar's mother was very sick. In the dream, she was asking Anvar why I had not yet gone to visit her. The story worked. My mother-in-law granted me permission to go to Anvar's and told me to go find out how Anvar and her mother were. My mother-in-law rarely minded me going to see Anvar. She had a very special relationship with Anvar and her mother, which showed that she was capable of loving and respecting others. And that was the reason I could not fathom why, after two and a half years of living together in the same mansion, she had developed no attachment or affection toward me.

Anvar and her mother had only a few friends and relatives. They were somewhat lonely. Anvar had lost her father when she was a small child. She had no sister, just one brother, who was a truck driver living with his in-laws 945 miles away in Kerman. He visited Anvar and his mother twice a year, and even though they had enough wealth to live a comfortable upper-middle-class life, he saw it as his duty to give them money.

In no time, I found myself in front of Anvar's house. Its front door, made of dark wood, always enraptured me. It was amazingly crafted, intricately decorated and designed, and reminded me of what my father often told Mashdi, "Remember to keep the front gate neat and clean. The front door is the salutation of the house. It should smile at all times." The knocker, made of authentic cast iron, was so beautifully designed that it added considerably to the door's personality.

I lifted the knocker and started to knock loudly. Between the front door and the building there was a very large courtyard. I wanted to make sure that Anvar heard the knock. I waited for her to open the door. She did not. I knocked twice more, and then I gave up and left. I was only a few steps away when I heard the entrance door to Anvar's house being unbolted. I immediately turned around. Anvar was calling my name, "Dorna, Dorna." I rushed toward her, and we kissed and hugged each other.

The courtyards of traditional Iranian houses are home to stunningly gorgeous ponds. Anvar's house had an elegant star-shaped pond in the middle of its courtyard, along with magnificent trees and gardens and pots of multicolored magical flowers. A huge hammered-edge, pure copper tray full of clothes was on the ground a few inches from the edge of the pond. I figured that Anvar was in the middle of washing clothes in the pond water. I told her that I was going to say hello to her mother first, and she went back to finish what she had started.

Anvar's mother was awake but relaxing in her bed. As soon as she saw me, her face broke into a radiant smile. She stood up, grabbed the sides of my face, and kissed my forehead. As a sign of respect, I kissed her hand. Anvar told her mom everything that I told her, and I knew that. So, after we sat down, she looked at me and said, "Dorna dear, you are astonishingly beautiful, blessed be the God, the best of creators. I cannot understand what Mirza Hadi is after. He has already hit the biggest jackpot of his life. Being so ungrateful to divine bounty is a sin." The way Anvar's mother used that gambling metaphor so naturally in the middle of those statements pertaining to divinity was quite interesting to me.

She changed the subject. "Dorna dear, you are no stranger, it is not concealed from God, let it not be concealed from you either. My biggest worry in life is that Anvar is still single and still rejects all suitors. It is not normal for a woman not to seek protection of God through a husband." She paused and sighed. "We had guests from my own hometown last week. They came and stayed for a few days. We gave them a warm welcome, entertained them day and night. They had come to ask for Anvar's hand in marriage for their son. The son himself had come, as well."

Anvar's mother suddenly stopped what she was saying and apologized for not being more hospitable toward me. She wanted to go and make me a cup of tea, but I stopped her. I asked her how did she like her guest's son. She responded, "He was tall, handsome, young, and moderately rich. In our town, his father was a well-to-do member of the community. However, Anvar did not even weigh out the pros and cons, and without wanting to know more about him and his family, she turned down the marriage proposal. The guests left dejected and dispirited, with their tails between their legs." Anvar's mother added that before they left, the guests showed her, privately, the two-and-a-half-carat diamond engagement ring that they had purchased for Anvar. From all that she described, I learned that Anvar had not told her mother anything about her intimate relationship with Kasra and her fiery, passionate love for him, of which Anvar's mother would have heartily disapproved.

After our conversation, I went back out to the courtyard to see Anvar. She was finished washing the laundry and was hanging the clothes on clothesline. I waited until she was done, and we sat down on a bench near the pond. After the usual pleasantries, I began to tell her all about Iris Coughlin. As I recounted what had happened, I found myself in tears. I sobbed when I told her about how Mirza Hadi had beaten me so hard that I had fallen down. I finished by confessing that I was worried that Mirza Hadi was growing cold in our marriage. Through thick and thin, I had been there for him, I said, but he had never connected with me on an emotional level. Neither had his mother.

When I was finished, Anvar fixed her eyes on me.

"There is an easy solution for your problem," she said. "There is an all-natural, plant-derived substance called the *affection drug*. Buy a bottle and pour ten to fifteen drops in your husband's and his mother's tea. After they drink the tea, in no time, that miracle drug will unharden their hearts. It will soften them so effectively that you shall see nothing but love and affection from them."

Anvar's words surprised me.

"Look Anvar dear, I am not a superstitious person," I replied. "In fact, not only do I not hold any superstitions, I despise them. Such things are for swindlers and charlatans to squeeze money from vulnerable and often poor or illiterate people."

"It is not like that at all. I am not talking about abracadabra and incantation. I, too, do not believe in magical means of warding off misfortunes and disasters. I have no use for clairvoyants, psychics, and palm readers. I am talking about herbal medicine, which has been used for thousands of years all over the world for medical treatments."

"I understand what you are saying, but I am skeptical that there is an herbal remedy for cruel-heartedness. That sounds illusory. Mirza Hadi and his mother have warm and loving relationships with many people—you are one of them. Their behavior toward *me* must have a psychological basis. There is no medicine for that."

"Don't argue, just try it," Anvar said. "You have nothing to lose. If it works, you have achieved your goal. If it does not, the current state of your relationship with them remains as it is. All I am proposing is a risk-free solution. Come back tomorrow, early in the morning, and I will take you to an experienced herbal expert on the other side of town. He is the only person in Tabriz who can make the affection drug."

As skeptical as I was, Anvar managed to convince me. She was very persistent, and saying no to her was like telling her that I did not trust her. She was the only friend with whom I was allowed to socialize and hang out. So, I needed to handle her trust in me as if it were a priceless gem, even if it meant going against some of my beliefs.

Before I left Anvar's house, she helped me come up with an excuse to give my mother-in-law. "In the morning, tell her, 'Anvar asked me to go today and help her choose fabric for a dress to wear to her cousin's wedding.'" With that excuse, Anvar was sure that my mother-in-law would allow me to go out with her.

The next morning, I woke up earlier than usual and went down for breakfast. Mirza Hadi and his mother were already at the dining table. As soon as my mother-in-law saw me, she said sarcastically, "Yippee, her ladyship has become an early riser." I smiled, said good morning, and sat next to Mirza Hadi. Mirza Hadi said he was in a hurry and that he had to rush out to an appointment. I always wondered what sort of appointment an idle, jobless person might have. It was too early for his daily rendezvous with his mistress, Irish Coughlin. For a moment, it occurred to me that perhaps he was taking Iris out for some countryside sightseeing, but then I remembered that it was not so easy to leave the city with the ongoing Soviet siege.

After Mirza Hadi left, I told my mother-in-law that Anvar had asked me to go fabric shopping with her that day. My mother-in-law's response, as expected, was mean.

"Has Anvar taken leave of her senses? How can your callow eyes and shallow taste for fashion help her? Plus, Mirza Hadi does not like his wife to bum around in the streets."

Because I had not been crazy about the idea of the affection drug in the first place, my mother-in-law's reluctance to let me go shopping was a good excuse for me not to participate in Anvar's scheme. So, I told my mother-in-law that her decision was wise and I understood it. She was shocked. She expected me to beg, but I did not, and to my dismay, she suddenly changed her mind. She did not want to displease or irritate Anvar, she said.

I was afraid that might happen. Years before, Anvar had saved one of my sisters-in-law's life, and ever since, my mother-in-law felt beholden to her.

I went to my room to change, and as I was leaving the house, my mother-in-law called to me, "Hey, you, the fashion expert lady! Listen, do your very best to return before Mirza Hadi. Every time he comes home and you are not here, he starts a commotion, and I hate that." Not knowing when Mirza Hadi would come home, it was impossible to obey. But I agreed anyway. As long as Iris was in Tabriz, he never came home before midnight.

Outside in the courtyard, I found the nature exceptionally beautiful. The warmth of the life-giving sun was pleasing, the trees and flowers awe-inspiring. The sound of running water coming from the fountain soothed me. Colorful, small birds flew between the trees, chirping and singing. I felt like I could meditate here. On impulse, I went and sat down on the fountain's edge. I closed my eyes, and soon, I was daydreaming.

In my daydream, the affection drug was highly effective. I mixed it with tea, and Mirza Hadi and his mother drank it. Soon after, their attitude toward me changed completely. My mother-in-law was no longer sarcastic and disrespectful. She called me by such endearing terms as Dorna dear, sweetheart, sweetie, pumpkin, and honey. Mirza Hadi metamorphosed into my eternal love, Nima, and called me princess, gorgeous, angel, and love. He did not beat me anymore. He cared about the baby I carried in my tummy, touched my belly to feel its movements. He treated me with dignity, celebrated my birthdays, and gave me gifts and flowers. We even had conversations together—actual conversations!

I was shaken out of my fantasy by my mother-in-law's voice. "Good grief, you are still here," she cried. "What the hell is wrong with you? Hurry up, Anvar is waiting for you. Get going!" I agreed and rushed to Anvar's house.

Anvar greeted me at the door. She complained that I was late and that we needed to rush. We got into a carriage, and Anvar told the coachman where to go. It was a very long ride. We passed through neighborhoods that I had never seen before and I could not have imagined existed, and we got off in a poor unfamiliar plaza. It was as if we had traveled to a different country. I attempted to pay the coachman, but Anvar beat me to it. She reminded me that I would have to give an account of my spending to my mother-in-law.

How this marriage has ruined my life, I thought. I, the mighty Moin-al-Tojjar's daughter, have reached a point at this young age that I cannot even pay a carriage fare without the humiliation of giving its account to my abusive mother-in-law!

Anvar went on and paid for everything on that day.

I was in unfamiliar territory. Everything was awkward; people were sitting on the ground or standing idly in groups of two or more all around. Most of the men were walking down the street with their heels flattening the back of their shoes. Four men leaned against a wall and stared at me and Anvar. Their gazes were distressing. One of them approached us and whistled.

"Hey, you are so cute," he said to me. "I could just eat you up."

Another of the men shouted after him, "Hey, Errol Flynn, ask the babe how would she like a real man."

I was scared to the bone, but I mustered up my courage, turned, frowned, and shot daggers at the man with my eyes. Like most of the other men there, he had taken his jacket off and had flung it over his right shoulder. As soon as he saw my face, he shouted aloud, "*Mamma mia*, look at those eyes!" Then he said, "Where have you been all these years? How would you like to be the mother of my future children?"

I asked Anvar to make him stop. She turned and screamed, "You are annoying us. Get lost or I will call the police." Then she told me to walk as fast as I could. The man followed us for a short while, then gave up. Anvar told me that people like this were not dangerous, they were just entertaining themselves, trying to bring some excitement to their idle lives.

"Why did they call that man Eroll Flynn," I asked Anvar.

"That is another amusement they have. They assign nicknames to each other," Anvar responded. "My brother knows some of them, and because of him, they usually don't bother me. They call that man Errol Flynn probably because Flynn is his favorite movie star. Among them, there are people who are called, *Hassan Chocolate, Javad Allora, Bijan Accelerator, Ali Istanbul, Bahram Tripe,* and *Ehsan Cinema*. My brother says that they are known with these nicknames since Hassan loves chocolate, Javad has somehow learned the Italian word 'allora' and enjoys using it frequently, Bijan drives extremely fast, Ali had once traveled to Istanbul and brags about that trip all the time, Bahram eats tripe almost every day for breakfast, and Ehsan frequents the movie theaters."

Anvar took me through narrow alleys. How did she know all these labyrinthine alleys so well? I wondered. What business did she have in such a place? The whole experience had made me suspicious, and I was afraid something bad was going to happen to me. I thought that if Mirza Hadi ever found out where I had gone that day, he would have broken my bones.

We arrived at a dark dead end where there was a house with an old ochre door. The door was open. Inside, a large number of shoes were clustered together near the entryway. Anvar and I took off our shoes and put them at a corner of the pile. Then we walked down a narrow corridor and into a waiting room.

In the waiting room, people sat on a rug spread out on the floor. There were no chairs. I counted seventeen women on one side of the room and four men on the other. They were customers, patients, clients—whatever you want to call them. The moment we entered, all eyes were on us. With all those people ahead of us, I got seriously worried that I would not return home on time.

The whole place was like a physician's clinic for the uneducated and superstitious. I was ashamed to be there. On one side of the room was a door that opened to the office of the so-called "herbal expert." Next to that door was a very low desk, behind which sat, cross legged, an obese, dark-complexioned, middle-aged woman with large hazel eyes and full lips. Anvar went toward her, bent so that she could see her face, winked at her, and said, in a loud voice so that everyone could hear, "Banu dear, please remember that, when we came earlier this morning, you told us to go and come back at 10:30. We are now back."

"Of course, I remember," Banu replied. "You are next."

People in the room began to grumble. One man yelled that "The rule is first-come, first-served. That is it." A woman shouted, "No one can jump the queue, even if her father is the king." Others chimed in, and it was impossible to understand what they were saying amid the commotion.

Banu got to her feet. "Silence, everyone," she cried. "These two women have a dying uncle in severe pain. They came early in the morning for medicine. I told them to go and come back at 10:30. I did not know when the Oracle would be in. Now he is in. Preventing a person from carrying medicine to a dying patient is a gravely sinful act. Don't ruin your next life."

When Banu had finished, everyone was silent.

I realized then how little I knew about ordinary people and how they lived. I had just observed something extraordinary. To violate the fair first-in, first-out discipline of serving clients, what Anvar and Banu did was a very calculated but not preplanned deception, something like a sleight of hand of the worst kind. Later on, I learned that Anvar's wink at Banu had been the key to the plot. It was a code to let Banu know that a large tip was coming her way.

When Anvar was done with her shenanigan, she told me, let us go sit beside the women. I was overwhelmed with shock. I had never seen anything like that place, not even in movies. The smell of that confining, oppressive space had made me nauseated, and I could not bring myself to sit down on that rug. I was standing there in a shocking state when Anvar grabbed my hand, pulled it down, and muttered, angrily but in a soft voice, to sit down. I sat down reluctantly in slow motion. That place was more crowded than a physician's clinic.

All the women who, moments ago, had been so agitated that we had jumped the queue had become very kind. One of them said, "I am very sorry for your uncle. What can one do? We were made out of dust, so we must return unto dust." Another woman sighed, "Azrael, the angle of death, always takes the most beautiful flowers first. God's garden must be spectacular." Others muttered that "God gives life, and he takes life away, we have no say"; "few live lucky lives, but all have death"; "death is the path to reach God"; "it is as natural to die as to be born."

These sayings were all clichés. But then one woman recited a beautiful poem, which I tried to memorize right away but could not. However, years later, I came across the following poem, which, I think conveys the same ideas:

"Come gentle Death, the ebb of care[21];
The ebb of care, the flood of life;
The flood of life, the joyful fare;
The joyful fare, the end of strife;

---

[21] Found in *Reviews of "Modern Science and Modern Thought," Etc. In a Series of Letters to a Lady*, by William Henry Goss (Stoke-upon-Trent: Vyse & Hill, Printers and Publishers, 1895), p. 158.

The end of strife; that thing wish I,
Wherefore come death, and let me die!"

The women began to discuss a couple of fundamental philosophical questions. Do human beings have the necessary tools for the comprehension of the mysteries of creation and of the universe? Can one be certain of anything but death? These women were a bunch of illiterate, unlearned, and unlettered women. Nevertheless, their philosophical discussions were profound.

I had yet to see any herbal medicine inside this strange place, nor had I figured out why we were there. Anvar was an intelligent woman, she did not belong here. Even after we visited the so-called "Oracle," as Banu referred to him, or "herbal expert," as Anvar called the man, my suspicion did not diminish. The Oracle had a muscular physique and was broad-shouldered with a fair complexion and large black eyes. He was probably in his late forties. He was nothing like what I had imagined—an old, thin man with white hair and long beard.

Anvar and I sat on the floor in front of the Oracle's low desk.

"What is it?" he asked. "I suppose that you cannot get pregnant. Is that why you are here?"

Anvar responded on my behalf. "No. There are major problems in her marriage." Then she told him almost everything I had told her about my issues with Mirza Hadi and his mother. The man did not ask many questions. After Anvar was done revealing my secrets to him, he stood up and walked toward a walk-in closet, went inside, and brought back some powder wrapped in a sachet. He gave the sachet to Anvar and told her to mix it with an orange-blossom drink and give it to me. Then he told me, "Every three days, take a teaspoon of the mix and put it in your husband's tea. Do the same for his mother. In no time, they will become the kindest husband and mother-in law in Tabriz."

Anvar paid the man the equivalent of fifty American cents, and we left his office.[22] We passed through the narrow corridor, and when we were back at the main entrance with the ochre door, Anvar shouted, "Banu, could you please come out and help us find our shoes?"

"Our shoes are right here," I said, pointing to our pairs in the pile.

---

[22] The value of $0.50 in 1943 is approximately $7.30 is 2020.

"Shush," Anvar said.

A moment later, Banu came out. Looking around to make sure nobody else was there, Anvar gave Banu equivalent of one American dollar, twice as much as she had given to the Oracle. Banu took it and put it in her pocket right away. Anvar hugged her and told her, "See you next time."

I followed Anvar through the labyrinth of dark and narrow alleys until we reached the plaza where we had encountered "Errol Flynn" and his friends. There we took a carriage and went home. At Anvar's request, the coachman dropped me off first, and Anvar told me that she would prepare the herbal medicine and deliver it to me the next day. It was half past noon. Mirza Hadi was not yet home.

The next morning, after breakfast, I went to my room and kept myself busy by reading. I knew that when Anvar arrived, we would need to find someplace discreet to hand off the so-called affection drug. She could not give it to me in front of my mother-in-law.

I grew anxious until finally she showed up. I told her that she was late. She replied that she had gotten here more than an hour ago. "I was downstairs talking to your mother-in-law," she said. "You know her, she is a conversationalist." Then Anvar withdrew a small bottle from the pocket of her long skirt and handed it to me. She said that I knew all the instructions already. We hugged and kissed, and she left. I never saw Anvar again.

# CHAPTER 6

## IMPRISONED IN A DUNGEON

### 1

The small bottle containing the so-called affection drug stayed in my pocket for two days. I had thought about not using the drug and telling Anvar that I had. However, on the third day, somehow, I was not myself. I was dreamily and eerily out of touch with reality, and I was no longer thinking about the consequences of pouring an unknown drug made by a hustler into Mirza Hadi and his mother's tea.

It was a day in early September, 1943. Mirza Hadi returned home around three o'clock in the afternoon, a sign that Iris Coughlin had left town, otherwise, he would have returned after midnight. He looked emotionally distraught. Before my mother-in-law and I could do or say anything, Mirza Hadi threw himself on a chair, closed his eyes for a long time, then confessed that he was absolutely terrified. He went on to explain that Iris was scheduled to fly to Paris from Tehran the next day, and that he had taken her to the bus station a couple of hours earlier. He watched her board the bus, and after it departed for Tehran, he followed it all the way to the Soviet checkpoint on the outskirts of Tabriz. He wanted to make sure that the bus passed through with no problems.

Mirza Hadi stopped and watched from afar, and once the bus cleared the checkpoint, he made a U-turn and drove back to Tabriz. On his drive back, he saw a small crowd circled around a corpse. He parked his car and got out to see what was going on. He recognized the corpse. It was that of a close friend, one of those men who never missed Mirza

Hadi's infamous all-male parties. Apparently, at the Soviet patrol checkpoint, the man had asked for permission to travel, and the soldiers had not given him a pass. He got into an argument with them, and they smashed him in the head repeatedly with the butts of their rifles. Mirza Hadi described how both of his friend's eyes were almost popped out of their sockets.

"Those bastards," he said. "Their monstrous crime was unfathomable. Why didn't they just pump bullets into his chest? Why did those savage animals have to shatter his skull?"

I took advantage of the situation and said, "Let me go and make you some tea. That will calm you down." I went down to the kitchen and made a pot of tea. No one was there. I filled a cup with tea and mixed in a teaspoon of the affection drug. Then I filled a second cup with tea, and as I began to slowly and carefully pour the affection drug into the teaspoon, my mother-in-law grabbed my wrist from behind and shouted as loud as she could, "Mirza Hadi, son, come here at once! Your wife wants to murder us both!"

Mirza Hadi rushed to the kitchen. He was confused.

"Who wants to kill us? What is going on?"

"Your wife, the mother of your unborn child," replied my mother-in-law. "Look, she was pouring rat poison into our tea when I caught her."

I was so afraid that all I could do was stutter. At last, I managed to say, "Ask Anvar. This is an affection drug, not poison."

My mother-in-law, with rage bursting from her eyes responded, "It was Anvar who saved our lives. She came here three days ago and informed me that the day you two went shopping, the whole time, you slandered us and vilified the entire Heshmat Mirza family. And on your way back home, you stopped by a department store and purchased rat poison." She turned to Mirza Hadi. "Dorna had told Anvar that she had seen rats in her painting room and wanted to get rid of them. Anvar grew suspicious, and that's why she warned me to make sure that Dorna never hangs around the kitchen with no one else present."

She pulled the bottle out of my hand and poured some of its content into a saucer.

"Does this look like an herb to you?" she cried. The liquid in the saucer bore no resemblance, whatsoever, with orange-blossom drink. I was in disbelief.

"If it was not for Anvar," my mother-in-law say, "Mirza Hadi and I would be dead by now. Anvar is correct that you want us dead so that your unborn child inherits all of the immense wealth of Heshmat Mirza."

"I swear on my father's soul that Anvar, herself, gave me the bottle and assured me that it was pure affection drug," I said. I was confused and terrified.

Mirza Hadi suddenly took off his belt and while yelling at me to shut up raised it above his head, aiming to whip me in the face. My mother-in-law stopped him.

"Don't beat her. She is pregnant and might lose your child. We have no choice but to keep her until she delivers. Then we will throw her out of the house. We will not have her arrested by the police. I do not want her to deliver our baby in the state prison. That is not good for our family.

"Leave it to me to punish her," she went on. "I know what to do." Then she looked at me and thundered, "I shall make you so miserable that even the birds in the sky will weep for you!"

Mirza Hadi left the kitchen, and his mother emptied the cups and the pot of tea. She took the saucer and the bottle with her, shut the kitchen door, and locked it from the outside. I sat on the floor and tried to fight the waves of intense fear I was feeling. Everything had gone wrong, and I was worried about what would happen to me. I felt that my doom was sealed. I badly needed help from Dena and Habib, but I had no access to them.

Anvar had framed me masterfully. Her plot was sinister, and with a simple neglect on my mother-in-law's part, I could have killed her and Mirza Hadi. She was atrociously wicked. She was not a wolf in sheep's clothing, she was Lucifer in a woman's cover, and I had been far too naïve and trusting. Why had she done this to me? How had her deep-seated animosity developed? Why had I seen no sign of it? I was amazed at what an actor this devilish woman was! I had done nothing to expect revenge. I had only shown her affection and given her love.

My anxious brain repeated these thoughts over and over again, and I could not calm my mind. I was overthinking and constantly shifting gears and could not focus and put things into perspective. Anvar's plot had dealt a heavy blow to me, and I could not blame myself for not being able to focus and figure out what was happening.

I do not know how long I sat on the floor of the kitchen before my mother-in-law opened the door and came in, flanked by the servants Afra, Ali, and Esmat. Looking at me, my illiterate mother-in-law, who was prosecutor and judge at the same time, explained the severity of the charges against me. Then she delivered her verdict.

"You attempted double homicide, and you were arrested at the scene of crime. Until your baby is born you are my prisoner, and you will be imprisoned in one of the basements of the mansion. Esmat will check on you every hour to see if you need to go to the toilet, whether you are thirsty and need water, or if you have any other demands. Every night, at bed time, she will carry her bedding to the basement and spread out her bedding on the floor next to your cot. Wake her up if you need to go to the bathroom or you have other urgent needs."

Then she divulged the most chilling part of my punishment: "Afra has already told Dena and Auntie that Mirza Hadi sent you to Paris to deliver there, so that his child would be a dual citizen of France and Iran. She told them that there was an exceptional situation and that you had to rush to accompany a female Parisian friend who was returning to France from a trip to Tabriz. That's why you had no time to say goodbye to them."

Then, for the first time, she insulted and belittled me in front of the servants. She had been careful not to do that before. "You damned bastard, do you get the picture?" she shouted. "Hurry up and get out of my sight."

She told Afra to throw me in "the dungeon." That was the correct word for where they were taking me.

Afra and Esmat first took me to the servants' area. I had gone to see that part of the mansion only once during my stay there. It had its own courtyard with a little pond at its center. Between the servants' houses was a small building, which had only toilets in it. A few feet from that building was Esmat's house. There, in the basement, was my dungeon.

We descended a flight of concrete steps to reach the basement. The door was locked. Afra unlocked it, and we went inside. It was a damp, moldy room with only one window, which was so high up that no one could out from it. The window provided very little light, but most of the time, it told me whether it was dark outside or light.

They had put an old rickety cot in a corner of the room. The cot was only a simple metal frame with a thin mattress and a pillow on top of it. A worn-out picnic blanket had been laid on the mattress. That was the bedding set. They had also laid a worn and tattered rug on the floor and had brought a basic wooden table and chair from storage and set it up near the bed. The table, which was dented and whose finish was worn, had a small mirror with many black spots. Looking at the ceiling, I could see water stains and spider webs all around.

Afra and Esmat did not stay there long. They asked whether I needed anything. I said no. They locked me in the dungeon and left. I was scared to death. I wished Mirza Hadi and his mother had drunk that tea mixed with rat poison.

I curled up on my side on a corner of the cot and fell into deep thought. It occurred to me that I could not refer to Mirza Hadi's mother as my mother-in-law anymore. I never used her name anyway; that was a misnomer. I pondered over this, and among the appropriate alternative ways to refer to her, I thought of "The Devilish One," "The Devilish Creature," "The Demonic Person," "The Wicked Jailer," and "The Diabolic Beast." I finally settled on "The Fiendish One." I thought that the various meanings of fiendish, such as "extremely inhumanly and wicked," "perversely diabolic," and "devilish," expressed Mirza Hadi's mother accurately. From then on, whenever I used "The Fiendish One," the servants—and, later on, my relatives and friends—knew who I was referring to. In this diary, too, from here on, I shall refer to her by this name.

I knew where I stood with the Fiendish One. What appalled me was that Mirza Hadi had not had an iota of decency to hear and examine my side of the events. I had never done anything to show even a hint of dishonesty or untruthfulness, and yet I was barred to express what had really happened and, not being heard, had severely eroded my sense of self-empowerment. That was not what I expected from Mirza Hadi. Even though we were not in love, I was still his wife, and we had experienced, hundreds of times, intense intimacy in the bedroom. That alone should have connected us deeply and should have enhanced our relationship. Furthermore, as a result of such intimacy, our baby was living inside my body. And yet, all of this did not mean anything to Mirza Hadi. To him, sex did not offer an emotional or intimate relationship. It was only a way to satisfy his urges.

Ali and Afra eventually came back in with two huge wicker baskets and one large suitcase. One of the baskets was full of my undergarments, and the other one was for dirty clothes. The suitcase contained my dresses, night gowns, toiletries, makeup, shoes, winter jackets, and such things.

After delivering the baskets and the suitcase, Ali left, but Afra stayed behind. She started to cry.

"Lady Dorna, what goes around comes around," she said. "The day will come when these godless people will pay for their atrocities. Ali and I have witnessed how they have treated you over the last two and a half years and how Mirza Hadi beats you so savagely. Now they tell us that you attempted to murder them. This accusation will leave another stain on their disgraceful conduct. It will follow them the rest of their lives. They have forgotten who you are, an angel and a beauty, the daughter of the great martyr Moin-al-Tojjar, our beloved hero, who gave his life for the independence of Iran." She added that the Fiendish One had gathered all the servants and had warned them that if they told anyone that I was imprisoned in one of the basements of the mansion, not only would she throw them out, but she would make sure that they never saw the light of the day again.

"The servants were all scared as hell since the Fiendish One sounded very serious," Afra said.

I thanked and hugged Afra, and I told her everything that had happened between me and Anvar. I was sure that the truth would flit from one person to another and eventually spread like wildfire. "When the lion is shot to death, even mice become fearless," I said to her. "If my father were alive, they would not have even dared to behave so discourteously. Anvar might have the brains of a fox, but she is playing with the paw of a lion." In the end, I assured Afra that I would survive delivering my child in that dungeon. I was a daughter of Moin-al-Tojjar. Like my father, I would die in the clutches of the lion, not under the tail of a jackass.

Ali and Afra were very close to me. They were two kind souls. Esmat, on the other hand, did not like me at all, and she was unhappy about the new duties assigned to her. She hated sleeping in the dungeon every night. I did not blame her. Once in a while a scorpion found its way to the dungeon, and either she or I smashed it by hammering it with the heel of a shoe. Often small lizards crawled here and there, but we left them alone. Esmat hated them.

Although I had told her the entire story of how Anvar had framed me, I sensed that she did not believe me. Unlike Ali and Afra, who were not too fond of Mirza Hadi and his mother's characters, Esmat was a pawn in the hands of the Fiendish One.

During the day, Esmat came to check on me every hour. She would knock on the dungeon door and ask, "Lady Dorna, do you need anything?" If my response was no, she left and came back, always on time, at the top of the next hour. It was Ali or Afra who usually brought me food and drinks. Unlike Esmat, who avoided me as much as she could, Afra would stay and talk with me and gossip about everyone and everything. She kept me abreast of all that was going on in the mansion and beyond.

For the first two days of my imprisonment, I stayed curled up in a fetal position on a corner of the bed. I thought about all the things that Anvar had told me since I'd known her. They replayed in my mind one by one: "Since I was young, I have been madly in love with one person, a man named Kasra, who left me and married the daughter of a very rich landowner . . . Before Kasra got married, he and I had a very close relationship with each other . . . Still, even after Kasra has married, I am fixated on him and gather as much information as I can about his life . . . Kasra is in my mind all the time everywhere, I can easily have an affair with him, but that is not what I want. I want him to myself . . . Life will always remain a gamble. We live only once, and I am determined to get Kasra back at any price . . . He is mine."

Suddenly, the pieces of the puzzle came together—everything fell into place. I had been surprised at how far Anvar and Kasra had managed to advance in their physical relationship without being married. In those days, and perhaps even now, in 1975, that sort of relationship violated the cultural core of the Iranian people—if it had come out, it would have put their lives in grave danger. I could only think of one man in Tabriz who would have taken such a risk . . .

It became crystal clear to me that there had never been a Kasra. Her lover had been Mirza Hadi.

Anvar had tricked me in order to ruin my marriage and win back Mirza Hadi. She had almost achieved her goal. All that was left to complete her devilish plan was to somehow make Mirza Hadi marry her.

Anvar had turned out to be a homewrecker after all.

When Ali came in to clean up my used dishes, I asked him if he would buy me a red pencil and a pencil sharpener. I told him that after I left that cursed mansion and got rid of its damned owners, I would reciprocate the favor.

"What is a worthless pencil, Lady Dorna?" he said while trying to hide his tears. "I would take a bullet for you. You are the daughter of our hero, the great Martyr Moin-al-Tojjar, who gave his life for the freedom of Azerbaijan and Iran. I will never forget his glorious funeral. Everyone from Tabriz is inspired by his lifelong service to our country. He is an example and a model for all generations of Azerbaijanis, now and in the future."

Later, he returned with what I had asked for, and every day I used the pencil to keep track of how long I was locked in that dungeon by drawing a line on the wall when I woke up in the morning.

Except for the days that they took me to the public bathhouse to bathe, my days were repetitive, with very few changes from one day to another, immobile, lethargic, sluggish, and torpid.

I did not know how to calculate the due date of my pregnancy. In those days, in Iran, it was a general belief that, from the moment of conception until the moment of birth, it would take exactly nine months, nine days, nine hours, nine minutes, and nine seconds. Based on that belief, I estimated that I had at least six months left before I delivered my baby, the baby who was already the love of my life, a real Moin-al-Tojjar.

On the seventh day of my imprisonment, being tired of sitting on the cot, I sat on the floor and leaned against the damp wall. I felt that I was a forgotten woman, treated like a leper, banned from seeing my friends and family. I missed them all. I missed Nima, who was in my heart all the time, and I missed my tailoring teacher, Ms. Suesan. I wanted to be like the wind, which I had not felt on my face for a week, a wind that howled through that dreary dungeon. I had the urge to howl again and again. I was dying for fresh air and the smell of grass.

Suddenly, I began to yell: "You bastards! I need the salubrious air of the mountains and of the verdant fields. I need to sit at the river's edge singing and dunking my feet. I am not asking for joy, just serenity. I have forgotten about joy. Joy left my life the day I married Mirza Hadi."

Being trapped, hopeless, and helpless, I became more and more agitated. Then I reached the boiling point, turned around and stood up facing the wall. Out of sheer frustration, I pounded my fists against it repeatedly until I exhausted myself. I was so distraught that I scraped my finger nails down the wall from the top to bottom and cried out, "Father, where are you to help me? Look at what they have done to me! Look at what your daughter has been reduced to!"

I collapsed. Next thing I know, I found myself in the middle of a garden, which went on, as far as the eye could see, in every direction. I thought the garden was as beautiful as the garden of Eden. It was as if I had found myself in paradise.

I turned around to see what was behind me. I saw my parents who were dressed in the most elegant clothes. My heart was bursting with such joy and happiness. My father approached me, embraced me and told me, "You are safe now, my daughter. No one can hurt you here. I will protect you forever." My father held me in his arms for a long time. Then he stepped back so that my mother, who was waiting, could hug and kiss me.

There was a wide and long table filled with the most appetizing fruits, pastries, and other delicacies. My father said that my Auntie and Hāji Darab were invited to join us. I asked where my brother, Sina, was, and neither of my parents responded. They lowered their heads and stared at the ground.

I reached for an apple from the table, and as I brought it to my mouth, it disappeared from my hand. I did that several times, and each time the result was the same.

A man came toward us from afar. I tried to place him. It was strange: one second, he was the Hollywood actor, Errol Flynn, and the next he was the Errol Flynn whom Anvar and I had encountered at the plaza on our way to the so-called herbal expert's clinic. The image just kept flipping back and forth between the two Errol Flynns. However, the whole time that he was walking, he never seemed to get any closer.

On our right side was the gypsy, whom I had met on the last day of my trip to Mirza Hadi's villages. Her many bracelets and bangles jingled, and she was screaming at the top of her lungs, "Your life's path is going to be constricted, narrow, and dark."

I asked my father what were the Errol Flynns and the gypsy doing over there, and he replied, "Which people are you talking about? There is no one here except you, me, and your mom."

I was confused. Then I saw my Auntie and Hāji Darab coming toward us. I ran to them, and as I was running, I fell down and woke up back in the dungeon. I wept for hours.

# 2

Afra had told me that, on the eighth day of my imprisonment, they would take me to the public bathhouse to bathe. Even though I knew that I would not be alone, I was excited that, for a few hours, I could be away from the dire dungeon and the damned mansion and that I could see the outside world.

In those days, in Tabriz, no house had its own bathtubs or showers, not even aristocratic houses or mansions. Everyone had to go to a public bathhouse to bathe. Bathhouses were open only to men from 5:00 A.M. until 8:00 A.M., after 5:00 P.M., and all day on Fridays. At all the other times, they were open only to women. There was a gorgeous bathhouse that my and Mirza Hadi's families both used. It was near Mirza Hadi's mansion. My sisters-in-law, Afra, Esmat, and I had to go to that public bath with the Fiendish One. Each of us packed everything we needed—all of our toiletries, towels, hair brushes, and change of clothes—into a bundle, which Afra and Esmat carried for us, since, in the eyes of the Fiendish One, it was beneath our dignity to carry our own bundles.

The Fiendish one also believed that taking a bath with ordinary people brought down her family's rank and reputation in the society, and for that reason, at the hours that we went to the bathhouse, she made sure that it remained closed to the general public. That was the case when Mirza Hadi went to that public bath, as well.

My father hated having the bathhouse closed to the public when he or his family were there. He used to say that nothing was more contemptible. He insisted that we remain part of the society at large and not separate ourselves just because we were rich.

Before getting married, when I went to the bathhouse with my mother and Dena, each of us carried our own bundle. Since we stayed in the bathhouse four to five hours, a maidservant carried enough snacks and seasonal fruits for all of us and for the people with whom we got into conversation on that particular day. The most common and popular fruit to eat in the bathhouse was pomegranate. During the pomegranate season, usually October to January, almost every woman brought one with her to the bathhouse. Two additional maidservants would accompany us carrying three large copper trays, which they handed to the workers at the entrance of the bathhouse. Since we bathed completely naked, for hygienic reasons, we did not sit on the floor. We put the trays upside down and sat on them.

After entering the bathhouse and passing through a corridor, we reached a large, vaulted, octagonal room with twisted columns, which had a fountain filled with coins in the middle. This was the dressing hall. There were stone benches all around the hall covered with beautiful Tabriz carpets. The lower half of the walls of the room were covered by turquoise and gold tiles showing birds and flowers, while the upper half were decorated with Persian miniature frescoes and the vaulted ceilings and archways were embellished all over with painted scenes from Persian mythology. Natural light illuminated the hall via ceiling ducts. Although it was not until I grew much older that I learned to appreciate the glory of Persian architecture, the amazing symmetrical beauty of this dazzling room never ceased to astonish me.

We undressed in the dressing hall and went to the bathing hall stark naked. In Iran, women did not mind seeing each other completely naked in bathhouses. However, men were ashamed to be seen by other men, and when they bathed, they wore loincloths that covered them from the waist to the knees.

In those days, showers had not yet been introduced in Tabriz. In the middle of the bathing hall, there was a gigantic basin placed on a metal-topped stove and filled with water. Inside the stove, a fire burned, and the fuel used by this particular bathhouse was a mixture of brushwood, leaves, and dung cakes. In a corner of the hall, there were a few small rooms in a row next to each other, where bathers went to have any excessive or unwanted body hair removed with a depilatory, which was readily available over there.

I loved to lie immersed for a long time in the hot water of the basin. There were several bathhouse masseurs called *dallacks* who helped clients wash. Each *dallack* used a sort of luffa covered with a cosmetic powder to scrub and exfoliate a client's body. Then she filled a bucket with water from the basin and poured its hot water over the client's head. After that, clients smoothed their soles with a natural volcanic pumice stone, and the *dallack* washed her client's hair and entire body with soap. Then she poured buckets of water down her head, back, and the rest of the body. For most women, the bath then ended with a nice massage or with getting their hair and nails colored with henna dye.

When we were done bathing, we sat on our copper trays for hours, relaxing, eating snacks and fruits, and conversing with the other bathers around us. We all knew each other. Bathhouses were places for socializing with neighbors and other fellow Tabrizis. There, people gossiped about their acquaintances, about their grocers, butchers, doctors, garbage collectors, and cobblers. Most of the time, the gossip was not malicious. To find brides for their sons, mothers often scanned young girls' bodies to see if they had good looks. Sisters did the same for their brothers. It was as if they were appraising a piece of merchandise.

Almost no topic was off limits. Women talked about their favorite foods and restaurants, about their family members' successes and achievements, about their plans for the future. Sometimes, controversial issues created misunderstandings, which erupted in loud quarrels. Among women, breakups and renewals of friendships in the bathhouses were not uncommon. Men, on the other hand, spent much less time in the bathhouses. Their discussions were about politics and the economy, and they rarely got into issues of daily life.

Today, in 1975, a great number of Iranian houses have their own showers, and most of the public bathhouses are no longer places to gather and socialize. Their role has changed substantially. However, there is evidence that public bathhouses have existed in Iran at least since 480 A.D. The fact that Persian literature is full of beautiful anecdotes, folk tales, poems, and aphorisms about bathhouses shows that they have been an integral part of Persian life and culture in its long history.

It was the morning of the eighth day of my imprisonment. Afra opened the door to the dungeon and asked whether I was ready to go to the bathhouse. I asked if she was the one who was going with me, and she responded positively. This made me happy—I had expected Esmat would be given the task of accompanying me.

I was ready to go, so Afra took my bundle, and we ascended the stairs and walked to the front gate of the mansion. There, one of Mirza Hadi's workers and a horse-drawn carriage were waiting for us. The worker came forward and, with a small bow, greeted me. He told me that we were going to a public bathhouse in a neighborhood that was quite far from us and that he and the carriage would wait in front of the bathhouse until Afra and I were finished.

The worker sat next to the coachman, and Afra and I sat inside the carriage. Our seat had a cover, and it was not easy for the passersby to see us. The forty-minute ride to the bathhouse was really delightful. I enjoyed every minute of it. Seeing people and passing by all the stores and offices was truly exhilarating. I was happy that, once a week, I could see part of the life inside the veins of my city.

The bathhouse that the Fiendish One had chosen for me to bathe in was a disaster. It was a dingy bathhouse in a poor neighborhood. Probably one of her servants who lived in that area had recommended it. There was no corridor leading to the dressing hall; instead, the front door opened directly onto it. In order to stop passersby from peering in, a line of loincloths had been hung from the ceiling like a screen. To enter the bathhouse, you had to walk through the hanging loincloths. The dressing hall was a large rectangular room, which had no fountain or pool nor any stone benches, only a few worn out, old wooden ones, none of which was covered with rugs or mats. It was all very plain and simple. The ceilings were low, and over time, the walls and ceilings had become discolored and covered in dark streaks and patches. There was not enough light due to the lack of windows. I did not belong there. I might have run out if Afra had not been there with me. Her presence gave me courage.

The bathing hall was not any better. The whole space was run down. The floors were covered with totally worn, crummy tiles. Looking at them made me nauseous, and I gagged at the thought of going barefoot on such a floor. Afra told me not to look down and instead to imagine that I was walking on high-quality Italian marble. I listened to her, and all those months that I went to that bathhouse, at all times, as much as possible, I avoided looking down at the floor.

Afra stayed in the dressing hall to guard my clothes and shoes, and I went to the bathing hall. There the basin was in acceptable condition.

However, depending on the type of the fuel used on a particular day, the water in the basin could be too hot or too cold to bathe. The bathhouse manager had told Afra that the fuel they used were chaff, hay, thorn and twigs and such. I soaked myself in the basin for only a couple of minutes. Then I asked a *dallack* to lay down a loincloth, and I sat on it and asked her to help me wash. Since she had not seen me before, she asked me whether I was new to the area. I told her that my husband and I had just moved from Mianeh to Tabriz, and she was shocked to hear that we had moved during a time when the "infidel" soldiers of the Soviet Union occupied our cities from all direction.

We went through all the stages of bathing, and I left the bathing hall in about half an hour. Afra could not believe how quickly I had finished. I dressed, and Afra paid the bathing fee to the bathhouse manager and tipped the *dallack*.

It seemed my humiliation had no end. Solitary confinement in a dungeon, along with all sorts of degrading treatments, has left scars on my psyche that remain to this day. Back in the carriage, I once again wished that the Fiendish One would soon be cast into the deepest part of hell, the Ninth Circle of Dante's Inferno.

A couple of days later, using her own money, Afra bought me a loincloth and sandals and gave them to me secretly without letting the Fiendish One and Esmat know. I included those in my bundle every time we went to the bathhouse. Having those items made it easier for me to bathe there. I would no longer have to step on the floor barefoot or sit on a stranger's loincloth.

# 3

My days were repetitive and full of misery. I was scared to the bones that I might rot in that dungeon. I wished that I was a freedom fighter fighting against the Soviets to free my beloved Azerbaijan. I was infuriated that, instead, I had been caged by an illiterate, despicable idiot of a jailer. At times, I had the urge to scream, as loud as I could: you, worthless bastards, I am pregnant, I should crave sweet, spicy, or salty food. Instead, I am craving music. I need music to trigger my feelings from anger, grief, and anxiety. Then I wanted to hit my head on the wall again and again until it was shattered.

Every so often, I had an urge to roar like a hungry lion, growl as powerful as the rumbling sound of thunder, and cause commotions more violent than the ocean storm tempest waves. And yet, at other times, I felt that I was a sacrificial lamb, calm and helpless. Unknowingly and inadvertently, my father had sacrificed me to strengthen our family's power and influence by establishing close ties with Heshmat Mirza's family.

My mood shifted several times each day. One hour I could be sad and helpless, and another hour defiant and contentious. One hour furious and revengeful, and another gentle and forgiving. When in wrath, I could not calm down. Instead, my wrath grew and my heart burned like a furnace. It was not easy to think rationally and logically when confined in a scary dungeon and deprived of sunlight day after day. I missed sun shine, I badly needed a room that was bathed in sunlight.

In that dungeon, I was not only a prisoner of the Fiendish One, I was a prisoner of my thoughts, too, thoughts that did not leave me alone even for a second.

In my perplexed and wandering state of mind, I wondered how much longer I could survive in that damp and moldy dungeon, curled up on my side on a corner of the cot, staring at the water stains, spider webs, and lizards all around me. Cursing people who commit evil deeds is very common in Iran. However, I always remembered the wise Arabic saying: a thousand curses never tore a shirt. I also agreed with the Danish proverb that said that a curse will not strike out an eye unless a fist goes with it. Whether or not I would ever get an opportunity to make a fist and knock out the Fiendish One, Anvar, and Mirza Hadi once and for all—that remained to be seen.

On rare occasions, I got a reprieve from my deplorable situation. The first time that it happened was early in September, on a really nice Friday, when Mirza Hadi and the rest of the family went out to a friend's village for an all-day picnic. The village was far away, and it was certain that they would not be back until late. Ali and Afra had come up with sound excuses not to go with them, so they took Esmat instead. Many of the others had the day off, since Friday is the weekend in Iran.

In those days, during the summer, it was common to set up a detached deck out in the courtyard. The deck at Mirza Hadi's mansion stood three feet off the ground, and it had rails made of intricately carved wood. It had been set up in a shady area of the courtyard, among the trees, and it had not yet been taken down for the cold season. Ali and Afra laid two carpets and a large rectangular wedge pillow on the deck, and then they opened the door to the dungeon and invited me to come outside and rest.

I went to the deck and sat against the pillow with my legs stretched out in front of me. All around me were flowers and trees, and the jubilant chirping of birds induced feelings of delight in me. Afra and Ali joined me on the deck, and we talked for many long hours. I told them stories from my childhood years and talked about my parents, Sina, Dena, Habib, Auntie, Hāji Darab, my cousins, Mashdi, my school teachers and friends, and my tailoring teacher, Ms. Suesan. They talked about their engagement and wedding, their village, and their difficult life over there.

That day, several times, I walked all around the main courtyard and each time I sat at the edge of the fountain for a while and relaxed listening to the sound of the waterfall. At lunch time, Afra wanted to spread a separate dining cloth, on the deck, before me. I asked her not to do that. I wanted to eat off the same dining cloth that they ate off. Afra had cooked two of my most favorite dishes.

Nearly thirty-two years have passed since that memorable day, and still I remember the details of all that we talked about and did on that day. Everything was just perfect—everything except for one thing that made my blood boil. Ali told me and Afra that some of the Soviet soldiers had gotten into the habit of leaving their posts, going to butcher's houses, and kidnapping the butchers. Then they took them to farmhouses around the city and forced them to take one of the animals, slaughter it, skin it, clean it, and prepare it to be grilled. The soldiers also made the family living in the farmhouse marinate and grill the meat for their feast. This happened regularly, and the repeated complaints to the intruders' supervisors fell on deaf ears. It was very likely that the Soviet leaders themselves were partaking in these feasts.

I stayed outside for nearly nine hours and returned to my prison well before Mirza Hadi and the rest of the family got home. If they had spotted me free outside, they would have fired Afra and Ali right away.

During my captivity, Afra and Ali released me several more times, bringing me to their house when it grew too cold outside to loaf on the deck. Each time, I had fun being with them. But no day was as exhilarating as that first day in September, when the sun shone brightly, and the birds sang, and the trees reached up to heaven.

# 4

Sometime in late October, something unexpected happened. Afra opened the door to the dungeon, and one of my sisters-in-law, Pegah, entered. She hugged me very hard, kissed me, and told me that she had wanted to come and see me for some time but had not been sure whether Afra and Esmat could be trusted. She confessed, "My mom will lash out at me, if she learns that I have come to see you." Eventually, Pegah had decided that she could trust Afra, and she asked her to open the dungeon door and let her in.

Pegah and I talked uninterruptedly for two hours, without running out of topics. She told me that my favorite writer, Sadegh Hedayat,[23] had written a new book called *The Stray Dog* and that she had purchased a copy for me. She gave me a very nice bag, which contained the book, a few pens and pencils, and a hardcover, fancy 250-page notebook. She told me that she knew how much I loved to read and write. I asked how she knew that Sadegh Hedayat was my favorite author, and she replied, "That was easy to find out. I checked your library in your room and found out that you had all of his books. I figured you must be in love with his writings. I know that a lot of people are. One of these days, I will begin reading his books, too."

Pegah said that, for her future visits, she wanted to know in advance what I needed so that she could purchase it for me. My reaction was to cry tears of joy. Pegah hugged and kissed me again. I told her that I always thought that she and her sister, Layla, did not care about me. Pegah confessed that she had always loved me but that any show of affection toward me would have enraged her mother.

Concerning the rat poison, Pegah had heard both her mother's version of events and mine, thanks to Afra. She believed my version fully.

---

[23] Sadegh Hedayat (1903-1951) was an Iranian writer, translator, and intellectual. He is widely considered to be the greatest Iranian author of the twentieth century.

She was convinced that I could not have possibly come up with all that story about visiting the so-called "herbal expert." Plus, it was crystal clear to her that I was incapable of even shooting a sparrow with a slingshot, let alone murdering two human beings.

"Few people are credulous enough to believe Anvar's story," she told me. "It is nonsense. We all love Anvar because once she saved Layla's life. However, she is a very sophisticated and complex person. Framing you the way she did must be part of a bigger plot." Then, showing an unbelievable sincerity, she explained how seriously her mother had wanted Mirza Hadi to marry Anvar and how severely her father had rejected the idea.

That day, Pegah revealed a side of herself that I could not have imagined before. She was not a robot or a puppet, as I used to think. She was an observant, intelligent, and thoughtful person. While in captivity, she came to visit me regularly, and I told her that if she ever needed help with her math or other subjects, I could tutor her. I also told her how much it meant to me that she believed in my innocence.

Pegah's visit was a morale-boosting event. I never knew that she was my friend, let alone a loyal one, one of those about whom the idiom, "A friend in need is a friend indeed," applied one hundred percent.

That day, after she left, I was floating on air. I had pens, pencils, and a notebook to write in; and most importantly, I had a new book by my idol, Sadegh Hedayat, to read. Moreover, I could hide them all from Esmat very easily. Each time that I wanted to use the bathroom, shortly before Esmat arrived, I put my book and stationery in the bag that Pegah had given me and hid the bag in the suitcase under my cloths. Except for the basket of dirty clothes, Esmat never touched my stuff.

I knew about Sadegh Hedayat's *The Stray Dog*. It had been published in Tehran one year earlier in 1942, but because of the Anglo-Soviet invasion of Iran, and especially the Soviet occupation of Azerbaijan, the book had not been distributed in Tabriz until mid-October of 1943. It was a collection of eight short stories, one of which, the title story, had a profound effect on me. I cannot possibly overestimate the extent to which "The Stray Dog" made me a better person and a more emotionally mature individual.

To explain why it had such a deep influence on me, allow me to retell the story here, in my own words.

# 5

"The Stray Dog" is about the disastrous fate of Pot, a full-blooded, purebred Scottish dog, who lived in the main plaza of a small beautiful town, Veramin, only twenty-two miles from Tehran. On the plaza were a bakery, a butcher, an herbal store, two coffeehouses that also serve food, and a barbershop. Under the burning sun, the people who worked there all had deeply tanned skins. In a corner of the plaza was an old sycamore tree with long crooked branches and large leaves that gave shade to a wide area. Under the tree, a teenager sold rice-pudding and another one sold pumpkin seeds. They worked long hours every day shouting their wares.

The afternoon heat of Veramin made everyone sleepy. Even the sparrows in their brick habitants dozed off during those hours, and silence fell on the entire plaza, except when it was pierced by the aggressive growling of poor Pot. He was a friendly, highly civilized, calm dog by nature. However, almost every day, the neighborhood children entertained themselves by throwing stones at him and torturing him.

Pot had a smoky gray snout and floppy ears, and his paws were covered in black. He was curly-coated with dirty, matted hair, and his eyes, which manifested hints of human intelligence, gleamed under his shaggy, mop-like coat. They say that the eyes are the windows to the soul, and deep gazes into Pot's eyes revealed a human soul within him. In the darkness that had overwhelmed his life, something endless surged in those brown eyes. They conveyed a message that was not possible to comprehend. They were full of such pain, agony, and patience that one can only see in the eyes of a stray dog. And yet, it seemed as if no one saw or understood those looks of suffering and beseeching.

In front of the bakery, the errand boy punched and slapped him, and in front of the butcher shop, the butcher's apprentice threw stones at him. If he took shelter in the shadow of a car, he would be kicked by the merciless drivers with their studded, hard-soled shoes. And when everyone else was finished with their atrocities, it was the turn of the teenager who sold rice pudding. That sadistic boy particularly enjoyed torturing Pot. Every time that the stone he threw hit Pot and Pot howled, he burst into laughter and yelled, "The damned filthy dog!" Then he threw another stone, while everyone around him, joined in his laughter and encouraged him to continue his devilish deed.

Pot had discovered a secret route, through meandering alleys, to the other side of Veramin, far away from the plaza, where a waterway led to a plantation. There, he could be safe. He liked to stay there all the time, but hunger always forced him back to town and to the plaza, where he could rummage through garbage for food and where the butcher sometimes threw him a bone or two or a passerby gave him a slice of bread from the bakery. Of all the smells in the plaza, nothing excited him more than the fragrant aroma of rice pudding. Even though all Pot's experiences with the boy who sold the rice pudding were frightening and utterly abusive, nevertheless, instinctively, Pot gravitated toward him. The smell of rice pudding triggered happy memories in his mind, memories of him and his siblings when they were fed their mother's milk.

At the plantation, Pot stretched out his forelegs facing the large groups of plants that were under cultivation. His body felt exhausted and his nerve pain never went away. He enjoyed looking at the beautiful scenery before him. The smells of the plants and all sorts of objects around him such as a dampened odd shoe, a scrap iron, or a torn handkerchief reminisced about the happy days of his past. The spectacular landscape and the inherent natural beauty of the plantation brought out Pot's instinctive desire to run and gambol on the plantation, just as his ancestors in Scotland had. However, he had been beaten so badly that his body had no energy for such activities.

Pot often found himself wandering down memory lane, thinking back on when he lived with this owner, in his owner's house. Back then, Pot had been well behaved, disciplined, sociable, and outgoing, and he did not shy away from meeting new people. He had been curious and imaginative, and he read his owner's emotions and behaved accordingly. He barked to let his owner know that somebody was at the door, and he received enormous love and affection from his owner's family.

He had had a perfect life and thought that all lives were like his. He could never have imagined the wretched life he led now, full of misery and contempt. In his owner's house, he had been fearless, bold, confident; in his new life, he had become timid and downtrodden, trembling with fear if he heard a sound or felt a movement around himself. Sometimes, he was even frightened by the sound of his own voice. Once in a while, he washed himself in the waterway, but in general, he had become accustomed to filth and lived with fleas and parasites on his body. People treated Pot like garbage, and he felt that, in a way, he had become garbage.

Since falling into this hellhole of a life two years before, Pot had not had one meal that satiated his hunger. Neither did he have a good night's sleep. His sexual desires and urges were suppressed, and his emotions and passions were stifled. Nobody petted, stroked, or caressed him. He had known no affection from anyone. While the people in the plaza and its surrounding resembled, physically, his owner and his owner's friends and associates, there was a world of difference between their behavior and disposition and his owner's. He wondered why their temperaments were based on sadism and savagery.

When Pot had eaten enough in the plaza to survive for another day, he rushed back to the plantation, where he could rest and be safe from malicious and abusive people. He reminisced about wrestling with his siblings when he had been a puppy and about playing with his owner's son. None of the members of his owner's family had ever hit him once; they petted him and fed him sugar cubes from their hands. But his favorite had been the son. The owner's son would run around the courtyard and the orchard on their property, and Pot would chase him and nibble gently at pantlegs and shirtsleeves.

At the dinner table, Pot walked around the table and enjoyed smelling the dishes. But he did not beg for food. His owner often gave him a piece of meat or a loaf of bread until the servant brought his food in a special bowl. Pot was fed homemade food only; he ate the same dishes that his owner's family ate.

It had been a strange set of freak events that had changed the course of Pot's life. One day, his owner was getting ready to travel somewhere far away. Pot loved car rides, and his owner wanted a companion, so he called Pot and sat him in the front passenger seat. After five hours of driving, they stopped in the plaza in Veramin to rest and have lunch. There was a female dog in heat in the vicinity, and the pheromones she emitted sent Pot into a frenzy. As soon as his owner opened the car door, he jumped out and began to run.

Pot followed the female dog's scent to an orchard surrounded by tall mud-and-straw walls. The entrance was closed. Pot walked along the walls until he found a narrow stream. Where the stream met the wall, there was a small circular opening for the water to pass through. Pot crawled through the opening and into the orchard. Pot found the female dog and spent all the afternoon with her. Shortly before sunset, he heard his owner's voice calling his name, "Pot! Pot!" As much as he felt obliged to follow his owner's command, an unearthly force made him stay with the female dog. Nevertheless, not long after, gardeners saw him and drove him out of the orchard with sticks and spade handles. After that, Pot looked for his owner all night with no luck, and that was how his new life in Veramin began.

Pot was the only stray dog who went to the plaza every day to find food. He had noticed that there were a few human beings whose conditions were not any different from his. They were homeless, and they searched in trash bags and trash bins for their meals. Sometimes, they begged for money and food from the travelers who stopped in the plaza and from the passersby. Pot was jealous of homeless people. No one ever threw stones at them, punched, slapped, or kicked them. By and large, they were ignored. People passed by them as if they did not exist. Things were very different in his case. Almost every man and boy who saw him considered it his duty to abuse Pot in one way or another.

The thing that tortured Pot the most was his need to be petted. His eyes begged for affection, and he was willing to give his life for a stroke on head. He needed to express his emotions, love, trust, and loyalty to someone. But he could not find anybody interested in him. All he knew from people were hostility and viciousness.

Two years after the scent of a female dog in heat had changed Pot's life, on a nice and sunny day, a car similar to his owner's car roared into the plaza and raised clouds of dust. The car stopped where Pot stood. A man got out and went directly toward Pot. The man knelt down and gave Pot a rub behind both ears. Pot started to wag his tail. The man was not his owner, and Pot stared at him in disbelief and astonishment. The man began to leave, but after taking a few steps, he turned back and petted Pot more. Pot was filled with wonder. This time, when the man left, Pot followed him.

The man went to one of the coffeehouses on the plaza and sat at a table outside. Pot sat on the ground beside him. The waiter came to kick

Pot and scare him away, but the man said that the dog was with him, telling the waiter, "Leave the poor animal alone. Like you, he is God's creature too." The waiter muttered something incoherent, probably a statement of disgust. The man ordered enough food for two people—lots of fresh bread, a big bowl of yogurt, fried eggs, and feta cheese—and fed Pot from his hand. He dipped pieces of bread in the yogurt, and placed eggs or cheese in the middle of small pieces of bread and gave them to Pot one after another. Pot's eyes were glued on the man in absolute disbelief. He was thanking him with his big brown attractive eyes.

That morning, for the first time in two years, he ate a bellyful of food without getting one single beating. He remembered that eating is not only for survival, it is also for enjoyment. He wondered whether he had found a new owner and whether he was awake or dreaming.

After breakfast, the man walked around for a while, and Pot followed him everywhere. At times he stopped and petted Pot, and each time, Pot wagged his tail and licked the man's hands. After he was finished strolling, he returned to the plaza, petted Pot, and went and sat in his car. Fear loomed large in Pot's mind. He did not dare to get in the car. Instead, he sat beside the car and looked fixedly at the man. All of a sudden, raising a big cloud of dust, the car pulled away, and there was not a second's hesitation before Pot began to run after it. He would not lose another kind man in his life.

Even though his entire body was in pain, he ran so swiftly that he covered more than a body length with each stride. While panting with his tongue hanging out, he ran with every bit of strength he had. The car drew from all of the villages in the vicinity of Veramin and passed through a country road when Pot nearly caught up with it. Nevertheless, the car drove too fast and Pot fell behind. But Pot did not resign himself to failure. He was determined to end his miserable life in that plaza, and by chasing the car, he was running away from his abominable present toward his glorious past. So, he continued to chase the car until he lost the last bit of his strength and collapsed.

With much difficulty, Pot dragged himself to the side of a river running through a farm and rested his body on hot, damp sand. Soon, everything went dark in his eyes. His body was paralyzed. He felt a severe pain in his stomach, and instinctively, he realized that he was not going to move from that spot.

The sun had not set yet when three hungry crows, who had smelled Pot from afar, started to circle overhead. One of them flew down, sat near Pot, and watched him carefully. When the crow was sure that Pot was not yet dead, it took off again. Those three crows had come a long way to peck out Pot's brown eyes.

# 6

On the day that Pegah gave me the new book by Sadegh Hedayat, I read "The Stray Dog" three times, and even during the first reading, I related to the story as though it were an allegory of my life.

I saw myself in Pot. Pot was a full-blooded purebred who, in the past, had lived a splendid life. Likewise, I was a blue-blooded, highborn woman raised in a huge luxurious home by highly cultured and distinguished parents.

Not all Iranians abused dogs. Many admired them. Some kept them inside their homes as pets, others kept them in their courtyards, orchards, or farms to guard their properties. However, Pot had ended up in a neighborhood whose inhabitants were merciless dog abusers. That was the same in my case. Of all my suitors, I wound up getting married to a sadistic wife-beater with a diabolical mother.

Both Pot and I lived in seclusion. Pot was forced to escape to a spot in the plantation and live a lonely life. I was imprisoned in a psychological torture chamber. We had both been separated from our own worlds and dragged into ones where we did not belong. We had fallen from the zenith of loftiness to the nadir of wretchedness. We both tried hard to adapt to our new menacing and hostile environment, and we both failed. Those environments were too tough and rigid to accept us.

At the end, three crows came a long way off and waited to peck out Pot's brown eyes. In my life, also, there were three "crows"—Mirza Hadi, his mother, and Anvar. But they were not waiting to peck my eyes. They were waiting to take my baby from me.

# 7

Every day, in that dungeon, I spent a few hours writing about my psychological condition. The more I tried to describe the emotional effects of my imprisonment, the more difficult it became. I tried to avoid repeating myself, so I always looked for new ways and new metaphors to explain my suffering. I wanted to connect with my future readers so strongly that they would feel, in their bones, the extent to which I was oppressed. I wanted them to feel the pain of a victim like me who was taken advantage of, her personal space and boundaries crossed and intruded. I wanted to convey that I would experience the trauma of having been so lethally violated for the rest of my days.

My life had become a dark, moonless winter night, my tears resembled the petals of withered water lilies, and I, myself, had been reduced to a rainless cloud of grief and gloom, or perhaps a thorn in the heart of a sunburned wasteland. Not long before, when I was not yet married, I wrote love songs for my Nima with lyrics that were specific to him. I wrote about his magical smiles, his elegant and luminous visage, and his angry ocean-blue eyes, which once jumped at me and set me ablaze in eternal flames of love. But in the dungeon, I wrote about how those hopes had turned to ash. Alas, lonesomeness! Alas, isolation! How desperately I yearned for my love.

Sometimes, I saw myself dispossessed and displaced, like a fire left behind at a campsite of a caravan traveling in a barren land. Other times, muffled and dejected, I felt that I was like a beautiful bud stripped of its petals by the wind of destiny before I'd had the chance to bloom. And that was my mood until, one morning in November, my father's voice echoed in my ears, reciting a line by Hafez that he used to recite often when he was alive.

> The sphere, I will dash together (and destroy); unless to my desire it come:[24]
> Not that one am I, to endure contempt from the sky's sphere.

---

[24] *The Divan-i Hafiz*, translated by H. Wilberforce Clarke, p. 607.

I suddenly understood those words in a way I never had before. My father was telling me to stop being in the doldrums all the time. His message was that I should fight against my condition and not be crushed underfoot.

I became excited. I got off the cot and began walking back and forth reciting poems by Hafez aloud:

> My eye, an ocean (of weeping) I make; to the desert, patience, I cast:[25]
> And, in this work, my heart into the ocean I cast.
> From the straitened heart the sinner, I heave such a sigh
> That, into the sin of Adam and of Eve, fire I cast.
> The sky's arrow,[26] I have endured; wine give, so that, intoxicated of head
> Into the girdle of the waist of the quiver of Jauza (Gemini), a knot I may cast.
> On this moving throne,[27] a draught of wine, I pour:
> Into this azure vault,[28] the resounding shout of strife, I cast.

In total ecstasy, I continued reciting other poems by Hafez:

> Come; so that the rose we may scatter, and, into the cup, the wine cast.[29]
> The roof of the sky we rend; and a new way, cast.
> If an army, that sheddeth the blood of lovers, grief raise
> Content together are I and the **Saki**;[30] and up its foundation, we cast
> Of reason, one boasteth; another idle talk weaveth:
> Come: before the just Ruler these disputes, let us cast.

Then I remembered that Mohammad-Taqi Bahar[31] also had a

---

[25] Ibid., p. 675.
[26] Arrow of affliction
[27] The revolving sky
[28] The sky
[29] Ibid., p. 638.
[30] The cupbearer
[31] Mohammad-Taqi Bahar (1886-1951), widely known as Malek o-Sho'ara Bahar

forceful, invigorating poem. Since I had forgotten its rhyme and rhythm and only remembered the concepts, I recited those concepts out loud, in my own words: "Rise and pick up the threads of your life, banish the sorrow that has enveloped your heart, and put grief away from your flesh. Be the rain and fall over dry and thirsty lands and over mountains, be a blaze and set the dry and wet on fire. Take a trip to a sugarcane plantation, cut and shape a reed flute from a hollow stalk of cane. Play the reed flute so that it fires up not an audience but the whole terrestrial globe. In the thick of the battle for enlightenment, be ready to come face to face with a growling lion. Fearless and determined, fight to beat the lion with your bare hands. Avenge the philosophers' sufferings against the graceless and wayward universe."

It is true that you cannot prepare for a marathon in a prison cell. However, I figured that if I walked the length of my dungeon back and forth 440 times, that added up to one mile. I set a goal to walk every day at least two miles, and I stuck to that goal with determination. I sang only happy songs, and I strived to fight the misery brought to me by the Fiendish One and her accomplice, Anvar, by laughing as much as I could. I triggered memories that made me laugh, and I recalled funny movies, which cheered me up, especially those with Charlie Chaplin. I changed my attitude toward the small lizards that lived with me in the dungeon. Even though I was scared to touch them, I looked at them as my friends, and I tried hard to tell them apart. I watched them move around with interest.

It was a pleasant surprise to find that what motivate me most was the stunning anthem of the Goal High School, my alma mater:

> Man survives on this earth, together and apart
> In light and splendor of sciences and art!
> On the foundation of culture and knowledge
> To build our destiny is our pledge!
> On this boundless earth, to achieve prosperity, bliss, and perfection
> We march toward the Goal, that is our direction!
> By taking any path toward the Goal

(the king of poets), is a prominent Iranian poet and scholar.

Immersed in arts and sciences will be our soul!
We, the youth of the Goal, carrying the torch of knowledge, shall
never digress,
Concordant and united, we shall progress, progress, progress!

I sang this anthem almost every day, and I never grew tired of it. It reminded me of the best days of my life. While singing the anthem, the beautiful faces of my high school friends, one after another, paraded before my eyes. I was happy that, in less than five months, I would see them all again. I knew where their parents' houses were, and I resolved to find and visit each one of them within the first two weeks of my freedom.

I had endured the Fiendish One and Mirza Hadi for too long. I should have left them right after my mother passed away. In Mirza Hadi's mansion, I had been a prisoner since day one, controlled and cut off from the outside world. Since getting married, I had not seen any of my high school friends, and I was dying to know what had become of them. That was no way to live. I had an obligation to rescue myself from this predicament. I would not leave my husband's house in a white death shroud.

In those days, there was a stigma surrounding divorce, but that wouldn't change without sacrifices. It was the responsibility of people like me to bite the bullet, get divorced, endure judgement, and little by little lessen the cultural stigmas associated with divorce until they vanished altogether. Toward that goal, I was ready and determined to do my part.

# 8

It was a cold December day, shortly after noon. Ali had just brought me a tray with my lunch. Even though I'd been hungry, as soon as I began to eat, I spat out the food. I felt like I was going to throw up. Dizzy, I got off the cot and began pounding on the dungeon door as hard as I could. But nobody answered. So I emptied the laundry basket and vomited yellow bile into it.

When Esmat came to check on me at one o'clock on the dot, I showed her the basket and asked her to take it out and clean it. She was not happy about that. Indifferent to my condition, without asking me questions or showing any concerns, she took the basket out, cleaned it, and brought it back along with a metal bowl. She told me to vomit in the bowl next time, since it was easier to clean it. Then she left.

When Ali returned to take the lunch tray, he noticed that I had not touched my lunch. I had a fever and abdominal pain just beneath my lower ribs. But I did not say anything about that to Ali. I just told him that I had no appetite.

I did not touch my dinner, either, and did not eat anything the next day. On the third day, after not touching my breakfast, Ali informed the Fiendish One that I was not eating. I was half asleep, wrapped in a blanket, when suddenly somebody punched me in the head. I opened my eyes to find the Fiendish One standing over me, yelling, "You bastard, you think that you can scare me by going on a hunger strike?" She pulled my blanket away so forcefully that I fell off the rickety cot, and the cot and the mattress tipped over, bringing the entire bed on top of me. Immediately, an excruciating pain began in my upper right arm and shoulder. The Fiendish One looked at me, and as soon as she saw my face, she left the dungeon in a hurry. As I tried to get up, I found limited range of motion in my right arm and shoulder. I felt that I was metamorphosing into Sadegh Hedayat's stray dog, Pot, and I thought about all the tortures and abuses that he endured.

Afra and Esmat entered the dungeon and told me that Ali had gone to hail a carriage and that the Fiendish One was taking me to see Doctor Sharif at his clinic.

As Afra and Esmat helped me dress, I told them about the agonizing pain in my right arm and shoulder. To avoid touching me there, Afra moved to my right side, put her left arm around my waist, made a fist with her right hand, and asked me to put the palm of my left hand over the top of her fist. We walked slowly out of the dungeon, ascended the narrow staircase, and, with some serious effort, went all the way to the front gate of the mansion.

Outside the gate, a carriage was waiting for us. In the carriage, Afra sat between me and the Fiendish One. I was in pain, half asleep, dizzy, and nauseous. I leaned my head on Afra's shoulder. All the way to the doctor's clinic, the Fiendish One talked on and on about how she had tried to convince Heshmat Mirza to let Mirza Hadi marry Anvar. "I wanted a bride for my son, not a cockroach," she said, talking about me without looking at me. "The yellowing of her damned skin is a sign of tuberculosis. She has probably spread the germ all over."

Doctor Sharif was a very close friend of my family. Sina, Dena, and I called him Uncle Sharif. We loved him. He was very kind to us, especially after my father's assassination. When we arrived at his office, he saw me promptly. He greeted us warmly, noted that I was pregnant, and expressed his sorrow that his friends, Heshmat Mirza and Moin-al-Tojjar, had not lived long enough to see their grandchild.

Afra helped me onto the examination table. While examining me, Doctor Sharif asked about my symptoms. I told him that I had lost my appetite, was nauseous almost all the time, I had abdominal pain, was feverish, itched at times, and my urine was dark. The Fiendish One asked Doctor Sharif if I had tuberculosis, and he responded, absolutely not. He said that the most important symptoms of tuberculosis were persistent cough for several weeks, coughing blood along with chest pain, which I had none of them. He explained that I had viral hepatitis A, which would gradually heal by itself. Then he told the Fiendish One that the baby was fine and that he could hear his or her heartbeat. That was a huge relief to know that my baby was not hurt when the Fiendish One threw me off the cot onto floor. Doctor Sharif advised that they should clean my mattress and bedsheets more often and told me that I should drink a lot of fruit juice and milk. He went into his office and returned with a few berries in his hand, which he put into my mouth one after another. He kissed my forehead and said, "My daughter, you are as beautiful as ever. I will prescribe a couple of tonics that will make you feel better. Nothing to worry about." I kissed his hand and told him, "Thank you, my dear Uncle Sharif."

On our way back, the Fiendish One did not say a word. I am sure that she was not happy to see all the attention and love that Doctor Sharif gave me. If she had known how close my family and I were to him, she would not have taken me to his clinic.

Back at the mansion, Afra took me to her house and asked me to rest there until Ali and the other servants replaced the cot with a real bed. Esmat brought me a large glass filled with carrot juice and another one full of pomegranate juice. Back in the dungeon, I noticed that the room was much cleaner. They had gotten rid of the spiderwebs and wall lizards, and the new bed was solid and sturdy with a thick mattress. They had replaced the worn-out, outdoor picnic blanket with a clean comforter and had provided me with bedsheets. Only God knows whether the Fiendish One was scared that I died in that dungeon, and she and her family got into serious trouble, or she wanted me to be healthy and deliver her a grandchild in tip-top condition.

A few days later, I realized that I should have told Doctor Sharif that I was imprisoned in a dungeon at Mirza Hadi's mansion and I should have asked him to tell Dena and Habib to come and rescue me. As I realized that I had missed a perfect opportunity to escape, I sank into painful emotions of remorse, guilt, self-reproach, and self-condemnation all at the same time. Not telling Doctor Sharif about my situation became a life regret, which I have tried hard to reconcile.

There is an idiom in Farsi that asks, why does a wise person do something he or she regrets later? In my case, it was not something that I did, it was something that I did not do. It was regret over inaction. All those days imprisoned in that dungeon, I had looked for opportunities to escape, and when one finally presented itself, I had failed to take it.

# 9

One day, Afra came to the dungeon and told me that the Fiendish One had sent her to ask for my wedding ring back. This did not bother me at all. I already considered my marriage with Mirza Hadi to be over. I had stopped giving a damn about him many weeks before. I told Afra that the wedding ring symbolized commitment to marriage, which I had not at all, and respect for husband, which I had none. Moreover, the ring constantly reminded me of my marriage, which was a terrifying nightmare. I told her that I had thrown the ring inside the suitcase, and while she searched the suitcase, she told me that, that morning, my sister's houseman, Uncle Verdi, had come by and spoken with the Fiendish One. My sister and Habib were worried about me. "Ever since she has gone to Paris, they have not heard from her even once," Afra heard Uncle Verdi say. "She has not sent them even one letter. That is just most uncharacteristic of Lady Dorna."

The Fiendish One responded that the Soviets were intercepting letters sent to the post office in Tabriz, and she assured Uncle Verdi that I was fine and enjoying my time in Paris. Unfortunately, Uncle Verdi did not think to ask the Fiendish One how she knew all of that. But in any case, I was glad to learn that Dena and Habib were concerned. It was most assuring that my family did not trust Mirza Hadi and his mother blindly. After all Dena knew all about my relationship with them.

When Afra found the ring in the suitcase, she said flatly, "To me, asking for your ring indicates that there are wheels within wheels. Oh God, have pity on all of us!" I told her not to worry at all. Lizards had found their way back to the dungeon, and I pointed to one that was crawling on the wall.

"Do you see that? You care more about that reptile than I care about Mirza Hadi. Soon, he will marry Anvar, and I will get rid of him immediately after my baby is born. I will be free as a bird. Let us face it, this mansion is like a glorious cloud that rains feces," I said.

Two days later, early in the morning, while Esmat escorted me to the bathroom, all around the servants' quarters, I saw women sitting on the ground with large round trays of rice on their laps. They were in the process of cleaning the rice. The uncleaned rice was piled on one side of the tray. Little by little, the women pushed small amounts of the rice to the middle of their trays and picked out any husks, grains of sand, and other debris. The rice that was cleaned was then pushed to the opposite side of the tray, and this process continued until all of the rice in the tray was cleaned. Except for one, all the women were so preoccupied with their work that they did not notice us pass by. That one woman saw me and immediately elbowed the woman next to her and whispered something in her ear. They both stared at me. I waved to them, but they ignored me.

I did not need to ask Esmat to know what was going on. This was the sort of scene you only saw at weddings and funerals, and because no one had died—at least, not that I knew of—I concluded that someone must be getting married soon. It could not have been Pegah or Layla's wedding since, in those cases, Afra would have informed me. They were preparing for the wedding of Mirza Hadi and Anvar. In Iran, polygamy was allowed then and is still allowed today. However, in those days, a man did not need permission from the previous nondivorced wives to marry again.

That day and the day after, every time that I was escorted to the
toilet, all I saw was the commotion of the wedding preparations. Women
sang wedding songs, and men hung marvelous lights throughout the
mansion. Mirza Hadi's marriage was so unimportant to me that, for the
few minutes that I was allowed out, I actually enjoyed hearing the songs
and looking at the decorations. The whole thing was a pleasant change
for a prisoner such as myself.

On the night of the wedding, Afra came in to bring me dinner and
told me angrily that, during the wedding ceremony, not only had Mirza
Hadi placed my ring on Anvar's finger, but the Fiendish One had given
her all of my jewelry. Those included my own personal pieces and the
wedding gifts my own relatives had given me. This news threw a wrench
in my plans for the future. I had tens of thousands of dollars' worth of
jewelry, expensive Persian carpets, and other precious items from my
dowry. I had been counting on those riches to lay a groundwork for my
future, without any idea that Mirza Hadi and the Fiendish One planned
to steal it all from me. They were going for broke by such shameless acts.

# 10

The day after Mirza Hadi's wedding with Anvar, around ten o'clock in
the morning, I was sitting on my bed and watching the lizards crawling
on the wall when suddenly I came to myself by the sound of a key into
the lock of the dungeon door. The door was opened and Mirza Hadi
entered. His presence in the dungeon upset me, but I remained calm by
staring at the lizards. I had prepared for this encounter for weeks.

Mirza Hadi sat on the chair and said, "So, this is your prison cell!
You are so lucky. If we had pressed the charge of attempted double-
murder against you, your cell would have been one hundred times worse.
You should be grateful to me and my mother for not throwing you in
the Tabriz jail. You owe it all to *my* baby." His slighting remarks made
me so angry that if I'd had a gun, I would have shot him in the head.
However, I kept my cool and said nothing.

"As a courtesy, I have come to tell you that, last night, I married
Anvar. I did not want you to hear it from someone else. Anvar has loved
me for a long time. Once she saved my sister's life, and as you know, she

recently saved the lives of me and my mother, as well. I am beholden to her. Plus, it was a lifelong wish of my mother that I marry Anvar. Finally, her dream has come true. You should have seen how happy she was."

"I hope that the pain of jealousy does not land you in trouble. What is done is done. Things cannot be altered. Let's face it, as soon as *my* baby is born, you can start a new life for yourself. You are still very young, only twenty-three, and still very beautiful. I am sure that you can find someone to marry."

Without looking at him even once, I smirked and replied, "All that you have told me is proof that you do not know me at all. There was never anything between us. We have not had one serious conversation about something that matters. You have no idea about my past. You do not know who I am and what my thoughts or ideas in life are. You have forgotten that I am a daughter of the great martyr Moin-al-Tojjar. I know all about you and Anvar. You should have married her to begin with. However, greed made you join all my suitors, who thronged like bees about the honey of my father's riches."

"Like your mother, my mother was also against our marriage, but for a totally different reason. My mother quarreled with my father long and hard to stop him from forcing me to marry you. She told my father that everyone in Tabriz knew that you are a self-indulgent playboy. She begged him not to compromise my happiness, welfare, and prosperity for a promise to a dead man. She argued that since your father had died, whatever agreement was between my father and yours was null and void. Nevertheless, my father was as adamant and determined to keep his promise as the insanely stubborn Captain Ahab was in seeking his vengeance on the white whale, Moby Dick."

I was glad that Mirza Hadi was still there and listening. I used a few other refences to famous western fictional characters to intentionally display my intellectual superiority over his. I had never seen him buy or read a book. He had no idea who those characters were.

"What you probably do not know yet," I went on, "is that I was and still am madly in love with a true gentleman, whose name is Nima. He darted like lightning through my life and ignited in my heart the flames of eternal love. He is the second coming of Joseph, the eleventh of Jacob's twelve sons, an epitome of physical beauty and inner virtue. He is a superb artist and musician. My and Nima's relationship was nothing like yours and Anvar's. Anvar gave you the fake name of Kasra and told me every detail of your physical relationship with her and how she stopped you so vehemently every time that you tried to go all the way. Do not even doubt that she is in love with you. More than that, she suffers from obsessive love. Once, she told me that she planned to do whatever she had to do to claw her way back into your life, ruin your marriage, and win you back. Well, she successfully carried out her plot, and last night, she achieved her lifelong goal. Good for her. To begin with, what business did Moin-al-Tojjar's daughter have in this mansion living with a degenerate man and his fiendish mother?"

Mirza Hadi broke in and told me to watch my tongue. But I had more to say.

"I never told my parents and siblings that I was in love with Nima. Only Auntie was aware. She is my confidant. Your mother pilfered all of the love letters that Nima had written to me from a hiding place in my room. You should read them. Nima's handwriting is master calligraphy. His choice of words and his fluency in composition have few rivals. I really deserved to have him as my husband. I deserved a camphorated candle with the most exquisite aroma, not a lantern with the awful smell of gasoline. I hope that you will ask your mother to return those letters to me. My and Nima's love for each other was beyond physical attraction. We trusted each other, and I chose his welfare over my own, just as he chose mine over his. We held space for each other.

"After Nima asked my father for my hand in marriage and my father rejected him, we only met once more to say goodbye forever. The great American poet Henry Wadsworth Longfellow[32] wrote that, 'Great is the art of beginning, but greater is the art of ending.' With that in mind, I held Nima's hands in a tight grip, and I swore by God, with every fiber of my being, that I had never loved, and would never love again, another man as I loved him."

At that point, I paused to gauge Mirza Hadi's reaction. He was still listening attentively. I am sure that he was taken aback by all these facts about his soon-to-be ex-wife. I knew that he did not want to listen to

---

[32] Henry Wadsworth Longfellow (1807-1882), one of the Fireside Poets from New England, was the first American to translate Dante Alighieri's Divine Comedy. Among his prominent works are "Paul Revere's Ride," The Song of Hiawatha, and Evangeline.

what I had to say from that point on; nevertheless, it was important to me to say all that I had carefully planned to tell him.

I talked much faster now. I had practiced speaking quickly and clearly. "This is the first and probably the last conversation between the two of us. I want to end our relationship, keeping in mind that greater than the art of beginning is the art of ending. So, you got married to the apple of Moin-al-Tojjar's eye, a girl born into an exceptionally privileged family, a girl who is highly educated and stunningly beautiful. You asked her father for her fine, delicate hand in marriage, and he gladly agreed. You married her, and she moved to your mansion. Did you ever think that, as her husband, you had serious responsibilities and obligations toward her? Of course not. You wanted me for my father's wealth and for the nights that you were not whoremongering. You left me every single day with your sadistic, soul-sucking mother. For me, your mansion is hell on earth. You are a wife-beater, an abuser, a ruffian. Your infidelity proved that you are an animal, and your openness about it showed that you are a wicked rascal. Your shameless swindling of your sister's properties and your robbery of their monies disgust me. My father did not allow me to marry Nima, the personification of goodness and embodiment of love and virtue; no, he forced me to marry you, the embodiment of vice and wickedness."

Suddenly, Mirza Hadi stood up and shouted at the top of his lungs, "Shut up, you fatherless bastard whore!" I got jump scared. My bones trembled with fear. Shaking with anger, he grabbed my hair, twisted my head toward himself, and slapped me across my face so hard that I saw stars. Then he left, locking the door of the dungeon behind him. Despite my agonizing condition, I broke into a smile! I felt that I had ended my miserable relationship with Mirza Hadi victoriously.

# 11

When Mirza Hadi came to visit me, I was still sick with viral hepatitis A, meaning he beat up a very sick, pregnant woman who could not defend herself. If I had been healthy and not pregnant, I would have kicked him in the testicles. The days were gone when Mirza Hadi could beat me without consequence.

After Mirza Hadi left, I tried to sleep. Afra brought my lunch at noon, and I ate a little while she waited. Then I told her everything that had happened between me and Mirza Hadi.

"The day will come when this godless man will pay for his atrocities," she burst out. "God is the perfect judge, the judge of all judges, a just and righteous judge. Lady Dorna, trust God and the glory of his majesty and refer Mirza Hadi for judgement to his mighty power." She said this and left, and I fell asleep.

A few hours later, the Fiendish One woke me up by bursting into the dungeon and talking gibberish. "I have come to set you on another fire, the fire of eternal jealousy!" she announced. "I have come to let you know that, last night, I personally placed Anvar's hand on the hand of my son, Mirza Hadi."

I cut her off. "I thought that my days of listening to your rubbish were over. You are a mentally feeble person, the type of illiterate who does not know her ass from her elbow. You are an embarrassment to the human race. Now shut up and leave this dungeon. Leave me alone."

For a moment, I thought that the Fiendish One saw red, but then she left the dungeon, cursing me and my family members with the obscenest words. That I expected since, by telling her that she was illiterate, I had hit her where it hurt most.

Mirza Hadi and his mother were too stupid to realize that things had changed and that Moin-al-Tojjar's lioness daughter was back.

# 12

Once I recovered from my bout of hepatitis, I began walking the length of my dungeon again, back and forth, 880 times almost every day. While walking, I sang happy songs and my alma mater's anthem. True, there were times that I was sad, but I fought hard not to fall into depression. What an agony loneliness is!

I was like the mythical phoenix; I was burned to ashes on the pyre of my doom, and I was being reborn from my ashes to begin a new life.

Even though Esmat slept in the dungeon every night, I never considered her company—she was just a prison guard. On the other hand, the few minutes that Afra spent with me each day, when she brought my meals, were a true blessing. Like Ali and Afra, Pegah was also a God-sent friend. Her visits boosted my morale. She came to see me infrequently, but when she did, she spent at least two hours with me. She brought me books and my favorites snacks—blackberry and plum rollups and dried sour black curd. Pegah's visits meant a lot to me since I knew that the lizards gave her the chills. It was not like visiting a prisoner in a city prison. For someone not used to the dungeon, it was next to impossible to endure that horrid environment for more than a few minutes. And yet, for my sake, she withstood all that repulsiveness for a relatively long time.

On a very cold February day, shortly after noon, while I was still having my lunch, Afra opened the dungeon door and Pegah entered. She had come for help with her mathematics homework. No matter how hard she tried, she said, she could not do the following problem:

> Draw the graphs of the below equations on the same Cartesian plane.

$$y = x^{\wedge}(2/3) + \sqrt{(1-x^{\wedge}2)},$$
$$y = x^{\wedge}(2/3) - \sqrt{(1-x^{\wedge}2)}.$$

It had been a long time since I had sketched the graph of an equation. My math skills in general were rusty, so, I began flipping through Pegah's textbook. Things came back to me quickly: how to find maximum and minimums of a curve and thus how to calculate the derivatives and also the second derivatives for the possible inflection points, and so forth. I kept reading and explaining the material to Pegah. We went over all of the examples of the relevant sections of the book together, and when I felt that I was ready, I tried to sketch the graphs of the equations. They were not easy to draw. At every step, I did something wrong, and it took me time to figure out what it was.

Our tutoring lesson lasted most of the afternoon.

I eventually managed to sketch both curves, and when I finished, I noticed that together they made the shape of a heart. The moment I completed that shape was one of the most rewarding moments in my entire life. I had solved a very beautiful calculus problem in captivity in a morbid dungeon after three years of total separation from any kind of studying. It was as if the graphs of these two equations took the shape of my own heart, with two arrows, the *x*-axis and the *y*-axis, piercing it in two directions—one vertically and one horizontally. Was there a better symbol of my wrecked life?

At 4:30 P.M., Afra came to see whether Pegah was ready to go. She was. She left with Afra, and I noticed that Afra forgot to lock the dungeon door. For the first time in all the months that I was imprisoned there, the dungeon door was unlocked and there was no one to guard me. This was my long-awaited opportunity to escape. I had only thirty minutes to make it out of the gate of the mansion before Esmat came to check on me—not a moment to lose.

With my heart racing, I put on my winter clothes and a pair of comfortable shoes and rushed out. I climbed a few steps, paused, and looked around to make sure that nobody was in the vicinity. The gardener was there, washing his hands and face with ice-cold water from the pond. I ducked down into the stairwell and stayed hidden until he was gone, then I walked through the servant quarters hugging the wall the whole way so.

At last, I reached the woods. I breathed a sigh of relief. There was no chance anybody would see me now: during the winter, no one went near the woods. I walked until I reached the clearing where Mirza Hadi parked his two vehicles. There were more trees beyond the parking area, but to get to them, I would have to pass through the clearing without attracting the attention of Mirza Hadi's chauffeur, who was pacing back and forth near the cars. When his back was turned, I held my pregnant belly and scurried behind one of the cars. From there, I quietly slipped into the woods.

I was inches from the gate when the gardener's wife spotted me. "Lady Dorna is trying to escape!" she cried. I rushed through the gate. I only made it several yards past the gate when it seemed as if the entire household had descended upon me. My heart sank. The workers stopped me and took me back to the mansion, where the Fiendish One was waiting.

She glared at me with hatred in her eyes. "You devil, do you think you could ever escape my custody? I am no ordinary person. No one can outsmart me. I am Heshmat Mirza's wife!"

The servants, the gardener and his wife, the chauffeur—all were present and watching us curiously. I turned to them and said, "Do not be deceived by this woman's bragging. It is all pretense. She is not a mastermind. In fact, she is so stupid that she cannot tell the difference between the letter A and the letter B. If the gardener's wife had not seen me, I would have made it to my sister's house in no time."

The Fiendish One was rooted to the spot, dumbstruck.

"Let's face it, you are of no value to society. You are nothing but a parasite. Do you see these people?" I asked, pointing to the workers. "I am sure that, in their hearts, every one of them hates you."

Finally, the Fiendish One found her voice and ordered Afra and Esmat to take me to the dungeon. Unaware of who had left the dungeon door unlocked, she blamed Esmat and told her that she would pay dearly for her mistake. Then, ashamed to have been outed as illiterate, she bowed her head and slunk away.

I was sad to be back in the dungeon, but I was glad that I had tried my best to escape. I had been so close to being reunited with Dena, Habib, and their five-year old daughter, Neda, whom I cherished.

The first few weeks of my imprisonment, I had been sure that one of the workers would anonymously inform Dena and Habib that I had not gone to Paris but that I was in fact there, in Mirza Hadi's mansion, locked in a cell. If that had happened, there was no way for the Fiendish One to know who had revealed her secret. The fact that it did not happen, was entirely antithetical to our cultural habits and practices. Given that most of the workers loved me, it was very difficult for me to cope with this fact on the top of the streak of bad luck that had overwhelmed me.

That evening, when Afra brought me my dinner, she expressed sorrow about my unsuccessful escape and regret that Esmat was to be punished for her own carelessness. Afra mentioned that what I told the Fiendish One, in front of all those workers, was very effective, and she was glad that "I paid her back in her own coin." Then she told me that, that afternoon, before my attempt to escape, the Fiendish One had announced that Anvar was pregnant. I was genuinely indifferent about this news, although it did make me a little hopeful that, with Anvar delivering a baby, I might be given custody of my own child.

That night, it took me a long time before I could sleep. The soft pillow under my head felt as hard as granite, and I could not stop rolling over. As soon as I settled on one side, I got uncomfortable and, immediately, I changed to the other side. This went on until I fell asleep. In sleep, I dreamt that I was standing in a verdant field at the foot of a mountain and that a prince was riding toward me from the summit on a white horse. As he got closer, I could see that he was a tall, handsome young man embodying athletic prowess with the image of a courageous, distinguished, and brave hero. He possessed valor and skills of the knights. He wore a surcoat over his silk clothing, a wide belt of gold, and his boots were elaborated with embellished decorations. I was standing nailed down and mesmerized by him. As he passed by, I waited for him to grab me, lift me onto the horse, and take me away with him. But he did not, and instead I chased behind him, yelling, "Nima, Nima." As I was running, Pot, the stray dog of Sadegh Hedayat, joined me, and we ran side by side, using every bit of strength we had, until I woke up.

# 13

From the day of my ill-fated escape attempt until April nothing unusual happened. I had my routines in captivity. I read, wrote, walked the length of my dungeon back and forth, sang happy songs when I could, and cried when I could not overcome the sorrow of my miserable life there. I looked forward to Pegah's visits, and the highlights of most of my days were when I talked with Afra for a few minutes. That was all.

All the months that I was imprisoned, I had no choice but to wash up and brush my teeth using the pond water. All the servants and their families did the same. We all shared the same pond. In winter months, when the water got much colder and ice covered the top of the pond, the servants broke the ice so that we could wash up using the freezing water underneath.

On April 12, 1943, before sleeping, I felt that my baby had dropped into a lower position in my pelvis. I did not know what to make of that. So, I ignored it and shortly after I fell asleep. On the morning of the next day, I woke up in full-blown labor. I immediately awakened Esmat, who rushed out to inform the Fiendish One. Shortly after, my water broke. Soon, I knew, I would hold my baby in my arms and breathe the air of freedom.

Esmat returned with Afra, and they helped me out of the dungeon, up the stairs, and to a nice guest room that had been prepared for my delivery.

In those days, in Tabriz, it was a tradition among well-to-do families to decorate the room where a baby would be delivered with indoor plants, containers of eye-catching, bushy basil, and an abundance of beautiful, colorful flower arrangements. The parents of the woman giving birth usually sent additional decorations and presents, and relatives and friends overwhelmed the delivery room with gifts. There was none of that in my delivery room. My baby was going to be born with no such welcoming gestures, and for me, that became another vexation on top of all the others.

My baby moved and kicked. I was filled with apprehension about the baby being harmed during birth. I was aware that giving birth could be dangerous for me and my baby, and it was sad that, aside from Afra and Ali, no one in that mansion seemed to care enough to worry about us.

They laid me down on a comfortable bed, and even though I was in excruciating pain, being in that guest room felt luxurious after all my months spent in the dungeon. They moved me to that nice room because it was extremely important to the Fiendish One not to tarnish her family's image in the society at large. Plus, the midwife would not have stayed in the dungeon for hours until my baby was born.

The midwife came in with an assistant, and she immediately asked Afra and Esmat to leave the room. She told them that she hated it when people gathered in the delivery room. I became somewhat concerned, but I tried not to be paranoid. I told myself that there was no plot to kill me or my baby. And even if there were, there was nothing I could do about it.

My contractions grew stronger, longer, and more frequent. Eventually, I felt an urge to push. While pushing, I did not scream. I only grunted and yelled after each push. There were cramps in my abdomen, back, and groin. It was the most painful process I had ever gone through.

At last, I heard the midwife's assistant say, "It's a girl." The pain subsided. I was thrilled. I felt like God had given me a confidant, someone with whom I could discuss my problems and private matters without worry.

Suddenly, I realized that I had not heard the joyous sound of my daughter crying. I asked the midwife what was wrong, why couldn't I hear my baby. The midwife kissed my forehead and told me, with sadness in her eyes, that my baby was stillborn. I experienced such a deep sadness that words cannot express. Ever since my father was shot before my own eyes, I was not shocked so horrifically. I asked to see her, but the midwife explained that Mirza Hadi and his mother had given the strict order to bring them the baby as soon as the umbilical cord was cut.

"I obeyed their order," the midwife said. "Your husband was devasted when he saw that his daughter was stillborn. He has taken her to the family mausoleum to have her buried."

My eyes began to rain like nimbostratus clouds, and I thought of a line from Hafez, which I will paraphrase here: "The blanket of life of one who is stained with wretched fortune, not even the waters of paradise can wash clean."

Contrary to my wishes, I was in no condition to leave Mirza Hadi's home. Over the next few days, the midwife came and checked on me regularly. No one cared if I left, and they never locked the guest room door. Afra helped me with the nitty-gritty needs of my daily life. Esmat was happy to be rid of me and to be sleeping in her own room again. Ali had transferred all my belongings from the dungeon to the guest room. The Fiendish One had not asked any of the servants to sleep in my room at night to watch over me. However, Afra came and checked in every night.

At last, after nearly a week, I told Afra that I felt strong enough to say goodbye to that damned mansion forever and ever. Afra advised that it was not a good idea to leave that day, since, early in the morning, Soviet troops had occupied the town again and were plundering grocery stores, bakeries, butcheries, and anywhere that might have food, including restaurants.

"Lady Dorna, you know how those savages are," Afra said. "If they see you, every one of them would want to rape you. They are known for rapes and gang rapes."

I was scared to death. I thanked Afra for her blunt warning—there was no way I was stepping out of that place that day.

The rest of that day, I could not stop thinking about my child. Up to the last minutes, she had been moving and kicking. How had she died? Had the midwife suffocated her? "Unlikely," I told myself, remembering how badly Mirza Hadi wanted to have our baby and how determined he was to assume her full custody. Every time that I reflected on these questions, I ended up suspicious, but at the same time, I concluded that I could never know what happened. Better to forget about it, I thought.

The next day, the Soviet troops left town and returned to their stations on the outskirts. Afra helped me dress warmly and pack my bags. She gave me my birth certificate, which the Fiendish One had held onto, along with another piece of paper. Mirza Hadi had asked Afra to give me that paper on the day that I left. I read it. It was a divorce certification. He had divorced me.

In those days, in Iran, men were entitled to divorce their wives unilaterally without any legal proceedings. Men's decision to repudiate their wives were fully facilitated by law, and they were uncontestable.

Afra was curious to know what the paper was. I told her, "Afra dear, this is my divorce paper, my freedom certificate. That calls for celebration." Afra nodded and said, what you lose on the swings, you gain on the roundabouts.

A horse-drawn carriage waited for us at the gate. Ali carried my luggage to the carriage and sat beside the coachman. Afra and I sat together. I had a very strange feeling. I was sad and happy at the same time. I turned to Afra and told her, "I moved to this mansion in a white wedding dress, bringing with me tens of thousands of dollars' worth of jewelry, gold, the finest Persian carpets, the most expensive furniture, and tons of other precious goods. Now, I am leaving penniless—I even have to rely on you to pay for my carriage fare. But I am glad that I am not leaving in a white death shroud. I am only twenty-three years old, and all that happened during the last three years was a long dreadful nightmare. I am born again today."

On our way to Dena and Habib's house, we saw shops with shattered windows and smashed doors, grocery stores that were badly damaged and ransacked, and broken chairs and tables inside restaurants that were practically wrecked. That carriage ride was very different from the ones I took once a week to go to the dingy public bathhouse. This time, we saw quite a few seriously vandalized stores on our way, lots of destruction. The Soviets had done more than just loot—this was savagery.

When the carriage finally stopped at our destination, I was relieved. My broken boat had struggled against the worst whirlpool during the darkest night. And yet, I had made it to shore.

# CHAPTER 7

## FREEDOM

### 1

When we stopped in front of Dena and Habib's house, I jumped from the carriage with excitement. Afra and Ali got down, too. Using the knocker, Ali knocked on the entrance door. In no time, Dena's houseman, Uncle Verdi, opened. As soon as he saw me, he shouted the news that everyone in the house had longed to hear: "Lady Dorna is back! She is here!"

Soon, Dena, Neda, and Uncle Verdi's wife, Houri, rushed to greet us. There were hugs, kisses, and much delight.

"Welcome back, my dear sister, the lady of all ladies, we missed you so badly, so sorely," Dena chirped. "I was worried to death about your very long trip to Paris. When did you return?" As she pressed me tightly in her arms, I burst into tears.

My niece, Neda, grabbed my dress with her little hands and asked, "Aunt Dorna, where were you? Did you go abroad to buy me nice dolls?" I lifted her into my arms and kissed her.

Dena asked Uncle Verdi to go to Habib's carpet showroom and inform him that I had returned, and she asked Houri to go to Auntie's house and invite her and her family for lunch. Dena asked Houri to tell Auntie not to wait until noon but to come as soon as she, Hāji Darab, and his daughters could. Then Dena began asking about my trip and the whereabouts of my baby.

"Lady Dena, your sister was not in Paris," Afra said. "They lied to

163

you. During the last seven or eight months, she suffered a lot of hardship. She has had a miserable life. Please give her time to explain what she endured. May God bless her. She is a true angel."

Dena gave Ali and Afra a big tip, and Afra hugged me and promised to come see me often. Ali told me, "You are a true Moin-al-Tojjar. You were at your best during the entire time that you lived in Mirza Hadi's mansion. Your father's soul is proud of you."

Ali and Afra left, and we went inside. I could tell that Dena was confused. Neda, too, had sensed that things were unusual. She was holding my hand the entire time.

We settled in the living room. Neda sat on my knee, and Dena started to speak. "Before you tell me what is going on in your life, tell me about your health," she said. "Are you well? Was your baby born smoothly? Any complications? Did you give birth to a boy or a girl?"

I responded that the baby was a stillborn girl. I began to cry again as I explained how Mirza Hadi and his mother had imprisoned me in a damp, moldy dungeon in the basement of one of their servant's homes and how I had spent my days on an old, rickety cot among spiderwebs, lizards, and occasionally scorpions. My story astonished Dena. She was furious. She clenched her jaw and ground her teeth. She was shaking badly. A short while later, when I repeated my story to Habib, Auntie, Uncle Hāji Darab, my cousins, Uncle Verdi, and Houri, everyone's reaction was very similar to Dena's.

For lunch, Habib ordered *chelow kebab* from Hāji Samad's restaurant. I had not had *chelow kebab*, my and every Iranian's favorite dish, for a long time. We all ate, with pure pleasure, Hāji Samad's tastiest rice, mixed with butter and egg yolk, along with his lamb fillet kebab, which was melted in the mouth, and his moist, tender, and juicy chicken kebab.

Everybody gathered around me and showed me love as I told and retold the course of events. I explained how Mirza Hadi had abused me physically and psychologically. My stories about Iris Coughlin and Anvar shocked them. They were in disbelief when I told them that Mirza Hadi had embezzled his family's monies and that he and his mother had stolen all of my jewelry, gold coins, and exquisite Persian carpets, and they wanted to know how a couple of savages could imprison me in a dungeon for months without anyone daring to report them to the police.

Auntie, who could not stop kissing and hugging me, cried out, "May God damn the Soviets. If they had not killed my brother, the accursed Mirza Hadi and his evil mother would never have dared to miscalculate their authority so drastically, never in a million years!"

Several times, my Uncle Hāji Darab made such statements as, "By abusing and imprisoning our angel, Mirza Hadi and his mother have waged war against our family. At a most appropriate time, when an opportunity presents itself, we will hit them hard. We will make absolutely sure that their deeds will not remain unpunished." Habib agreed. "We will make them return all that they have stolen from my dear sister-in-law, who is as much a sister to me as to Dena," he said.

In the end, everyone was happy to hear that Mirza Hadi had divorced me. "We are all thrilled that you have returned to your own house," Habib said. "This is as much your house as it is mine and Dena's." I broke into tears of joy.

For months, I was thrown in a garbage bin like a piece of trash, and I felt unwanted. Having rejoined my family, I was overwhelmed with the tender passion that they were gushing out of their hearts for me. They infused and implanted new spirit in me. I told them about the unlimited kindness of Ali, Afra, and Pegah, and I was happy that I imported much love for them into the hearts of each of my family members present as well as Houri and Uncle Verdi.

# 2

The next morning, I woke up to find that Dena had left a substantial amount of cash on the coffee table for me. It was a strange feeling knowing that I could spend all that money without having to give an account of my expenditures to anyone. It was like old times, my sweet days in my parents' house.

After completing my morning routine, I went to the dining room, where Dena and Habib were waiting for me to have breakfast. Little Neda was extremely happy to see that I had spent the night in their house.

"Aunt Dorma, stay with us forever, okay?" she said.

I kissed her and replied, "Of course. I will never leave you!"

After breakfast, Habib and Dena showed me a large room, which they had in mind to turn into my bedroom, and another room adjacent to it, which would be converted into an arts room for my use, a place to paint and to practice the art of tailoring. Habib said that he remembered how much artistry I had imbued in all the details of the wedding dress that I had tailored myself. Dena and Habib were planning to keep me busy, and in no time, they furnished both rooms with the most elegant and expensive pieces of furniture and art supplies. In particular, I loved the two carpets that were laid in my bedroom. They were identical Esfahan rugs with designs that were colorful and rich in tone, inspired by the architectural motifs of remarkable building in the historical city of Esfahan. These carpets were a most exquisite mean to express the quintessence of Persian art.

Later on that day, Dena took me to several fabric shops, where she purchased quite a few fabrics for me. I insisted on paying for them with the money that she had left for me on the coffee table, but she did not let me. She paid for everything, not only for the fabrics but also for several pairs of shoes, which we bought afterward.

When we finished shopping, we took a horse-drawn carriage to the tailoring shop of my teacher, Ms. Suesan. She and her workers were so excited to see me that I became a little embarrassed.

"I heard that you were in Paris," Ms. Suesan said. "Otherwise, you would have come to see us, isn't that right?"

I answered loud, so that everyone could hear: "No, I was not in Paris. I was locked in a dark, horrifying dungeon in Mirza Hadi's mansion the whole time that you thought I was in France." Then I told her and her staff, concisely, all that had happened to me until the day before, the day I gained back my freedom. They were speechless.

At last, Ms. Suesan said, "Goodness gracious, your inner beauty and dazzling good looks are proof of the perfection of creation. Your beauty is a divine gift. How could anyone be so thankless, so ungrateful to God for such a wife, such a daughter-in-law, or such a friend? These people must be the direct descendants of Satan himself. Who else could be so antagonistic and so cruel to a divine gift?"

While I had been telling my story, Dena flipped through the fashion magazines that Ms. Suesan kept in her shop, choosing patterns and designs that she liked. In those days, the German magazine *Burda Style* had not yet existed, and I cannot remember what popular fashion magazines focused on sewing and were used for clothing and dress patterns. After 1952, almost all tailoring shops in Iran had many issues of Burda Style available for their customers' use.

Dena had good taste in fashion and picked out examples of dresses that she thought would look good on me. Ms. Suesan took my measurements, and we left all of the fabrics with her so she could make me custom dresses just like the ones Dena had seen in the magazine. Then, Dena and I set off for home.

# 3

On the third day of my freedom, Dena, Neda, Houri, and I went to our usual historical bathhouse to bathe. Having the experience of bathing in a dingy, dilapidated bathhouse in a shabby neighborhood for over seven months, our usual bathhouse looked much more magnificent than I had remembered. I used to think that it had a hint of the glory of Persian architecture, but on that day, I realized that, in fact, it *was* that very glory.

The manager of the bathhouse and her crew were glad to see me, and I was happy to see them. It was the first time that our little Neda and I were in the bathhouse together, and I could see how joyful she was. At one point she asked me, "Aunt Dorna, will you come to bathe with us every day?" I smiled and said, sure, and then I explained the difference between day and week and how we went to the bathhouse every week, not every day. I do not know if she understood, but she nodded in agreement.

After we left the bathhouse, I told Dena that I had an irresistible urge to visit our parents' and Sina's graves. She agreed that it was a good idea, and after we returned home, we left Neda with Houri, grabbed the key to our mausoleum, and took a carriage to the cemetery. Even before my imprisonment, the Fiendish One had prohibited me from visiting the tombs of my family members for at least a year and half. After such a long time, standing where my parents and Sina were buried, I had a strange feeling that I was attending a kind of family reunion. First, I kissed the graves of my parents and Sina. Then, for each of our grandparents and other relatives who were buried there, Dena and I recited the short prayer that we usually recite for our deceased ones.

Up until that point, I had been calm and composed. Suddenly, I started to cry, and I had the urge to sit beside my father's grave. I began to talk to him.

"My dear father, you were a remarkable person, a legendary man, a man so great that a humongous empire, that of the Soviet Union, saw you as a threat and had you brutally murdered by the agents of its forceful Red Army. To you, managing all those villages, farms, and businesses was as easy as strolling through a garden. To our eternal gratitude, you backed us under any circumstances. You were our support and security. You raised us to be creative. You were world famous for your honesty, patriotism, courage, and righteousness. You cared about us tremendously, but to our disappointment, our dreams were absent from your mind. You yourself decided what our dreams should be, and then you, not us, worked to accomplish those dreams for us."

Dena stood behind me, listening. I went on:

"Your philanthropic deeds have made major differences in many people's lives. And yet, you could not raise your only son to be a responsible, decent, and worthy person, and you utterly overestimated Heshmat Mirza family's prominence. My mother and Auntie told you many times that Mirza Hadi was corrupt to the core, but you did not believe them. Oh, father, you were not alive to see how they threw your daughter in the trash like she was a piece of garbage. If you had been alive, you, the lion of Tabriz, those worthless mice would never have dared to tyrannize your daughter. How could they treat a helpless orphan like that? How could they flaunt their wealth so blatantly, day and night, in her face and belittle her constantly for being destitute?"

"Father, Mirza Hadi and his mother crushed my spirit and shattered my pride beyond repair. What a happy and prosperous life I could have had if only you had let me marry Nima! Beside him, I would have been eternally blissful and joyful every minute of my life." As I spoke, my despair poured out in a flood of tears. Tears raced down Dena's cheeks as well. She grabbed my arms and made me stand up. Then she hugged me tight and kissed me many times. We left the cemetery, and I felt that our visit had mitigated my mental agony, at least for that day.

At home, after a late lunch, Dena inquired, "So, my beautiful sister, tell me, who is Nima? Why don't I know anything about him? Am I the only member of the family not in on the secret?"

I smiled. "No, it is kept secret from Neda and Habib, as well!" We both laughed. Then I told her the real story, all about how Nima and I had fallen in love at Hāji Morad's shop, the day that he had come in to buy a reed pen, inkpot, and ink. I told her about everything that had gone on between us and about how our parents and Sina had thought that Nima was just another suitor, a poor fiddler after father's wealth. Auntie, of course, had arranged for us to meet one last time, and I described to Dena that last rendezvous where I had held Nima's hands and declared my love for him.

Dena was shocked to hear all of this. She confessed that she never realized I was so courageous and had such a latitude in conduct. Until then, she had thought that her kid sister was in total compliance with the rules that society and tradition dictated. She said that she was proud of me, that I was a true Moin-al-Tojjar, and that she could not wait to tell Habib all about Nima. I did not object to that.

# 4

On the fourth day of my freedom, I told Dena that, while in captivity, I had resolved to find and visit each of my high school friends within the first two weeks of my freedom. I wanted to check on them and see how they were doing. I badly needed to reconnect with old friends and let them know that I was back. To me, no friendship is more genuine, more precious, or longer lasting than school friendship. I could trust my old friends no matter how much time passed.

I told Dena I would be back for lunch, and I set off in the direction of my best friend Atoosa's house. Or so I thought. My mind wandered as I walked, and I eventually found myself not at Atoosa's house but at the place where Nima and I had had our secret rendezvous, under the sycamore tree beside the stream. Nothing had changed. That place was still a perfect location for secret meetings. Being there gave me great pleasure. I fancied that Nima was there leaning against the tree, as he always did, his angry ocean-blue eyes looking at me. My thoughts set my heart ablaze once more.

After that day, I would regularly frequent that secluded place, perhaps hoping that someday Nima would also get nostalgic and set out for that spot. I also frequented the mansion where I was raised. I would stand across the street and stare at its gate, lost in recollection. Perhaps the song "Those Were the Days," sung by the Welsh folk singer Mary Hopkin, described best my state of mind:

> Once upon a time there was a tavern
> Where we used to raise a glass or two
> Remember how we laughed away the hours
> And think of all the great things we would do
>
> Those were the days my friend
> We thought they'd never end
> We'd sing and dance forever and a day
> We'd live the life we choose
> We'd fight and never lose
> For we were young and sure to have our way . . .
> Then the busy years went rushing by us
> We lost our starry notions on the way . . .
>
> Just tonight I stood before the tavern
> Nothing seemed the way it used to be
> In the glass I saw a strange reflection
> Was that lonely woman really me . . .

Many years after my freedom from Mirza Hadi's prison, during one of my trips to Tehran, I stopped in a music shop and purchased a collection on cassette tape of the newest songs that had been released in the UK. Among them was this song, one of my all-time favorites. It infiltrated my soul and dug deeply into my times with Nima before getting married to Mirza Hadi, and my days at my parents' house. I still hum that song now and then.

That day, I stayed at that gorgeous private place for about an hour and then went to where Atoosa's parents lived. I knocked on the entrance door, and Atoosa's sister and older brother opened. They both wore all-black outfits, which shocked me. I thought perhaps one of their parents had passed away.

Atoosa's sister hugged me and began to cry. "Where are you my beautiful sister to see that your best friend has come to see you?" she wailed. That indicated that it was Atoosa herself who had passed away. Soon, Atoosa's mother joined us, and all of us wept and mourned.

"Where have you been my dear daughter?" Atoosa's mother asked. "I missed you at the funeral. I wanted so badly for you to be there and say your goodbyes to Atoosa. Her love for you was boundless."

They invited me into their living room, where they asked me about my trip to Paris. I responded that I never went to Paris, that I had been in captivity in Mirza Hadi's mansion. I said that I would tell them all about my life as Mirza Hadi's wife later, but first I wanted to hear about my beloved Atoosa.

Atoosa's sister explained that a month before, Atoosa had come to visit her parents and stayed with them until after dark. She decided to walk home alone, and after a few blocks, she noticed a Soviet four-wheel drive GAZ-64 following her. She was scared to death and rushed to a narrow alley to hide. But the three godless criminal soldiers parked the car in front of the alley in order to block it, and then they ran after Atoosa and captured her. They dragged her inside their vehicle, drove her out of Tabriz, and took turns raping her inside the car. When they were done, they returned Atoosa back to the alley where they had kidnapped her.

Atoosa did not tell her husband what had happened. The next morning, she went to a bathhouse, where she took a considerable amount of hair removal mixture from one of the small depilatory rooms and, when no one was watching, put it in her mouth and swallowed it. The depilatory used in Iran was a putty-like substance created by mixing lime and arsenic and dissolving it in water. It was toxic and could be deadly if ingested. Consuming a tablespoon or two of this depilatory substance was a not uncommon method of suicide among Iranians.

Atoosa left a long letter explaining what the Soviets had done to her. She did not want that violent crime to go untold, but at the same time, she could not bear the humiliation. Atoosa had ended her letter with these words: "I will take my life for a cause. I do not want to die in vain.

Let my case be a record of the acts committed by that satanic army that invaded my beloved country." Word spread in Tabriz, and soon everyone knew why Atoosa had taken her own life. For many years, she was an example of a brave, righteous Azerbaijani heroine.

As is our tradition, when someone dies, usually his or her immediate family wear only black clothes for a year, close friends and relatives for four months and ten days, and other friends and relatives for forty days. From that day on, I wore black and visited Atoosa's family regularly. Four months and ten days after Atoosa's death, her mother and sister came to see me at Dena and Habib's house, and they brought me a length of sky-blue fabric, more than enough to sew a dress. They thanked me for wearing black and standing by them during their time of great sorrow. Then, following the tradition, they asked me to stop wearing black from that day onward. Bringing me a fabric of a color other than black symbolized their wish that I begin wearing non-black cloths. I kept in touch with Atoosa's parents until they passed away, and I still see Atoosa's sister once a while.

On the fifth day of my freedom from Mirza Hadi's mansion, I stayed home, mournful and depressed, lamenting Atoosa's death. I was too sad to go and see my other school friends. But on the sixth day, I began visiting the rest. I found and reconnected with each and every one of them. I revealed to them what Mirza Hadi and the Fiendish One had done to me, and they all understood why I had disappeared all that time. My friends were all married and had good lives. Some had one or two children, and two of them were still childfree.

One day, after I returned home from visiting a friend, Dena told me that she had sent Uncle Verdi to Mirza Hadi's house to arrange for the transfer of my belongings. Then she called Uncle Verdi to come and tell me himself what had happened. He recounted his meeting with the Fiendish One carefully: "Lady Dorna, I talked with Mirza Hadi's mother face to face. I told her that Lady Dena had sent me to arrange a time for me to go there with a truck and transfer Lady Dorna's carpets, furniture, and other possessions to our own house. I offered that I could wait for her to put Lady Dorna's gold and jewelry pieces all in a bag so that might I take them with me right then." Uncle Verdi shook his head. The Fiendish One's reaction had been absolutely shameful. He repeated her words exactly as she had uttered them: "Go tell Lady Pauper and her sister to hold out their begging bowl to someone else. I do not throw spare change at people who can earn money by doing some work. Tell them that a lot of families need washerwomen. That job best matches their character and social status."

This did not surprise me at all—that was the Fiendish One, alright. Dena told me that one way or another, she would not let those thieves steal my riches.

# 5

What happened to me in Mirza Hadi's mansion continued to disturb me. While awake, I could keep myself distracted. However, when sleeping, I had no control over what went through my mind. I had nightmares and dysphoric dreams about my life being in immediate danger and my hopeless efforts to save myself from jeopardy and harm. Sometimes, the vivid images produced in my nightmares were exact replays of my past traumas; other times, they were only related to those traumas. For example, in one recurrent nightmare, I lay on the rickety cot in the Fiendish One's dungeon while an army of scorpions attacked me from all directions. Each time, I woke up screaming.

My shouts also woke up Dena and Habib. Dena would immediately rush to check on me. She would caress my forehead, kiss me, and stay until I fell asleep again. During the night, she checked on me at random times, as well. She had observed that, in my sleep, I screamed aloud, made abnormal movements, and gave long inarticulate speeches and that my breathing paused repeatedly. Those nightmares also caused distress in my daily life. I suffered from intense anxiety, sleepiness, and fatigue during the day.

Habib knew a doctor of neurology, Doctor Mir, who was educated at the University of Tübingen in Germany, which was one of the most prestigious places in the world to study neurology. Doctor Mir was his customer and had purchased several of his finest Esfahan and Tabriz carpets. Habib made an appointment for me to see Doctor Mir, and after the initial visit, I began seeing him regularly. We talked a lot about my past, and even though he was only a medical doctor, he provided me therapy, too. In a few weeks, the intramuscular injections that he gave me every other day, as well as all the therapy that he provided, improved my condition considerably. Dena told me that most of my sleep behavior disorders had either disappeared or considerably lessened. I had nightmares only once a week, sometimes only every other week.

On a gorgeous spring day, engrossed in painting in the garden, I suddenly noticed that Dena, Doctor Mir, and Uncle Verdi were standing beside me. I stood up and shook hands with Doctor Mir and welcomed him. Uncle Verdi had carried two folding chairs with him. He set up the chairs next to me and left. Doctor Mir and Dena sat down, and we chatted about the trees and flowers around us, about the food shortage due to the Soviet occupation, and about how the soldiers regularly violated the agreement that they stay outside the city. They often entered Tabriz, in groups of three to five, raped women, plundered restaurants and grocery stores, and left.

After a while, Dena left, and Doctor Mir told me that it was a great idea that I channel some of my energy into painting. He explained that, through art, I released myself from living with all the physical and emotional abuses that I had endured in the past. As we talked, two pigeons that had been perched on a tree branch spread their wings and flew in freedom toward the unlimited horizon. I got excited and said that I wished I could freely fly with those beautiful pigeons.

Doctor Mir put his hand on my hand and said, "Dorna dear, if you want to fly, let us fly together to the summit of happiness and the height of glory."

I immediately pulled my hand away from his. "Doctor, I hope you do not mean what I never want to hear from anyone," I replied.

Staring into my eyes, he urged me to marry him. He admitted that he had fallen in love with me, and he asked for my permission to allow his mother and sister to come that evening to ask Dena and Habib for my hand in marriage. I could not believe what I was hearing. The doctor's proposal disgusted me. The world began to spin around my head, and I began to shiver. Before my eyes, it was as if Doctor Mir had metamorphosed into Mirza Hadi. I thought that he was trying to grab my hair, twist my head, and slap me hard across the face. I realized that I had instinctively lifted my hands to guard myself.

I suddenly screamed "no" at the top of my lungs, and I began to run away from the Doctor. He rushed to his car and came back with his medical bag. Dena and Houri caught me. They took me to my room, and Doctor Mir gave me an intramuscular injection, which put me to sleep right away.

When I woke up, Neda was sitting on a corner of my bed with a solemn look on her pretty face. I sat up against the headrest and told her, "Neda, sweetie, I love you to bits. Thanks for watching me."

"Aunt Dorna, did that man hit you?" she asked.

"No, honey, I thought he was going to hit me. But he did not."

I was so unbelievably smitten with Neda. I hugged her, then I got out of bed, lifted her in my arms, and carried her to the family room, where Dena was sitting by herself. I had a long conversation with Dena. I told her, "If you or Habib want to get rid of me by finding me a husband, you should say so. I can go and live with Auntie's family until I find a teaching job. Then I will rent a room somewhere and live independently by myself." That made Dena extremely upset. She swore on our father's soul that she had let Doctor Mir talk to me directly only because he had practically implored her to let him.

"There is a king sitting on the throne of my heart," I replied, "and that king is Nima. All these years, I have been captivated by the perfection of his physique, as well as his unblemished moral character. When immersed in thoughts about him, my soul separates from my body and I refashion to pure love, a transcendental state that is hard to explain. You see, sis, my life is a never-ending poem, and each stanza is made up of feverish lines about Nima. No man deserves to marry a woman whose heart and soul yearns for another man like this."

Dena understood my reasoning and agreed that there was a great deal of logic and humanism in my argument. She promised that she would reject, firmly but respectfully, all of my future suitors with the exception of Nima, if he ever showed up. Thereafter, every now and then, Dena mentioned that I had another suitor, but that was all, nothing specific. I was never curious to know who they were.

The most difficult marriage proposal I ever received directly was from Atoosa's brother. I sat down with him and told him, very kindly, that I loved him like a brother and that I could not possibly marry him.

I also mentioned that I had a long-lost suitor for whom no flood could drown my love. At some point, Atoosa's widower also asked me directly for my hand in marriage. I was so utterly disgusted that I could not bear listening to him. I asked him to leave and never ever again make such a proposal. I told him that he was the last man in the world that I would marry. I knew that, by asking me to marry him, he was not doing any wrong *per se*. Nevertheless, there was nothing more aggravating than the thought of getting married to my deceased best friend's widower.

# 6

A few days after Doctor Mir's proposal, at the dinner table, Habib revealed that he had a business proposition for me.

"You want to go into business with me?" I asked incredulously. "You must be joking. How could a business partnership be established between a twenty-three-year old penniless woman with no experience or education in business and a master businessman such as yourself?"

He replied that it was very easy. He owned a beautiful, unused property in a good location of Tabriz. He had decided to convert it to the largest tailor shop and tailoring school in Azerbaijan, and he wanted me to run it. I would be fully in charge and pay him half of the total profit every month. He was planning to begin renovating the property soon, and he wanted me, Ms. Suesan, and Dena to help him with the reconfigurations.

I could tell he was sincere, and I knew exactly why he was making me this offer. After my encounter with Doctor Mir, Habib and Dena were determined not to let the abuse that I had endured in Mirza Hadi's home destroy me. Toward that goal, they had come up with the solution of keeping me occupied with the work of running a huge tailor shop. Their solution would prove to be highly effective.

The next day, Dena and I went to see Ms. Suesan, and we asked her to join us in establishing a grand, state-of-the-art tailor shop and tailoring school. We offered her a monthly salary equal to her highest net monthly income of the past twelve months. Ms. Suesan was tired of running her own shop, and she needed a change. The idea of coming and working for us appealed to her, especially because we wanted her to teach in addition to tailoring. She asked for a fair amount of goodwill money to transfer her entire business to us. Habib paid her what she asked for without haggling, and we hired all of Ms. Suesan's dressmakers, as well as her errand boy and her cleaning person.

Habib converted his property into a nice, modern tailor shop. We named it *Atoosa's Tailoring*. It had an elegant showroom, a huge workshop for the dressmakers, a well-equipped classroom, a small kitchen, and a spacious lavatory. In no time, thanks to Ms. Suesan's help and mentoring, I became a competent manager. Her customers all transferred their business to our shop, and we attracted a considerable number of new clients, too. By the third month of our operation, we came up with a good net-profit margin, and from there, our business took off.

In less than three years, I became relatively rich from the tailor shop. Habib was a serious businessman, and I was a serious partner. I kept excellent records, which Habib meticulously reviewed once a month. He was very proud of me. A few times, I proposed to have a real estate agent appraise the rental value of our shop so that every month I could pay half of the rent to Habib, but he rejected the idea every time that I brought it up. He emphasized that, as far as he was concerned, the property belonged to both of us.

It was hard to imagine that, only three years before, I had lived in utter despair. How miraculous that the chains had been broken and I had been freed from the claws of the devil; how lucky I was that my sister and brother-in-law, the angels of my life, had taken me under their wings, protected, healed, and guided me with unconditional love. And how true was the saying by Hafez: "When the demon goeth out, the angel within may come."[33]

# 7

At times Afra came to see me. So did Pegah. First, they came to Dena and Habib's house, later they visited me at my tailor shop. Pegah never mentioned anything about her family, but Afra liked to gossip about

---

[33] *The Divan-i Hafiz*, translated by H. Wilberforce Clarke, p. 312.

them, and even though I was not interested in hearing about Mirza Hadi, the Fiendish One, and Anvar, I didn't stop her. I learned from Afra that Mirza Hadi and Anvar had gone to Tehran so that Anvar could deliver her baby in the best hospital of the capital. Anvar gave birth to a girl in her seventh month of pregnancy, and they stayed another seven months in Tehran before returning to Tabriz.

Shortly after Mirza Hadi returned from Tehran, my Uncle Hāji Darab encountered him in a religious ceremony at the Jameh Mosque of Tabriz. I was told that before the clergy began to deliver the sermon, Hāji Darab went and stood behind the microphone stand of the loudspeaker and said, "Dear compatriots, you all remember our national hero, Martyr Moin-al-Tojjar, a lion of Iran who gave his life for our country and died the death of the righteous. A man in whom we all found a true source of dignity and pride. Martyr Moin-al-Tojjar is survived by his two daughters, Lady Dena and Lady Dorna. Lady Dorna, his younger daughter, is of matchless inner and outer beauty. She is well educated, well read, and a true intellectual and artist. She is the pride of all Azerbaijani women. And guess what: of all the suitors who were willing to devote themselves and their lives to her, Martyr Moin-al-Tojjar chose Heshmat Mirza's son, Mirza Hadi, a man who turned out to be a relentless womanizer. Not only was he unfaithful to his wife, but he became physically intimate with his Irish mistress in front of her."

"Mirza Hadi and his diabolical mother accused Lady Dorna, who was only twenty-three years old, of attempted murder, and they imprisoned her in a damp, moldy dungeon in the basement of one of their servant's homes. Our pregnant angel, carrying our hero's grandchild, spent seven months on an old rickety cot among the spiderwebs, lizards, and scorpions. After seven months, Lady Dorna gave birth to a stillborn child. At that point, thank God, Mirza Hadi divorced her. But he and his mother embezzled over one hundred thousand dollars' worth of her jewelry, gold, gold coins, Persian carpets, and other belongings. It is true that legally we cannot do much about these extortions and those abuses, but we, the heroic people of Tabriz, should not sit idly by and let Mirza Hadi and his mother get away with stealing Lady Dorna's riches."

I was informed that after Hāji Darab's passionate plea to the people of Tabriz, everyone in the mosque stood up and began to chant, "Death to the faithless, death to the faithless." Scared for his life, Mirza Hadi fled the mosque. His chauffeur rushed him to his mansion.

The day that I left Mirza Hadi's mansion, Hāji Darab had said that, "Mirza Hadi and his mother have waged a war against our family. When an opportunity presents itself, we will hit them hard." I had not understood what Hāji Darab had meant, but after I learned about his speech at the mosque, I knew that his words were not hollow. He was a man of action who kept his promises. I was proud of him and the rest of my family. Then I thought of Pot, the protagonist of Sadegh Hedayat's "The Stray Dog," and about all the similarities between my time at Mirza Hadi's mansion and Pot's time in the main plaza of the town Veramin. In the end, my fate was very different from Pot's. It was a shame that there had been no Habib, Dena, Auntie, or Hāji Darab in Pot's life.

I learned from Afra that, when Mirza Hadi returned to his mansion from the mosque, he was sweating, trembling, and out of breath. He ordered his servants to keep the gates locked and not to open them unless they knew who was knocking. Then he called the Fiendish One and Anvar and told them what had happened. Then he yelled at his mother and told her that her actions had almost gotten him killed at the mosque.

"I wish you had an iota of wisdom," he thundered. "Why should God give me a mother who is so thoughtless? Did you think that you could embezzle all the riches of Moin-al-Tojjar's daughter without consequences? Did you forget about Hāji Darab, that pious man, who has enormous influence and respect among the merchants of Tabriz? He and Habib have been waiting for me to return from Tehran. They have drawn their daggers. What a stupid idea it was to imprison Moin-al-Tojjar's daughter like that. What happened today at the mosque marks the end of our prominence in Tabriz. We have been humiliated and disgraced forever."

According to Afra, at that point, Anvar hugged Mirza Hadi and tried to calm him down by telling him that, "First thing tomorrow, I will ask Ali to go to Habib's showroom and then to Hāji Darab's chamber in the Tabriz Bazaar and tell them that we were in Tehran and have just returned. He will tell them that we have no intention of embezzling Dorna's riches and that we would like them to come to our mansion and collect her belongings as soon as possible. I will also ask Ali to tell them that we will invite a few honorable merchants to come and witness the transfer of the riches." The Fiendish One did not say a word.

The next day, a huge truck arrived carrying everything that I had left in Mirza Hadi's mansion. I was mostly excited about my jewelry and gold coins, which had been given to me by my parents, and about my lavishly elegant Persian carpets. What amazed me, however, was that none of the jewelry that I had received from Mirza Hadi, his family members, relatives, and friends had been included. Even though I did not want anything from Mirza Hadi's side of the family or from his friends, I was astonished that the Fiendish One had clearly kept an accurate record of which gifts had come from their side and which had come from mine.

Soon after Hāji Darab's speech at the mosque, the owner of the gorgeous bathhouse that Mirza Hadi's family bathed in visited Hāji Darab at his chamber in the Tabriz Bazaar. He told Hāji Darab that he would no longer close his bathhouse to the general public when Mirza Hadi and his family bathed there. He cursed Mirza Hadi and his mother for what they had done to me. "The late Moin-al-Tojjar stood firm against Soviet occupation," he exclaimed. "With that resolute character, he was the backbone of the Tabrizis. Mirza Hadi and his mother must have been born from a demon. How else to explain such satanic behavior?"

Even after Mirza Hadi returned my possessions, the people of Tabriz treated him and his mother with contempt. They sent them hate messages via intermediaries, mostly their servants, chauffeur, gardeners, and relatives. When Mirza Hadi and his mother appeared in the streets, people came up to them and said things like, "Death to the faithless." Mirza Hadi and the Fiendish One were reaping what they had sown. For a long time, they stopped appearing in public. I was happy to learn from Afra that, for the most part, people left Mirza Hadi's sisters alone.

Three years after my divorce, with all my savings from the ever-flourishing tailoring business, I could afford to buy a small house in the neighborhood where Habib and Dena lived. I told them of my intentions, but they were strongly opposed. They did not want me to live by myself and told me that, as long as I was single, it was better for me to live with them. Plus, leaving their house would have been a big blow to Neda's morale. She was attached to me, and we loved each other limitlessly. Dena argued that we were all happy living together and it was stupid to disturb such happiness. I was convinced.

# 8

The atrocities committed by the Soviet troops in Azerbaijan and elsewhere in Iran never diminished. Every day, they found a new way to harass people. One of their most threatening actions was to suddenly and without any stated reason station soldiers on the rooftops of certain residential houses around the city. Those soldiers fired shots at random to scare passersby, and at times, they went down inside the houses where they were stationed and took whatever they could find: money, watches, clocks, jewelry, jewelry boxes, men's opal or turquoise rings, shah maghsoud[34] prayer beads, and other valuables. They created a climate of fear all over the city.

Then one day, all of a sudden, someone fired at a Soviet soldier who was pacing back and forth on a rooftop. The shot hit the soldier in the arm. Even though it was never discovered who had shot the soldier, the Soviets took their revenge by going to the cemetery and shooting a woman in the head as she grieved beside her son's grave. It was suspected that the attack on the Soviet soldier had been arranged by the Soviets themselves, since it gave the commander of the occupying forces an excuse to demand a $3,000[35] fine from the people of Tabriz. The commander gave us, the Tabrizis, forty-eight hours to pay the fine or else face the total destruction of our city. Everyone panicked, and some of the merchants of the Tabriz Bazaar contributed and collected a sum of $900[36] and gave it to the commander. He took the money and commanded his soldiers to abandon their posts on the rooftops and return to the outskirts of the city.

Shenanigans like these became easy to spot, and most of us avoided being fooled. That was why, even when the Soviets used cannons to

---

[34] A precious stone extracted from mines in Afghanistan.
[35] Approximately $52,000 in 2020.
[36] Approximately $15,600 in 2020.

launch fire at the business and homes of prominent Iranian officials, instead of fighting back, people tried to ignore them. They knew that the Soviets were looking for excuses to start a conflict in order to extort more money. This is how Tabriz and other occupied cities were until the end of World War II.

In the south of Iran, American troops had joined the British troops stationed there. In 1942, a treaty had been signed by Iran, Britain, the United States, and the Soviet Union that set a deadline for the withdrawal of all foreign forces from Iran within six months of the end of the war. Once the war ended, that deadline was set to March 2, 1946. The British and American forces respected the treaty and departed Iran ahead of the deadline. The Soviet forces, on the other hand, refused to leave, citing the preposterous pretext that they were concerned for the security of the Soviet oil fields near the borders of Iran. This alarmed the Iranian army and the Western powers. A new political party backed by the Soviets emerged in the province of Azerbaijan, the Democratic Party of Azerbaijan (DPA), which advocated a serious secession movement, and the Red Army began referring to the occupied regions as "liberated territories under its control." These were clear indications that the Soviets planned to disintegrate Iran, and Tehran's military was not strong enough to fight back.

In 1946, an able, eminent, and pragmatic statesman, Qavam al-Saltaneh, became the prime minister of Iran. At the urging of the United States and Britain, Qavam complained to the United Nations about the Soviets' interferences in Iran's internal affairs. In March of that year, Qavam flew to Moscow and directly negotiated with Stalin. He and Stalin signed an agreement that a Soviet-Iranian joint oil company be created to produce oil from the oil fields of Iran's northern provinces, pending ratification by the Iranian parliament. Iran would retain a 51 percent stake in the company, and the Soviet Union 49 percent. In exchange, Stalin would withdraw the Red Army from the Iranian provinces.

In May of 1946, the Soviet Union pulled out of Iran, and amid jubilant celebrations, our beloved Azerbaijan was freed from the hands of its savage occupiers. On December 12, 1946, Qavam's government dispatched troops to Azerbaijan, crushed the resistance movement, and took full control of the province. The remaining leaders of the DPA all fled to the Soviet Union.

In October of 1947, the bill to create a joint Soviet-Iranian oil company was presented to the parliament by the Qavam government. It was pronounced dead on arrival. Qavam had known that the agreement that the Soviets control 49 percent of the oil reserves in Iran's northern territories had zero chance of being ratified by parliament. His negotiations with Stalin had been a stroke of genius. He just simply deceived Stalin. Iranians have given Qavam a great deal of credit for this historical achievement.

# 9

In June of 1946, while the DPA was in control of Azerbaijan, the party established the University of Azerabadegan in Tabriz, the second university to be established in Iran, the first being Tehran University, which was officially inaugurated in 1934. Attending a university had always been a dream of mine. Aside from marrying my beloved Nima, I longed for nothing more than pursuing higher education. Up until that point, that wish had been a castle in the air. Dena and Habib knew how passionate I was about attending university, and they helped me reschedule my time so that I could both run my business and take classes.

I applied for admission and was admitted to Azerabadegan University. I became one of the first students to attend the institution in its inaugural year, and of the three areas of study that it offered, medicine, agriculture, and pedagogy, I chose to pursue pedagogy. Things went smoothly until December 1946, when the Iranian government crushed the DPA and took control of the Azerbaijan province. At that time the university was shut down, and the government did not plan to reopen it. At the behest of a grand clergyman, the government reopened the university in November 1947 as Tabriz University. The clergyman had warned the Iranian government that if they did not reopen the university, it would become a historical fact that the DPA established a university in Tabriz, but the Iranian government closed it. The new university refused to enroll those who had attended the previous one until its president, Doctor Khanbaba Bayani, ordered to readmit the students who were not members or sympathizers of the DPA. I was among the students who were readmitted.

I graduated valedictorian from Tabriz University in 1950 and was given a part-time teaching assistant position at the school. Dena, Habib, Auntie, Hāji Darab, and the rest of the family were unbelievably proud of me. They regretted that my father was not alive to see his daughter become a university graduate and university instructor. Nothing would have made him happier.

On my graduation ceremony, I wished Nima was there, and I wondered why our paths had not crossed all those years. Pegah was among the friends who attended my commencement. She gave me a beautiful eighteen-karat gold fountainpen as present. I wondered how in the world a demon had given birth to an angel!

I greatly enjoyed my time as a student; and even more, I enjoyed my time as a teacher. The only thing that annoyed me was that, almost every month, someone proposed to me, usually younger men who were sometimes very handsome. If I had never met Nima, I was sure that I would have fallen in love with one of these suitors.

Curiously enough, I did not feel sexual or emotional attraction to any of these fine gentlemen. That was probably why, in a strange dream I had one night, my shadow took me quite seriously to task. Why my shadow, I cannot say.

In my dream, I was walking in a wide empty street at sunset. The air was cool and crisp, and the sunset had cast my longest shadow of the day. Suddenly, my shadow rose up before me and began to talk.

"Let us go to a tavern. I really need to get drunk," she said.

"I have never been to a tavern. That is not a place for women."

"I know one that is open to women."

My shadow took me to the tavern, a working-class place where everyone was drunk. We sat across from each other, and my shadow ordered a bottle of wine. When the waitress brought her the wine, she grabbed the bottle and a glass, filled it to the rim, and gulped down one glass after another until she was dead drunk.

"Now that I'm drunk, I can be blunt," she said. "Tonight, I want to vent my wrath. You have made my life miserable. You are in a position of honor, and yet you are utterly deplorable. Let's face it: in the book of your life, Nima and his love are a chapter whose pages are turned forever. Why don't you get that? You cannot fish in a dry river."

"The more Nima is inaccessible, the more fervent my love becomes," I replied. "Each true love story is a complex journey, and I do not know anyone who went through it smoothly. Do you know a case where a person in love was in control of their love? You must have sensed that Nima and I are one soul in two bodies. We are kindred spirits. I will remain loyal to love and its command. 'Be thou faithful unto the end.'"[37]

"You take your love too seriously. Love comes and love goes, as simple as that. Fall in love with one of those handsome suitors, and the new love will replace your old love for Nima. Don't stunt your sexual growth. By remaining loyal to a married man you haven't seen for years, you've deprived yourself of the joy and pleasure of sex and of all the feelings and emotions that are associated with motherhood. Eternal love is nonsense. I doubt it very much that you still love Nima. Your love for Nima is a bubble, but not over water, a bubble over a mirage. And not a mirage seen by a sober person, a mirage seen by a passed-out-cold drunk. Your illusion of your love for Nima is that far removed from reality. I am not saying that you are not in love—what I know is that you are in love with love itself. That is what gives you pleasure."

"You have waited for Nima much longer than you should. You are longing for a married man who might not even be alive anymore. Life is like nectar, and time is like bees. Do you know how greedily and hungrily bees eat nectar? Do not waste your life waiting for Nima. Be wise. I do not want you to die in complete hopelessness."

"You know, I would rather be the sweeper of this tavern than to be your shadow," she began to shout. "That is how tired I am of you!" At that moment, I woke up, calm but confused. I looked for the shadow, but I could not find her anywhere. I realized I had been dreaming."

I turned on the light and wrote everything that I could recall from the dream. The next day, I analyzed what I had recorded. I was convinced that the shadow was not my subconscious mind speaking to me—I was sure that my subconscious was in full support of my love for Nima.

As for what the shadow told me, it was true that I was able to live without Nima's physical presence in my life, but I knew that I could not

---

[37] New Testament, Revelation 2:10.

live without loving him and thinking about him. That love was an inseparable aspect of my character. After all those years, I could still hear his voice, and hoping to find him someday had given a purpose to my life.

In my dream, my shadow had been concerned that I would die in hopelessness. "If death is a departure to the spirit world," I told myself, "then I would die full of hope, since I would be joining my beloved Nima in the afterlife. But if death is a departure to extinction, then thinking about Nima will continue to bring me joy until I breathe my last breath."

I continued arguing with myself: "Perhaps my destiny is to never see Nima again. Or I find him, but he has married, and our physical union will be impossible. In either case, I will continue to float on the spell of my love for him, which lifts my spirits. And that is something that I would never give up."

My shadow urged me to be wise. But as the great Sa'di wrote in 1258, it is impossible to be wise and in love at the same time. However, my love for Nima was not the sort of love that could make me, as Persians say, so deranged that I flew to the mountain. In the end, I concluded that a love that comes and goes was not a real love. A true love is love forever!

My shadow could not change my mind. My love for Nima was not a matter of choice—it was beyond my control. My heart would remain loyal to Nima for the rest of my life, and to me, there was something sacred about that.

# CHAPTER 8

## THE SECRET REVEALED

### 1

Between 1950 and 1960, I made myself as busy as can be by teaching part time as an instructor at the university and by running the tailor shop. I continued to live with Dena, Habib, and Neda. We traveled together a lot, and I spent time with friends and relatives. And yet, no one, not even Dena, was aware that I was constantly fighting for my sanity. I was trying hard to be happy, and sometimes I was. However, all the abuse that I had endured had left me deeply scarred. And as if all of that was not bad enough, finding no trace of Nima anywhere in Tabriz just made my emotional condition worse.

Afra kept me informed of everything that happened in Mirza Hadi's household. In 1957, Anvar died of breast cancer. After Anvar's death, the Fiendish One requested to meet with me. She had told Afra to tell me that, on her deathbed, Anvar had confessed that she had framed me. I refused to meet with her.

Two years later, Mirza Hadi died of a heart attack. He had suffered for a long time from complications related to syphilis. He had been too embarrassed to seek treatment until it was too late. A physician friend told me that it was possible that Mirza Hadi's heart attack was related to his syphilis, but only his doctors could determine for sure.

Before Mirza Hadi's death, Afra had never mentioned his and Anvar's daughter. But after he died, she told me, "I never felt that Mirza Hadi loved anyone. Not his parents or sisters, not you or Anvar. But there was no limit to his affection for his daughter, Parla. As selfish and self centered as he was, he probably loved Parla more than himself. He gave her all of his attention and care and never said no to anything that Parla asked for. On his deathbed, he transferred everything that he owned to her."

According to Afra, after Mirza Hadi's death, Parla hired an accountant and an appraiser to help her determine how much of her inheritance rightfully belonged to her aunts, Jaleh, Pegah, and Layla. Then she paid them their shares in cash. She kept the mansion and all the other assets for herself. The Fiendish One had not asked for anything. She wanted her share of her husband's inheritance to be divided between her daughters and Parla so that no inheritance disputes would arise after her death.

It was late September, 1960, when Afra came to me with a message: "Mirza Hadi's mother is dying, and she says that she wants to see you. If she does not, she is afraid that she will burn eternally in hell. She says that she knows a secret and that if she tells you, you will forgive her."

Afra begged me to go and see the Fiendish One and allow her to ask me for a pardon. But I could not. I simply could not forgive her or Mirza Hadi or Anvar, never!

Afra returned twice more with the same message and same plea, but I refused to go and see the Fiendish One. A couple of weeks later, she died. I was only 39 when the last of the three demons, who had appeared in my life, and had damaged my mental health permanently, joined the other evil spirits in the depths of hell.

# 2

It was Thursday on the third week of October 1960 when there was quite a hubbub in Dena and Habib's house front yard. All the friends and relatives, old and young, big and small, had arrived to prepare for the next day's festivities—the party that would be held in honor of the mysterious guest.

After recognizing the violinist in the neighbor's yard as none other than Nima, I had lain down on the upstairs floor of Dena and Habib's house. Fifteen minutes went by, and I rose and rushed downstairs. I looked for Auntie everywhere. Finally, I found her in the front yard talking with one of our relatives. I pulled her aside.

"I just saw Nima from a window on the second floor. He is at the neighbor's house. He was playing violin."

"What are you waiting for!" Auntie cried. "Hurry up and go! Do you realize how long you have been waiting for this moment? I know that women should not chase after men. But given your love and the sacrifices that you have made in the hopes of finding this man, I wouldn't worry about being culturally correct at the moment. Go follow your heart! Hurry!"

I was over there in less than a minute. Not knowing what to do, I knocked at the door. A man opened up. Before he had the chance to speak, I said, "I am sorry to bother you. I have come to see Nima. I am his old friend."

The man turned around and yelled, "Nima, there is a lady here at the door asking for you." In no time Nima was standing before me. I was breathing rapidly. My heart was pounding. Nima was shocked. He was as red as a beet, and his neck was covered in splotches.

"Oh, my God, Dorna, am I dreaming? Is that really you?" He wiped his palms on his pants and shook my hand. There were butterflies in my stomach.

"I thought I will never see you again," I said. "I saw you playing violin from the window of my sister's house. I have been living with my sister's family for sixteen years now."

Nima was sweating. He drew a handkerchief from his pocket and wiped his face. "Such excitement has made me forget my manners," he said. "'The chamber of vision of my eye is the dwelling of Thine: Show courtesy, and alight, for this house is the House of Thine.'[38] Please, come in."

I entered the house, and Nima introduced me to his companions as a dear friend he had not seen for more than twenty years. Then, we went to the living room to talk privately.

"Dorna dear, my love for you never diminished, not an iota, not even when my wife was alive." He had regained his eloquence. "I have been burning in your love all along. I have written so many poems for you that I could publish a volume. You know better than anyone else that love knows no reason, no measure, no law. Just as my marriage with a fine, innocent lady did not affect my love for you, I know that your

---

[38] *The Divan-i Hafiz*, translated by H. Wilberforce Clarke, p. 73. It is common to recite this poem when inviting someone very dear to enter your house.

marriage with Mirza Hadi could not have changed your feelings for me. Otherwise, you would not be here right now. We have always belonged to each other. You are the embodiment of virtue and goodness. We may not have had each other, but we have had one another's hearts all along."

Talking with Nima, I fell into ecstasy. He talked about how he had spent years thinking of me and how I was beauty and purity personified. I told him about how finding him was the main reason for my existence and how the vacillation between despair and hope had carried away my peace for years. I explained that, whenever I was full of despair, I found solace in the thought that Nima actually lived within me and that I was looking elsewhere for what I already possessed myself.

That day, we talked for three hours—but there was so much to say that we would have needed days to catch up. I learned that a few years after Nima got married, his wife died of ovarian cancer. They had a son together, Dara, who was now eighteen, and Nima never remarried. He worked as a music teacher, and for many years, he taught in Tehran, where he also played violin for the Tehran Symphony Orchestra. Only recently had he and Dara returned to Tabriz. That explained why our paths had not crossed all those years.

Briefly, I told Nima my story in turn. He was infuriated to learn how I had been treated in Mirza Hadi's home. He said that it was a mistake to believe that human beings evolved from savagery to civilization—there were still savages among us. He was delighted when I told him that I had rejected plenty of suitors during the last sixteen years in hopes of finding him.

He told me that the last time he had seen me was at my father's funeral. I had always wondered, given how my father had treated him and his mother, whether or not he had attended the funeral.

"I saw you from afar, walking with Mirza Hadi behind the coffin," he told me. "I was there walking side by side with my compatriots and shouting, 'Martyr Moin-al-Tojjar, you a lion of Iran, your legacy will live on.' I envied Mirza Hadi. Not only did he have you, but he got to be the son-in-law of our great patriot and freedom fighter, the Moin-al-Tojjar." Obviously, Nima had forgiven my father.

Neither Nima nor I wanted to leave, but it was getting late. Nima told me that he would come pick me up the next morning at 8:00 A.M.

I told him about the splendid party at Dena and Habib's house. So he said he would come on Saturday instead. I invited him and his son to the party and told him that, "My entire family knows you, and they would be thrilled to meet you. This is a great opportunity for you and your son to come and get to know everyone. I promise that Dena and Habib will not treat you and Dara the way my father treated you and your mother." We laughed. He was reluctant to accept my invitation, but eventually he agreed to come.

When I went back home, Neda, Dena, Habib, Auntie, my cousins, and Hāji Darab were all waiting. Auntie had told them where I had gone. They surrounded me, hugged me, and kissed me. They were overjoyed that I had finally found Nima.

"Dorna dear, is Nima still married?" Auntie asked. I jumped up and down and responded, no! The female relatives broke into a chorus of ululation.[39] They were all excited that I had invited Nima and his son to the party the next day.

# 3

The next morning, all the guests, more than a hundred people, arrived by ten o'clock. The guest of honor was supposed to arrive at eleven o'clock. At my request, Nima and Dara arrived at nine to get acquainted with my family before the party began.

Habib and Hāji Darab hugged and kissed Nima and Dara as if they were greeting two of their own family members, while Dena, Auntie, Neda, and my cousins all shook hands with them and said how happy and honored they were to meet them. Dara was a carbon copy of his father: he looked exactly as Nima had when I first met him twenty-one years before, handsome and with the same ocean-blue eyes. I loved him immediately, as if he were my own son. He kissed my hand and said, "Seeing you is a dream come true. My father is my best friend, and he hides nothing from me. He was very loyal to my mother, truly a loving husband. However, after her death, he poured his heart out to me. You should read the love poems that he has written for you. He talks about

---

[39] In Iran, ululation, a high-pitched trilling of the tongue, is practiced at weddings and other occasions as an expression of joy.

you almost every day. I lost my mother to cancer, but I feel like I just found a new one." I told him that the feeling was mutual.

It was around 9:40 A.M. when Dena and Habib took me, Nima, Dara, Neda, Auntie, my cousins, and my Uncle Hāji Darab to their family room. They locked the door from inside so that nobody could interrupt us.

Dena sat next to me, held my hand, and began to talk. "Dorna dear, my love, please listen carefully and try to be calm," she said. "Your ex-mother-in-law, on her deathbed, sent Afra to you three times begging you to go and see her. You refused. She wanted to reveal a secret to you and ask for your forgiveness. She thought that if you forgave her for all that she had done, she might have a chance to be forgiven by God on the day of her judgement.

"After you rejected her, she asked me to go in your stead. I agreed. When I got to her home, there was a girl there. As soon as I saw her, I knew that she was your daughter. She was the spitting image of you. Without thinking, I went and wrapped my arms around her and kissed her. Your ex-mother-in-law said what I already knew to be true: 'Dena dear, this is Parla, your niece!'

"Parla was shaken. She was confused and did not know what to make of the situation. She asked, 'Grandma, what are you talking about? Is this lady my mother Anvar's sister? I didn't know that mother had a sister.' Her grandma murmured, 'No, my sweet angel, she is your real mother's sister. You have never met your mother, the one who gave birth to you.'"

I was numb. Dena realized that she might be overwhelming me, and she paused for a few minutes.

Nima took advantage of the silence. "Dorna dear, your sister is giving you fabulous news!" he said. "You have a daughter. Isn't that fantastic?"

"Yes, I am following what Dena is saying," I replied. "But these turns in my life are huge shocks. I found you yesterday after twenty years, and now I am learning that I have a daughter who I was deprived of raising."

Everything was so surreal. I was no longer sure of what was true. Dena kissed me and put a glass of cold water against my lips. As I drank, she went on to say that the Fiendish One had told Parla, "I have to tell you a long and shocking story before I die. I wanted to do it in front of your real mother, but she refused to come and see me. I understand why. I pray that one day she forgives me. Instead, I will tell you everything in front of your aunt, Lady Dena. I am thankful that she is here."

At that point, according to Dena, Parla got out of her chair and sat at her grandma's side, holding her hand. The Fiendish One began to tell her story with regrets and tears. She told her, in detail, how Anvar had framed me.

"My dear Parla, I imprisoned your mother in a dungeon for seven months," the Fiendish One has said. "I made sure that she suffered every minute of her time there. I tell you all of this so that you know how vicious I was and how much pain and torture your real mother endured in your father's home. Your mother was held captive in that dreary basement room until she gave birth to you. I had bribed the midwife, and as soon as you were born, she placed a towel over your mouth to muffle the sound of your crying. Her assistant cut the umbilical cord at once, and you were whisked out of the room and delivered into my arms, after which I brought you, along with your father and Anvar, to a hotel room. The midwife played her role masterfully. She kissed your mother's forehead and told her that her baby was stillborn. You mother believed her. Your father divorced your mother on that same day, and we freed her. The next day, your father and Anvar took you to Tehran."

"Three months before your birth, we had announced that Anvar was pregnant, which she was not. After four months living in Tehran, we announced that Anvar had given birth to a daughter—you. When you returned with your parents to Tabriz, no one was the wiser."

Dena observed that, while listening to her grandma, Parla was visibly distressed. But she wanted to hear her full confession. Afterward, she wanted to see me right away, but Dena told her to wait for a few weeks so that she could arrange a big party, a huge celebration to welcome her to the family—and to surprise me with the news. Dena had a very hard time convincing Parla to be patient, but in the end, she agreed to wait at most three weeks.

During that time, Dena and Neda met with her regularly, almost every day. Habib and Auntie had also joined them a couple of times. They had told Parla everything that they knew about my life, my love story with Nima, my marriage with her father, my days in the dungeon, my education, and my tailoring business. They told me that Parla was very proud of me and that she thought I was a true lioness. Dena had also told Parla about my father and his immense wealth, about his patriotism and how he heroically resisted the Soviet occupation until he was martyred. And they told her, too, about how after my father was killed, my brother, Sina, gambled away everything we had and then committed suicide.

# 4

Parla was coming to the party prepared. But I was there in a state of shock. Tears streamed down my face nonstop. I was brimming with excitement, and also resentment. The satanic trio had struck another heavy blow, and it made my blood boil to realize what a huge oxymoron my life had been, what a painful and arduous fairytale.

Around 10:30 A.M., we all went outside. I stood between Dena and Auntie at the end of the long walkway that began at the gate. Dena then told the rest of the guests what the afternoon's celebration was really all about.

"Dorna has a sixteen-year-old daughter, Parla, whom she has never met," she announced. Everybody grew silent. Dena explained all that happened after Parla was born and how I never knew that I had a daughter until that very morning. She talked about the deathbed confessions of the Fiendish One and mentioned that it was her and Parla's decision to have that grand surprise party. Then Dena asked the guests to form a line on each side of the walkway. Uncle Verdi and Houri distributed flowers among the guests so that they could toss them in the air when Parla arrived.

Parla's car came right on time. She got out of her car outside the gate, and I got my first glance at my daughter. I wanted to run toward her, but Dena and Auntie grabbed my arms and held me back.

"What are you doing? Are you crazy? Do you want to ruin the entire ceremony?" Dena murmured.

The butcher, whom Habib had hired, had already tied all four feet of the snow-colored sheep, the sheep with the cherubic face that I had petted the day before. He carried the sheep, laid it down beside Parla's feet, and slaughtered it. That was a ritual in Abrahamic tradition. Habib and Dena sacrificed a sheep in Parla's honor and would later give its meat to the poor.

After the sheep was slaughtered, Parla stepped on its blood and passed through the gate. The guests began to ululate. They tossed the flowers at her. Parla's aunts, Jaleh, Pegah, and Layla, and their husbands and children, as well as Ali and Afra and Parla's chauffeur, followed behind. Dena had invited them all.

When I at last saw Parla's face, I immediately recognized myself in her. She was my daughter, without a doubt, the mirror image of my sixteen-year-old self. The ululating continued until Parla reached me. I greeted her with open arms, and we hugged for a very long time. Parla then hugged Auntie, Dena, and Neda, and I introduced her to Hāji Darab, Nima, and Dara.

Then I told her about how I had accidentally found Nima the day before. Parla told Nima that she was happy that she was not the only new person to join her mother's family. She bent to kiss his hand, but Nima stopped her and kissed her forehead instead. Parla and Dara faced each other, and they both blushed. "History is repeating itself," I thought. "If I am not mistaken, they have just fallen into the trap of each other's love."

That day was one of the happiest days of my life. After years of separation from my love, Nima, and my gorgeous daughter, Parla, everything had fallen into place. I owed all of that and, in particular, my survival to the three angels in my life, Dena, Neda, and Habib. Because of them, I could be happy in spite of all that I had suffered in Mirza Hadi's mansion.

On that Friday, the guests indulged themselves in music, dancing, singing, and endless assortments of heavenly food, drinks, desserts, and fruits. I spent some time with Jaleh, Pegah, and Layla. Jaleh told me that, a few weeks before his death, Mirza Hadi had said to her, "Jaleh dear, I know that all of you have known, from the beginning, that Parla is not Anvar's daughter. Of everything we tried to keep secret, we could never hide her true nature. It is obvious where she got her looks and her manners. I have appreciated immensely that no one ever told Parla anything about her real mother. However, after my mother's death, I want you to tell Parla that she is a granddaughter of the hero of Azerbaijan, the great Moin-al-Tojjar. It is important for her to know that Moin-al-Tojjar's blood flows in her."

"If we had a wise and thoughtful mother, things would not have gone the way they did," Mirza Hadi had told Jaleh.

Pegah, Layla, Afra, and Ali, all confessed to me, separately and in different ways, that they had suspected that Parla was my daughter. But they never said anything because they did not want to upset Parla's happy life.

Parla and I hugged each other many times that day. Our hugs never seemed long enough. Parla told me that when she was in seventh grade, one day, during a quarrel with one of her classmates, she was told that she was obviously a bastard because she bore no resemblance whatsoever to her mother, Anvar. When she got home, she flipped through Anvar's old photo albums and looked at Anvar's childhood photos and did not find any picture that resembled her.

"Since that day, I had felt like a square peg in a round hole whenever I was among Anvar's relatives," she told me.

Parla was clearly still in a state of shock. She felt as if her life had been a big lie. She felt betrayed. Nevertheless, she was happy that she had found me, her real mother. Looking dreamily into my eyes, she said that when she hugged me in the morning, she felt that her soul was inseparable from mine.

Eventually, the guests began to leave, but Auntie's family, Parla, and her chauffeur stayed. We did not let Nima and Dara leave either. We asked them to stay for dinner, and we gathered inside the house and talked until midnight.

It was amazing that everyone living or working in Mirza Hadi's mansion had figured out that Parla was my daughter; and yet, during those sixteen long years, none of them, not even Ali or Afra, had revealed the secret to me. Not only that, no one had even bothered to anonymously drop hints that my daughter was alive. This was another anomaly entirely antithetical to our cultural habits and practices. However, I was reasonably confident that my bad luck was coming to an end.

# 5

Monday morning at 10:00 A.M. sharp, Nima came to pick me up in his car. He was all dressed up. I asked him to come in and have a tea, but he said, "No, we should rush."

I sat next to him in the passenger's seat, and he began to drive. He had told me that he wanted to take me to a very important exhibition, one where they did not let anyone in without a birth certificate as identification. I had found that strange. But I was excited to spend time with him, so I had not questioned it.

The car stopped. I looked out the window. We were in front of a marriage registry office.

"Guess why we're here," he said.

"You don't want us to get married right now without a wedding party, do you?" I replied.

He reminded me what I had told him during our last secret rendezvous all those years ago. He recited my words verbatim: "I swear by God, with every fiber of my being, that I have never loved, and will never love again, another man as I love you. You are my only love. You are my first love, and in my dreams, in the wide expanse of imagination, where my thought bird takes flight freely and without fear, I will always be with you, with you alone. Wherever I am and wherever I go, I will carry your heart with me. I carry it in my heart. You are my kindred spirit."

He smiled at me. "I have been reciting these words two or three times a week for the last twenty years. I do not want to lose you again. Let us join in marriage right away."

He parked the car. We went inside the marriage registry office, and a clergy married us. Less than two days after finding Nima, we were husband and wife, as simple as that.

When we were back in the car, Nima kissed me for the first time. I told him that I would like for us to go to our secret rendezvous location, since I always wanted to see him there again. He drove to that location and immediately went and leaned against the sycamore tree beside the stream of water. He was as handsome as ever. I could not believe that he was mine.

We stayed there a long time. I told him about how I had gone there at random times, hoping that I might see him. He was ashamed that it did not occur to him to do the same. Several times, we indulged in lusty, passionate French kisses. After a very long period of longing for each other, in the words of Hafez, "The bird of fortune went into the snare of ours,"[40] and "The world's work hath gone to the desires of ours."[41]

---

[40] *The Divan-i Hafiz*, translated by H. Wilberforce Clarke, p. 23.
[41] Ibid., p. 20.

From our secret rendezvous location, we went back to Dena and Habib's house. I introduced Nima to Dena as my beloved husband. She did not believe me, but I showed her my birth certificate. The clergy had recorded there that I was married to Nima. Dena was surprised. She hugged me, then she hugged Nima and told him, "Welcome to the Moin-al-Tojjar family."

"No honor surpasses that of being our national hero's son-in-law," Nima said.

Dena called Uncle Verdi and Houri and told them, "Dorna and Nima just got married. That calls for another celebration. But for now, we will just have the family gather and celebrate their union." Houri hugged me and Uncle Verdi kissed Nima. Uncle Verdi left for Habib's showroom to give him the news, and Dena asked Houri to go to Auntie's house and give her the same message. Then she told me and Nima that it was our job to inform Parla and Dara that we were gathering that night for a celebration.

In those days, schools closed at noon and reopened at 2:00 P.M. We had to catch Parla during that period. We did not know which school she attended, and it was next to impossible for me to go to Parla's mansion. Nima told me that I had no choice. It was unfeasible for me to avoid my daughter's residence.

"Bite the bullet, and let's get it over with," he said. As hard as that was, I agreed. There I was, a tortured victim visiting her torture chamber on her wedding day. Only a child's love can entice such an action.

We arrived at Parla's mansion, and Ali and Afra rushed to greet us. They had already met Nima the day before. The gardener and his wife came next. The gardener's wife kissed my hand and apologized for not having let me to escape the mansion. She was the one who caught me on the day I almost fled.

"I realized the consequences of the evil thing I did much later, when Lady Parla was three years old," she told me. "At that time, I noticed that she was not Lady Anvar's daughter, and if I had let you escape, you would have given birth to her in your sister's house, and you could have raised her yourself. May you and the God almighty both forgive me." I told her not to worry about it. What had happened was water under bridge.

While Nima and I were talking with the gardener and his wife, Afra went and informed Parla that we were there. Parla rushed out and hugged me.

"Mother, what a pleasant surprise! Welcome to *your* mansion." Every time that she called me "mother," I was overcome with delight. Then Parla hugged Nima and told him again how pleased she was that her mother had found him.

"Parla dear, your mother and I just got married," Nima announced to her. "From now on, nothing and no one can stand between us, not even our shadows."

Parla was thrilled, she hugged both of us again. She invited us to have lunch with her, and we accepted.

At lunch she told us this: "Over the last three weeks, I have heard the sad story of so many obstacles that came together and kept the two of you apart. It is amazing that your deep, pure, and genuine love for one another has remained so strong and not diminished in spite of all the heartache you had to endure. With every fiber of my being, I believe that you should have a child of your own, who would be an expression of your rare and profound love."

She turned to me and went on speaking: "Mother, I am only sixteen years old, and I have inherited this mansion with all its workers, not to mention an enormous amount of money and other properties. My father did not want anyone to assume guardianship over me, out of fear that they might try and get at my wealth. When my grandma was alive, she guided me and helped me manage my financial affairs. I need someone I trust to help me. Moreover, I am not comfortable living in this huge mansion by myself. I can rely on Ali and Afra, and I trust the gardener and his wife. My chauffeur is a kind and gentle soul, as well. Nevertheless, I need to live with family members. If we had remained unaware of each other's existence, I would have asked Aunt Pegah and her husband to move here and live with me. However, now that I have my own mother and my new father, I want you to come and live with me. I know that this mansion was a prison and torture chamber for you. But I want you to build unforgettable pleasant memories over the ashes of those dreary ones. I want you and Nima to raise your future children and grandchildren in this place." Then she added that she had dismissed Esmat, the guard of my prison, and given her enough money to have a comfortable life back in her village.

Parla put me and Nima between a rock and a hard place. I hated that mansion, and Nima did not want an aristocratic home. We were faced with the most difficult decision we ever had to make. After agonizing over all of the possible options, we decided that, because of our unlimited and unconditional love for Parla, we could not refuse her wishes, and Nima and I soon moved in with Parla.

Dara preferred to stay in his father's house, and although he continued to live there, he came to see us often. His relation with Parla was very warm. Even though none of them ever mentioned it, I always thought that they were madly in love.

One day, about three years after Nima and I moved in with her, Parla told me, "Mother, I do not know why Dara is not asking for my hand in marriage. As you know, I have rejected all of my suitors expecting Dara to propose." I mentioned this to Nima, and he said that he knew why. Dara thought that he did not have even one star in the seven skies,[42] while Parla was the richest woman in Azerbaijan, perhaps in Iran. When it came to wealth, there was a mountain between them.

Nima and I met with Dara several times and argued that true love and devotion for one another overrides everything else. I said to him, "Look, my father thought that between a husband and his wife there must be economical parity, and that separated me from your dad for twenty years. I would have preferred to be with Nima, even if it meant not inheriting any portion of my father's wealth. Parla has more than enough for her and her children and even her grandchildren to live like queens and kings. Why should she desire a rich husband? That is ridiculous! She needs a husband whom she loves."

After much discussion, we finally convinced Dara to propose to Parla. He did, and they have been happily married for twelve years now.

---

[42] A Persian expression meaning "very poor."

# CHAPTER 9

# GHEYSAR

Now that I am completing these notes, I am fifty-four years old, and Nima is sixty. The year is 1975. Nima and I live with our thirteen- and fourteen-year-old sons, Kaveh and Behzad, and with Parla, Dara, and our three beautiful grandchildren in Parla's mansion. We have an amicable relationship with Parla's aunts, Pegah, Layla, and Jaleh. They are all married and live in their own houses. However, we see each other often. We love them, and Pegah is my best friend.

We have lost Auntie and my Uncle Hāji Darab, but thank God, Uncle Verdi is still with us. All four of my cousins are married, and our loving relationship with them is as strong as ever. Neda is also married and has two sons. They are the cherished apples of Dena and Habib's eyes, and I love them as much as I love my own grandchildren.

The mansion sometimes reminds me of the worst days of my life, and I have been trying very hard to substitute all those tortured memories with the merry ones that I have made during the last fifteen years. They say that in love there is no lack, and I feel that there is nothing I lack in my life. They say that love is love's reward, and I feel that because of my endless love for Nima, I have been rewarded a life full of love. In the last fifteen years, to me, the world has been as colorful and joyous as it was during my days with my parents, siblings, Mashdi, and Auntie.

Sex with Mirza Hadi was mechanical. It was all about techniques that maximized pleasure. Even though it led to the birth of Parla, another love of my life, it never was anything more than a means to fulfill sexual desire. However, sex with Nima is the expression of our mutual feelings

201

for each other—it is true lovemaking. It is the mystical union of two bodies with one soul, the state of being unified, the oneness of Nima and I. With Nima, sex is a lot more than a physical activity. I give him all that I have, and while having sex, I feel like I am floating on air. The joy of our sex goes even beyond unifying us and way beyond sensual pleasure. It produces a sense of merging with the universe.

I feel that, with all the changes in my life, I am as happy as a woman can be. However, even with my new life in total harmony and happiness, I am saddened to report that my towering hatred of Mirza Hadi and his mother and of Anvar has diminished not all. Even though they have all been dead for nearly sixteen years, my feelings toward them are tightly entangled in my psyche. I have not been able to totally free myself from their physical and psychological effects.

I cannot possibly finish my book without addressing the need for vengeance that has come from all of this scarring. This is a need I have kept secret from almost everyone in my life. In order to understand it, I must first tell you about a movie.

In 1969, a prominent Iranian filmmaker, Masoud Kimiai, made a *sui generis* movie called *Gheysar*.[43] It starred the legendary Iranian actor Behrooz Vossoughi in the role of Gheysar, an immortal protagonist. The movie begins with a scene in which an ambulance rushes a young woman, Fati, to the hospital. Fati, who has taken a great amount of poison, dies in the hospital but leaves her grieving family a suicide note. The note indicates that she was raped by Mansour, the brother of one of her friends, and could not cope with shame. Fati's older brother, Farman, is a penitent ex-roughneck who has turned his life around to become an honorable man running a butcher shop. Farman confronts Mansour, the rapist, and in no time, they grapple with each other while the rapist's two brothers watch on. As Farman is strangling the rapist to death, one of the brothers pulls a switchblade from his pocket and stabs Farman to death.

Gheysar, Farman's younger brother, works in the south of Iran. When he returns to Tehran for a visit and finds out that his brother has been killed and his sister was raped and later committed suicide, he flies into a rage. He vows revenge, but he knows that to slaughter the three brothers who destroyed his family, he needs to hide his wrath and remain

---

[43] An Iranian name for Caesar.

discreet. One day, he learns that one of the brothers, Karim, has gone to bathe in a public bathhouse. Gheysar goes there right away and finds Karim in a shower cubicle, where, he repeatedly stabs Karim and finishes him off by slicing his jugular vein with a sharp blade.

They say that the noblest vengeance is to forgive, and Persian poets have urged this point repeatedly. However, I should confess that, each time I see the movie, it gives me enormous pleasure to watch Gheysar stab the empty-handed, naked murderer. As a victim, I should identify myself with Fati and Farman, but instead, I identify with Ghaysar. I immerse in his character, and find him within myself. Then I imagine that I am him, but not stabbing Karim, stabbing Mirza Hadi's sadistic evil mother. How hedonically rewarding is taking revenge on those who made my life a living hell when I was in my prime. I feel that vengeance is sweet, as the Greeks say, and there is a Latin proverb that states that to take revenge on an enemy is to obtain a second life. Unfortunately, I never took my revenge on Mirza Hadi, the Fiendish One, or Anvar. Perhaps that is why I have never felt that I obtained a second life.

As the movie continues, Gheysar finds Rahim, the other brother of the rapist, working in a slaughterhouse. He butchers Rahim, leaving his corpse among the cattle before fleeing the scene. When watching those scenes, I do not see Gheysar butchering Rahim, I see myself butchering Mirza Hadi, and how appropriate is it for Mirza Hadi to be finished off that way.

Once, I was an innocent person and all that was in my life was love. I was as peaceful as a sparrow; a mere drop of blood could send a shudder down my spine. But then I witnessed the Soviet invasion of Tabriz, their atrocities and cruelty, their cowardly murder of my father and thousands of other patriots. Add to that the cruelty perpetrated against me by Mirza Hadi, the Fiendish One, and Anvar, and it starts to become clear why I see myself in someone like Gheysar. Even though I could never do what Gheysar does in the film, I cannot help but dream of bloody revenge. Such dreams bring me satisfaction, even if, in real life, I am an ardent student of the teachings of Mahatma Gandhi and Dr. Martin Luther King. Such are the contradictions I live with.

In the movie, after Gheysar kills the second brother, things do not go smoothly. Mansour, the rapist, goes into hiding. Gheysar tracks down Mansour at his hideout, and they fight. Mansour stabs Gheysar and tries to escape, only to find that the police have surrounded him. He runs back the other way. Still alive, Gheysar strains every nerve and summons all of his strength to kill Mansour. As Gheysar inserts his sharp knife into Mansour's heart, I do not see Mansour on screen. What I see is Anvar, slumping to the ground and drowning in her own blood.

The movie ends with Gheysar trying to flee. But the police shoot him in the leg, and he goes to an abandoned train wagon to hide. The last thing we see are the officers making their way to his hiding spot.

Once upon a time there was a content teenager, full of charm and beauty and charisma. People were fascinated by her glamor and elegance. She was raised in a moral household to be creative and intelligent. One day, this angel was forced into an arranged marriage, and in her husband's house, she was reduced to an object, toppled from the peak of grace to the abyss of disgrace. She was tortured body and soul.

Years have passed since her liberation, but still a hidden sore remains. And no matter how blissful her days are now, that sore, "Like a canker, gnaws at the soul in solitude and diminishes it."[44] What you have read is the story of that girl's life, my story.

---

[44] Sadeq Hedayat, The Blind Owl, 3rd ed., translated by Iraj Bashiri (Bashiri Working Papers on Central Asia and Iran, 2013), p. 16.

www.ingramcontent.com/pod-product-compliance
Lightning Source LLC
Chambersburg PA
CBHW031453260626

47154CB00017B/2617